Indulgence

K.A. BERG

Indulgence

K.A. Berg

Copyright © 2021 by K.A. Berg

All rights reserved.

No part of this book may be reproduced or transmitted in any form or by any means, electronic or mechanical, including photocopying, recording, or by any information storage and retrieval system without the written permission of the author, except for the use of brief quotations in a book review.

This book is a work of fiction. Names, characters, places, and incidents either are products of the author's imagination or are used fictitiously. Any resemblance to actual persons, living or dead, events, or locales is entirely coincidental.

VISIT MY WEBSITE AT WWW.BERGBOOKS.COM

COVER DESIGN: T.E. Black Designs; www.teblackdesigns.com

EDITOR: Ashley Williams, AW Editing; www.awediting.com

INTERIOR FORMATTING & DESIGN: T.E. Black Designs, www.teblackdesigns.com

Something was missing. Deep down, I wasn't satisfied.

It all started with dinner and a blindfold. We led each other down a path we didn't know if we'd be able to return from. We saw a side of each other we'd never seen before. What's more . . . we liked it.

Indulging in our sexuality was the best thing we'd done for our marriage, for ourselves.

Until it wasn't.

Some lines couldn't be uncrossed. Some things couldn't be undone. What happened when you've indulged too much? How could you ever fix it?

Dangerous Woman—Ariana Grande

Hard For Me—Michele Morrone

Every Time We Touch—Cascada

Adore You—Harry Styles

The Bones—Maren Morris

Past Life—Trevor Daniel & Selena Gomez

It Feels So Good—Sonique

Nobody's Love—Maroon 5

Need You Now—Lady A

Say Something—A Great Big World

ONE

NATALIE

"MOM, HAVE YOU SEEN MY lacrosse cleats?"

If I'd told him once, I'd told him a million times. Put your lacrosse stuff in your lacrosse bag in the garage when you come home from practice.

"Did you put them in your lacrosse bag like you were supposed to?" I called back as I tried to get everyone's lunches into the correct lunchboxes.

Turkey for Jackson.

Ham and cheese for Emma.

Chicken salad for Matteo.

And a garden salad for me.

"Mom, Saturn's rings fell off," Emma screeched from the end of the hall. "I need you to help me put them back on. I worked too hard to get anything less than an A."

Oh, my little perfectionist. No wonder she was always so stressed. She couldn't accept anything less than the best. I felt sorry for her future husband.

"And hurry. The bus will be here in ten minutes," she added as if I weren't already aware of the time her bus came every morning or what time it currently was.

"I still can't find my cleats, Mom," Jackson called out

again. I felt equally sorry for his future wife as I did for my future son-in-law. That boy was a mess of disorganization and food crumbs. "I need them for practice after school."

I took a deep breath and then let it out. In and out.

His cologne—Curve, the same it had been since college—invaded my senses before he kissed the top of my head and snatched a banana muffin from the plate on the counter.

"Jackson," he called out to our son. "Your cleats are in the back of my car. Emma, get the glue gun. I'll be there in a minute."

"Thank you." I exhaled heavily. How was I so exhausted already? It was only seven thirty. "It's as if they are completely incapable of verbalizing the word Dad when they feel the tiniest bit of crisis. It's always Mom. Mom. Mom. Mom."

I loved my children, but from the moments of their births, which happened six minutes apart, they hadn't stopped. Some days, like this one, I woke up drained.

Matteo smiled the grin that always grounded me. "They just know who is better at everything."

I rolled my eyes as my lips tipped up on one side. "You don't need to lay it on so thick this early in the morning, babe."

His forest-green eyes twinkled. "But it got a half a smile out of you."

"Dadddd!" Emma yelled, the inflection of her voice showcasing her panic. "The glue gun is ready. We don't have much time."

Matteo shook his head. "I better go before she has a heart attack."

The rest of the day wasn't any less hectic.

It was actually a day from hell.

Metro was a gallery in downtown Seattle that was run by a

brother and sister duo from France and featured art from all over the world. Bastien Bisset was an abstract expressionist painter and Annetta managed his career. I managed the gallery.

"Phillip, how does a painting just go missing?" I asked exasperatedly because, how could a shipping company lose a giant painting? We had a new exhibition starting next week, *Emergence*, which was a showing of emerging artists, and it would run for two weeks.

Phillip clicked and typed on his end while I stood on the loading dock in the back of the gallery with a driver who did not have the painting on his truck. "It has not been scanned off the truck, Mrs. Collins."

"The only boxes left on this truck are not large enough to house the painting, Phillip," I told him. "I assure you it is not on this truck. If this is the new standard of service at Echo Logistics, Metro is going to have to move our business elsewhere."

If the artist got wind that his painting had gone missing, it could have a catastrophic impact on the gallery's reputation. No one would want to let us handle their work if we couldn't guarantee safe arrival.

I hadn't wanted to think about the fact this particular piece was Alek Devereaux's highlight painting in his debut collection. It was supposed to make its rounds up and down the coast over the next three months.

The threat of moving our business elsewhere, seemed to light a fire under Phillip's ass. "Give me an hour, and I'll have your asset located."

I sighed. "That would be great, Phillip. Not as great as having the painting here now, like it was supposed to be, but at least we are moving in the right direction. I'll await your call."

As soon as I disconnect the call with him, the driver's phone rang. He stepped away, probably getting yelled at by

Phillip, and I counted the crates on the loading dock that contained the other pieces that *had* arrived.

"Let's get these moved inside," I called to Pete, the head of our in-house moving team.

Just as we finished checking the last box of the delivery, my phone rang. I was expecting Phillip, not a frantic Emma.

"Hello?"

"Mom, I was so distracted fixing my science project that I forgot my piano folder, " Emma rushed out.

I glanced down at my watch and sighed. Only two hours to get her folder to her. That meant heading across town and back in the beginning of rush hour traffic. Wonderful. "I'll bring it to your music lesson."

She exhaled, sounding relieved. "Thanks, Mom."

Traffic wouldn't help ward off the migraine knocking on my door or the seventeen new gray hairs I'd have by morning.

"Great job, team." I nodded at the men as they covered the last box with the wool blanket.

From my office, I scooped up the stack of paperwork on the corner of my desk. I still had so much left to do.

Where was Phillip with my painting?

Speak of the devil. My phone rang as I rushed to my car.

I skipped the greeting. I didn't have much left in me today. "Tell me you've found it, Phillip."

"It's at the University of Oregon."

Great, my piece was five hours away at a college art museum. Phillip assured me that my painting would be at the gallery first thing tomorrow morning as I drove home.

I was over the day by the time I ran into the house grabbed the folder and then ran back downtown to drop it off to Emma. Her shoulders visibly relaxed the moment she was prepared for her lesson. Matteo and I needed to sit with her to discuss her anxiety and stress levels. I knew it wasn't healthy for a child to be as concerned about perfection as Emma was.

While I waited for Emma's lesson to end and Jackson's

lacrosse practice to finish, I ran the slew of errands on my to-do list throughout town.

I dropped off new dry cleaning while picking up the previous batch I dropped off last week. Then I stopped at the UPS store to send back our Amazon returns. The drapes I ordered looked great online but not so great in person. Last was the grocery store. It seemed as if I lived at the grocery store. We were always running out of something. Either bread or milk or the protein bars that Jackson liked to eat before practice.

Lately, my life felt as if it was a tornado, spinning around knocking down everything in its path or, in my case, the never-ending to-do list. I was Mom, Mrs. Collins, and the gallery manager. All at the same time on some days. Once in a while, I just wanted to be Natalie, and be Natalie in a place that was all about making Natalie happy. On the heels of that thought was always guilt. I had great kids, a wonderful husband, and a good job. I was happy. Truly I was, but I figured I was just tired of the monotony of everyday life.

I finished at the store right on time. After packing everything into the trunk of my Jeep Cherokee, I swung back to pick up Emma before shooting to school to grab Jackson.

Turned out, Jackson's best friend, Scotty, needed a ride home, and Jackson volunteered me without bothering to check first. Not that I minded necessarily because I loved Scotty, but I was tired and Scotty lived on the other side of town, which meant twenty minutes in the opposite direction during the thick of rush hour.

Emma glowered at the boys in the backseat, all the while complaining about having a lot of homework and how she would be way behind and miss *Riverdale*. As if missing *Riverdale* were the end of the world, but I assumed that to a twelve-year-old who would undoubtedly hear spoilers tomorrow, it was.

It was after six when I pulled into the garage. "Can you

each grab a bag before you rush into the house, please?" I asked the kids as I popped the trunk. I did not feel like making a second trip back out for the groceries.

Emma let out a garbled protest while Jackson smiled. "Sure, Mom."

With the mood swings and anxiety raging through Emma's body, I was sure her impending first period wasn't too far off. God, please, anything but that. If Emma was about to start PMSing, I was going to move out.

Exhaling a deep breath for what had to be the thousandth time that day, I gathered the remaining bags and headed into the house, needing to get dinner started.

"Guys . . . get started on your homework," I called as I dropped the bags onto the counter. "Jackson, please make sure you shower first. Dinner should be ready in about forty-five minutes."

While putting away the groceries, I also started dinner. Life wasn't possible without multi-tasking. I pulled out the sauce from two nights ago to heat while I started the water for the lasagna noodles. I had just slid it into the oven and had begun working on the salad when Matteo came in the garage door.

"Hey." He smiled at me as he strolled into the kitchen "It smells so good in here."

"Thank you," I replied, turning my head toward him for a kiss.

Matteo was probably the world's best husband. He was kind, patient, and level-headed. He listened and never failed to kiss me hello or good-bye. I knew that, no matter what, I could always count on him.

He picked a cherry tomato from the bowl before asking, "How was your day?"

"Long, but all right. Yours?"

"Same old, same old." Matteo was an actuary. He assessed risks for a living. Like the guy Ben Stiller played in the movie

Along Came Polly. He analyzed the financial costs of risk and uncertainty, using a bunch of math stuff way beyond my comprehension, to judge the likelihood of an event happening, and then he helped his clients develop policies that minimized the cost of that risk. "The kids in their rooms?"

I nodded as I gave the salad a final toss before bringing it to the table. "Can you make sure Jackson showered? Oh, and fair warning, Emma is pissy because we had to take Scotty home and now she'll miss her show."

He took a deep breath. "Oh boy. Okay, I'll talk to her. How much longer?"

"About ten more minutes."

Matteo killed Emma's bad mood, a skill he excelled at. She was such a Daddy's girl. Dinner passed smoothly with even a few smiles from our daughter. Man, no one told us how hard this parenting gig would be when the teenage years loomed over our heads. It was exhausting.

As I stood in front of my dresser hours later, pulling out a pair of pajamas, warm hands slipped under my top and rubbed along the waist of my skirt. "We made it through another day," Matteo said, kissing my neck. "How about a little after-dark fun?"

I turned in my husband's arms and kissed him. I wasn't particularly in the mood for sex, but I wasn't not in the mood either. Sex had become the same things on repeat lately. It almost felt like a chore. Not one that I necessarily dreaded, like folding the laundry, but a chore nonetheless. It felt as though we were always on a time limit. There was the bare minimum amount of foreplay. Some kissing, a bit of petting, and then one of us was on top of the other.

Still, I pulled my top over my head while he unbuttoned his shirt. We had to be quick because we never knew when the kids would remember a permission slip that needed signing or needed a shirt that couldn't be found but they needed for tomorrow. Both things had happened to us before. Nothing kills an orgasm faster than the sound of your child calling your name while you have a dick inside you.

Maybe that was part of the rut as well. We were always waiting for the other shoe to drop. Or at least, I was.

I kissed Matteo's neck under his ear where he liked it the most as he shucked off his dress shirt. His dick stiffened against my hip as I stepped into him. He unzipped the zipper in the back of my skirt, and it dropped to the floor while I pulled his undershirt over his head.

A few moments later, we were both naked and laying on the bed. Matteo reached down and strummed me just where he needed to while I stroked him up and down. He licked my nipple before pulling it into his mouth. As if we could actually hear the ever-ticking clock, Matteo shifted his hand from my body to his as I let him go. He lined himself up at my entrance and pushed in. I wished I could say that I felt all the sparks and fireworks that I read about in my stories, but unfortunately, no. It felt like a penis slipping into a vagina. The same as the last one hundred times. It felt the same as always . . . good.

He moaned softly in my ear.

I scratched my nails down his back and wrapped my legs around his waist, trying to pull him deeper into me. It had been getting harder and harder to quiet my mind during sex enough to come. My brain was too busy worrying about what needed to be done next that I wasn't able to enjoy what was happening in the moment.

Did I wash Jackson's lacrosse uniform for his game tomorrow?

Did Emma have play practice Tuesday or Thursday this week?

Did I mail out Matteo's mother's birthday card?

Shit, I needed to focus or I wouldn't be able to *at least* try to come.

Maybe if Matteo gave my ass a little slap it would keep my attention in the moment.

That was a whole other issue I had going on lately. I kept picturing the kinky sex where the girl was being hammered into in oblivion or tied up while she came over and over. It was hard to come when thinking about that while having sex missionary style.

Sweat dotted Matteo's hairline. His forearms strained on either side of me as he held himself up and his hips thrust back and forth. He was so sexy as he loomed over me, his abs flexing as he got close to his climax. Unfortunately, I wasn't any closer than I was while still dressed. A twinge of guilt hit me deep in my gut. I wanted to come with my husband; I did. I loved him. I was attracted to him. He made me feel special, but during the actual sex part, I felt nothing. Zip. Zilch. Nada.

What was wrong with me?

I raised my hips and met Matteo's thrusts. I panted. I mewled softly. I even squeeze my muscles together like I was doing Kegels to make it feel real as I faked my orgasm with my amazing husband, and he came with a grunt.

Matteo smiled down at me and kissed the tip of my nose. "I love you."

God, I felt like the worst wife in the world. I just faked an orgasm with my husband who only ever tried to make me happy. I wished I had a way to tell him that this wasn't working for me anymore, but the last thing I wanted was to make Matteo feel as if he weren't enough. He was everything. I just had to try to figure out what was happening on my end. Then I could fix myself, and we would go back to being the way we were.

That was it. That was all.

"I love you too."

We rolled out of bed, and I headed for the shower first.

With Matteo's back turned to me while he grabbed a pair of sleep pants from his drawer, I swiped my phone from my dresser and slipped into the bathroom. After turning on the shower, I typed in the name of my favorite porn site and pulled up a tag that I knew would help me get the job done quickest.

I stepped into the shower and let the hot water hit my back while I watched a pretty brunette get both of her holes filled by two large dicks. Her face twisted in pleasure as they worked in and out of her. My fingers found my clit and rubbed back and forth, up and down. The sensations began building quickly, and a few minutes later while I watched the muted girl screamed out her pleasure, I bit my lip and came from my own hand.

The guilt from deceiving my husband crept back in, and I felt that shame that washed over me every time this happened, but a girl had to do what a girl had to do.

Chapter Two

Matteo

If I didn't know my wife the way I did, if I was insecure in our relationship, then I would have thought she was having an affair. But I knew Natalie better than any other person on this planet did, so I knew that, without a doubt, she was not cheating on me.

Not that knowing that did anything to help me understand what Natalie was going through or why there was a disconnection between us in the bedroom. It seemed to be the only part of our relationship that had shifted. Everything was fine, and then it wasn't. Or at least that was how it felt to me.

I questioned myself over and over, forcing my mind to think back, find signs I missed. How could I claim to know everything about my wife—like how she wouldn't eat Oreos without peanut butter or that she twirled her hair around her finger when she was nervous—but not understand why she suddenly couldn't come during sex?

She did her best to pretend, but she also didn't realize she squeezed her eyes closed while she faked her orgasms. Watching her eyes as she climaxed was my favorite part of making love to Natalie. Her eyes were a unique shade of brown that was mixed with a deep honey. Watching the way her eyes rolled back and how the flecks of gold in her irises glowed made my dick swell.

When Natalie faked it, she closed her eyes. She was overthinking the act, making it sellable. When she came, she didn't think about it, and her eyes just followed the sensations of the release.

As soon as she closed her eyes, it was like looking at the side-by-side photo in the kids' *Highlights* magazine where you had to find the six differences between the photos. She overarched her back, pitched her moans a notch too high, and squeezed her eyes closed.

When it happened the first time, I waited for her to tell me what went wrong and why she couldn't get off. But she didn't say a word and acted as if it were business as usual. I didn't bring it up for fear of embarrassing her. Maybe she didn't want to discuss it at that moment. Maybe she needed time to process what happened and why she didn't finish. Typically, the only other times that happened were because we'd been interrupted.

After that first time I noticed it, the faking became more of a regular thing than coming. It wasn't all the time, but it was far more often than not.

I couldn't figure out what was going on with her, and it was driving me crazy. For me, sex had always been more than just getting off. It was about the connection. I didn't care how much of a wuss that made me. I loved my wife more than anything, except for Jackson and Emma, and I cherished those moments where we were one.

The instant I met her, I knew she was different. She hated math, and I was trying to help her understand it, which never really happened, so that smile I desperately craved from her seemed unobtainable. The urge to soothe her worries consumed me, so I kept at it. She was stressed and wound tight, but she drew me in.

When Nat came to our tutoring session after passing the

first test she took with my studying help, she graced me with the biggest, brightest smile I'd ever seen. It was beautiful, and I was addicted. Her smile was my drug. We had been working together for a few weeks by that point, and I was already crushing on her, but after seeing the way her happiness could light up my world, I was a goner.

I had no doubts that Natalie was the one for me. She was the one I wanted by my side always. A life with her and everything it had to offer us.

We've been thrown some curve balls along the way, but we always came out stronger. I liked to believe that was because we had this way of understanding each other. Yin and yang. Natalie was the anxious one while I was the calm one. She had the temper where I could defuse the situation. Emma was a mini Natalie in every way possible, except math skills. Emma was almost better with numbers than I was. We understood our differences, embraced and leaned on each other, talked about things, which was why her lack of openness with our bedroom issue confused me.

I was fairly certain it wasn't an attraction problem either. Natalie was still attracted to me. I could feel it in her touch. Plus, it wasn't as though she was turning down sex, which I assumed would have been the case if she didn't want to be with me. She just wasn't climaxing during sex. She was getting herself off in the bathroom alone instead.

It was hard not to feel hurt after I saw her in the shower last week. We had finished making love, and she went to shower, which wasn't out of the ordinary. Except, when I popped into the bathroom to grab my glasses and contact case, I saw what she was doing.

Through the frosted glass of the shower doors, I could see Nat's silhouette. She was holding her hand out in front of her. I couldn't quite figure out what the hell she was doing until I saw where her other hand was and where it stayed long past washing. Natalie was rubbing one out in the shower, watching something on her phone, porn I presumed.

We had just finished having sex, where she faked her orgasm, only for her to go flick her bean in the shower. I had a ton of questions, mainly I wanted to know why. Why not ask me? If the dick wasn't working, why not ask for my tongue or fingers? Why wasn't my wife talking to me about this?

If she wasn't discussing the issue with me, she had to be talking to someone, which was why I broke the cardinal marriage rule: No snooping through the other's electronics.

I needed to know what was going on, and I wasn't going to wait any longer. I'd been patient for three months. It was long enough.

Natalie's new exhibition opened tomorrow so she was working late, and Scotty's mom was dropping the kids off from their after-school activities, so I had some time alone.

We kept our laptops and tablets in the bedroom. Our tablets sat on our nightstands. Natalie liked the read before bed, and I had an addiction to Words with Friends and 2048 because, well, I loved numbers. I'd play one for a little while as Natalie watched a show or read her books.

I went for the tablet first. Natalie's entire life tied into one device—her phone, iPad, and computer.

The first place I thought to check was her messages. I searched my name in the search bar and scanned through the conversations where my name was present, hoping to find some answers.

She wouldn't have discussed bedroom issues with any of our parents, so I scrolled passed those. My sister was out because I doubted Nat would discuss our sex life with Isabella. She might discuss it with her sister, though, but only if there was no one else in the world to speak with, so I doubted Deanna knew anything. I scrolled through, looking for anything sex related over the last three months, but came up empty. There was nothing in her conversations with her two best friends, Norah and Penelope either.

Maybe it was in an email. I checked her email next, searching Norah and Penelope's names first, thinking they would most likely be her confidants for something like this. They'd been close since college, and I was fairly certain nothing was a secret between them—those three had no boundaries.

But, again, I came up empty. I checked her sister's email address next, but nothing was there either.

The image of Nat in the shower, touching herself, flickered in the back of my mind. I clicked the Safari app and checked her search history. Scrolling back to the week before, I found something useful—Natalie's porn views in the browser history. Link after link of videos she'd clicked on.

I felt guilty, as if I were invading her privacy, but I pushed through it and clicked on the first link.

Holy shit.

The video was of a woman sandwiched between two men, each one thrusting in and out of her body. I clicked back and found links for a few more of those. Then I found one of a woman tied to a bed with a man using toys on her, making her come over and over. There were videos of anal and even a few threesomes with two women and a guy.

Jesus, I would have never guessed that was what Natalie was getting off to. Was this what she wanted? Threesomes, anal sex, and bondage? No wonder she wasn't getting off during regular sex. She wanted more.

A conversation I walked into a few weeks ago dinged in my mind. Penelope and Norah were here, and the girls were discussing some book. When I entered the living room, they were gushing over a woman being collared by two men.

When I asked what that meant, I got more than I expected in an explanation. They rambled on about the inner workings of the relationship then fawned over the way she was loved by two men, blah, blah. I wished I had paid a bit more attention since this was what my wife seemed to be into. At least to two parts, I didn't think Natalie was looking for a BDSM relationship.

I closed out the Safari app and opened the Kindle app. Maybe I should see what kind of books she was reading. That may shed some more light on the things Natalie found enticing. I made note of the title she was reading and the last few she read. I grabbed my iPad and opened my Kindle app. We shared the Amazon account, so I had access to all her books and she mine. I downloaded the ones she read most recently before closing out of the app and returning her iPad to her nightstand. She'd be none the wiser that I had snooped through it.

The porn was an eye-opener. The books would be helpful too. She was always talking to Norah and Penelope about how sexy these book boyfriends were, so there was no harm in seeing what made these men so damn appealing. If they were anything like the porn scenarios she was watching, I sure had my work cut out for me.

Chapter THREE

NATALIE

With having to run a few extra errands after work, it was close to seven when I finally pulled into the driveway. The house was oddly quiet as I walked in, yet the scent of something delicious filled the air.

There was no fighting over who would set the table for dinner coming from the kitchen.

The kids' backpacks weren't abandoned on the floor for me to step over as I hung my jacket on its hook.

No sound heard from any of the televisions.

I didn't hear any TikTok music coming from phones.

Matteo's car was in the garage, so I knew he was definitely back from picking Jackson up from practice and Emma from the library. Maybe he took them out for a quick bike ride or walk or something. Maybe I should enjoy the rare moment and embrace the quiet.

"Matteo? Emma? Jackson?" I called as I entered the living room.

"In here," Matteo answered from the kitchen.

I followed his voice and the scent of garlic to find him standing in front of the stove cooking. The table had been set for two, complete with wine ready to be poured and a single red rose in a vase sitting in the center.

"What's this?" I asked, wracking my brain to see if I'd forgotten some important date. It wasn't our anniversary, a romantic holiday, or my birthday. I had no idea what the occasion was.

He turned from whatever he was making in the skillet, looking casual in his jeans and gray T-shirt, and smiled. "Dinner."

Well, the table settings and smell of food gave that away.

"Where are the kids?" I asked. Fridays were typically a free-for-all after a week's worth of school, activities, emotions, and exhaustion.

A gleam I hadn't seen before shone bright and sneaky in his green eyes. "I dropped them off at my parents' for a sleepover."

"Oh?" I couldn't keep the surprise out of my voice. Matteo didn't typically make plans for the children without checking with me first. Not that I required him to check with me, but we worked as a team and kept each other in the loop. "But Jackson has a lacrosse game tomorrow."

"I know." That was all he said. No elaboration as to why plans had changed or how Jackson was getting to his game. He just turned back to the stove and turned off the burner as though his making us dinner with no kids was an everyday occurrence.

He was acting super weird. I didn't know whether to be frightened or intrigued.

"Why the change in plans?"

He grabbed the skillet from the stove and made his way to the kitchen table. "I have plans with you," he answered ominously as he plated what looks like shrimp scampi. My favorite.

Hmm. Dinner. No kids. My favorite meal. It almost felt as though he was buttering me up for something—or apologizing, but nothing had happened. At least, nothing that I was aware of.

"Plans with me?" I asked like a dolt because I had no damn clue what was going on.

"Yes." He nodded. He was being succinct, not giving anything more than the bare minimum of information. As if he held a secret he was protecting. Nothing like Matteo usually was.

The golden-brown flecks in his green eyes melted a bit as he pinned me with a stare. "Now, sit, please. Dinner is ready."

Was I in the damn twilight zone? Matteo, who was always easygoing and soft-spoken, was ordering me around with a bit of bite in his tone? What the hell was going on?

I sat, mostly because the deep timber of his voice had me following his orders as if I were conditioned to obey his command. "Shouldn't I be aware of the plans too?"

He heaped a generous helping of pasta and shrimp onto my plate. His eyes zeroed in on mine as if he was trying to convey some kind of message, but I wasn't getting it. "You'll find out soon enough."

"Matteo, what's going on?" I was starting to get a bit worried. Everything was so out of the ordinary. "What's this all about?"

Moving from my plate to his, he filled it before answering. "I said"—his voice was rugged and authoritative—"you'll find out soon enough."

That was unsettling and appealing at the same time.

Matteo and I had been together since our sophomore year of college. I'd never been a math person. Okay, I hated it, so I put off starting my requirements until second year. After I miserably failed the first test of statistics, I bit the bullet and got a tutor. Taking the class once was bad enough, having to retake it wasn't something I wanted to do. The school assigned Matteo as my stats tutor. He was patient and calm. He never laughed at my dumb mistakes or batted an eyelash when I threw a fit as I tried to figure out the odds of certain outcomes at the roulette table. Who asked questions like that anyway? Bookies and gambling addicts.

He had this way of settling me from the very beginning. He'd done it during our study sessions and then again eleven months after barely passing stats when the second line appeared on the pregnancy test I took in the bathroom of his college apartment he shared with two of his friends Adam and Trevor. It was the spring semester of our junior year. Then he kept me sane, again, when the doctor told us we were expecting not one but two children. His ability to soothe me continued through summer courses and online fall courses, all so I could graduate with my art history degree before the babies came in January. It was there and stronger than ever when we threw the shotgun wedding into that crazy mix.

Matteo had always been the calm to my storm.

So, seeing this gruff, short, and commanding side of him was new. While I wasn't entirely sure what to make of it, it made something flutter deep in my belly.

"How was work?" he asked as he picked up the bottle of wine, poured me a glass, and then one for himself.

I followed his every move as he took the seat across from me. "The *Emergence* exhibition finished today. The crew was working on getting everything ready to be shipped out as I left. Oh, and Bastien has decided that he will use the Portland Gallery opening as a platform to reveal his newest collection."

"That doesn't sound all too surprising." He sipped his wine. "It's been about two years since his last show, hasn't it? The new location makes the perfect setting."

"It has, and yes, it does," I replied, spinning linguine around my fork. It smelled so good; my mouth watered in anticipation. "But the collection isn't finished yet. He just started working on it and wants it to be a ten-piece collection on life in reverse. We open in August, which is only five months away. What if the main show piece isn't ready? We know that Bastien works in his own off the wall way, but it doesn't always result in rapid productivity."

"Bastien loves the pressure. He thrives on it. He'll have it all ready." Matteo watched me chew with a tilt of his head as he gripped his wine glass by the stem. "Good?" he asked over the rim.

With my mouth full, I nodded.

His lips pursed as he tipped the glass up to sip the wine. As soon as he swallowed, he grinned with a certain something extra I couldn't quite put my finger on. "Fantastic."

The entire setup felt like something I would read in one of my romance novels. The alpha-ish behavior. The stares. The dinner. The no kids.

What the hell was happening?

He clearly had something up his sleeve that he didn't want to tell me about, so I just rolled with it.

We finished dinner with a bit of light conversation, ignoring the giant elephant of Matteo's behavior. He filled me in on Jackson's lacrosse practice and Emma's progress on her group project she was working on at the library. As soon as I ate the last piece of shrimp from my plate, Matteo stood and removed it from the table.

"Did you enjoy dinner?" he asked as he rinsed my dish and then his before opening the dishwasher and setting them inside.

God, there was something sexy about a man loading the dishwasher. There was no tearing my eyes away as I watched, riveted. "I did. It was delicious. Thank you very much."

He smiled at me, this time with a very conspiratorial tip of his lips. "You're most welcome. Now, finish your wine so we can have dessert."

Wow, he really went all out on this. "You made dessert, too?"

He shook his head as his grin grew wider and wider. I swore that if it were possible for the corners of his lips to twirl like the Grinch's, they would've. "No, my dear. You are the dessert."

I was the dessert?

A jolt of shock zipped through my body as the wine left my glass and slid over my tongue. I tried my best to swallow it and not choke as I stared at the man who looked like my husband but was clearly embodying the persona of someone else tonight.

FOUR

Matteo

MY VERY PERPLEXED WIFE GULPED. I swore I heard the sound almost as much as I could see her throat work to get that sip of wine down without choking on it.

"I'm the dessert?" Her voice had a quiver to it. Not of fear but of uncertainty. She didn't know what was going on, which was the point. I wanted her off her game. I didn't want it to be a regular night of our married sex. The jig was up. I knew what she wanted. What she fantasized about when she touched herself. My wife—my beautiful, sexy, secretly dirty wife—wanted more. She wanted different. She wanted adventure. What we were doing didn't work for her anymore, and if she wasn't happy, I couldn't be happy. So, Matteo 2.0 was created.

It'd been a little over two weeks since I snooped through her iPad, and the time had come and gone for her to bring it up.

So, from then on, the only thing Nat would be thinking about during sex was how many times she would come and how hard.

Time and time again, Natalie made me the happiest man in the world—in and out of the bedroom. It was my turn to step up to the plate before this turned into something that ruined our marriage. Sex was an important part of a healthy marriage alongside trust and communication. If one of them started slipping, everything started to crumble in its wake. All the components tied together for success. She wasn't satisfied with our sex and wasn't confident enough or didn't trust me enough to communicate her needs. I analyzed risks for a living, and not fixing this little rift in our life was a risk I wasn't willing to take.

"Yes, you are," I confirmed, stalking toward her, eating up the span of our kitchen in just a few strides. "You are the only thing left to eat tonight."

Her forehead scrunched, and the V that appeared between her eyebrows every time she thought too hard about something popped up as if on cue. "You're being weird. What's going on?"

I gripped her hand in mine and led her from the kitchen and down the hall of our simple ranch-style home to our bedroom. "It's more like what's going down, Nat, and that will be me on you until you come on my tongue." I looked back at her shocked face over my shoulder and added, "You'll be begging for me to stop making you come today."

She stumbled a bit, stunned, and, yes, the lust was there, whether or not she wanted to admit it, she was turned on. Her pupils dilated and a pink flush spread up her neck as she sucked in a quick gasp.

"Matteo." She breathed my name as if she didn't know what to say.

"Natalie?" I mocked as I opened the door to our room.

I may have gone a little overboard on the romantic side of things, but I didn't care. She deserved candles and flowers even if I'd been thinking about unique ways to defile her body, how to touch her in ways she had never been touched before, as I set them up. I only wished I had known sooner that this was what she wanted. What husband wouldn't be willing to try all the things his wife was reading about and watching on porn sites?

My wife would have her fantasies come true.

Tonight, though, we would start off simple.

Natalie and I had a lot to discuss before we did some things she was looking at. I didn't know what she actually wanted to try versus what she was just intrigued by. Plus, I hadn't done any of this shit before, and I needed to start off slow my-damn-self. You didn't jump on the black diamond after years of only sliding down the bunny slope.

I watched as her eyes took in the room. The vanilla-scented candle flickering on the dresser. The rose petals on the bedspread. The red satin strip lying across the bed.

When she looked back at me over her shoulder, I was still standing in the doorway.

"What's the ribbon for?" she questioned, walking toward the bed.

I made my way to her and picked up the piece of material. I stepped behind her and raised the strip over her head, then across her eyes.

"This," I explained as I tied it into a knot behind her head.

She sucked in a quick breath. "And what are you planning to do while I'm blindfolded?"

Her voice was still shaky, but if her nipples were any indication, the blindfold turned her on. I could see the stiff peaks standing at attention under her thin top.

I leaned down, kissing her neck first. I made my way to her ear and whispered, "Whatever I want."

My name fell from her lips like a prayer.

Her shirt had a little tie in the front just above her breasts. I pulled the string, and it opened, giving me enough room to slip a hand in. My fingers slid under the lace of her bra, and I found her pebbled nipple just begging for my touch. Her body jerked against mine as I pinched the nub between my index and middle finger like it was a cigarette. Her breathing sped up when I released it and traced the skin around it

"Do you like that?"

"You know I do." And I did. I knew she liked her nipples played with.

I pulled my hand from her shirt, wanting to get my mouth on them instead. Gently, but with a bit of urgency, I tugged her shirt from the waist of her pants and pulled it up over her head, careful not to knock off her blindfold. She looked sexy as sin with the red blindfold a stark contrast to her fair skin and the white lace covering her breasts.

It all needed to go. The need to have her bare before me consumed me like a wildfire, her already bared skin the sparks taking off in the wind, spreading the flames over more ground. I needed to see all of her. Her shoes went first, followed by her pants. They fell nicely down her legs, leaving her standing before me in just her panties and bra and the blindfold.

She stood stock still, letting me dictate each move, each step. What was going through her mind? Was she wondering if I had a stroke and my brain was malfunctioning? I didn't know if there had ever been a point when I really took my time with her body. We were kids when we first started dating, discovering, fumbling, and having fun. Then the kids were born, and life swept us away. We treasured every moment we got to have sex. I knew I cherished the intimacy, but I couldn't really remember us necessarily appreciating each other's bodies.

"God, you're stunning," I praised when I finally had her bra and panties off and she stood before me completely bare, her long waves of hair hanging over her shoulders. Her cheeks pinked, making me question when the last time I truly complimented my wife was. I often told her I loved her. That her butt looked great in her pants. I noticed when she changed her hairstyle. But I couldn't remember the last time I made her feel like a wanted woman. Like the beautiful woman she was. And I had to ask why she didn't feel comfortable enough to tell me that things sucked in the sack?

Kneeling, I picked up her left leg. "I don't tell you that enough, do I?" I asked before I leaned down and placed my lips on her ankle. She squeaked but said nothing as I continued up her leg to her hip then paused at her navel. "You are the sexiest woman I've ever laid my eyes on, Natalie. You were fourteen years ago, and you are now."

She whispered my name, her voice laced with thick emotion.

Continuing my ascent, I kissed the soft flesh of her stomach and then each breast. Her skin was smooth under my lips and smelled like the jasmine lotion she loved to use. Finding the hollow of her neck, I pressed my lips into the little divot before dragging my tongue up to her ear. "The sight of you when you first wake up, when you've just gotten home from a long day at work, when you're all dolled up for the company Christmas party, every single version of you makes my dick hard."

To prove my point, I took her hand and placed it on the bulge that was making my pants snug. My dick jerked and practically begged for me to let him inside her.

Dropping her hand, I swung mine back and slapped her ass. Not too hard, but hard enough. "Now, get your fine ass on the bed. On all fours. I want to see all of your pretty pussy before I eat it for my dessert."

When this idea of making her fantasies a reality first started to take root, I didn't truly know how I felt about it. I wasn't much of a dirty talker. I hadn't been much of a take-charge man. I was always subdued and respectful. I didn't know if I could step into the role of a dominant man, but I enjoyed the way the deeper tone of my voice made goose bumps dance across Natalie's skin. The way her movements were eager, and her breathing was faster than it had been in a while. I was getting off on exciting my wife, and we hadn't started the fun stuff yet.

Natalie on her hands and knees on the bed was a vision. The red splotch of color in the middle of her right ass cheek sent a zing straight to my dick. Damn, it was erotic as hell seeing my mark on her like that. I climbed onto the bed behind her and rubbed my hand down the curve of her ass.

She fidgeted, and I couldn't help but smirk. She really was enjoying herself.

My fingers itched to touch her lower, to feel if she liked this as much as I thought she did. Pressing my lips to the handprint on her skin, I dipped my fingers down and ran one through her slit.

Nat moaned as her back arched a bit. "You're wet, love." She was soaked. My finger slipped right through her. I dragged it back up and then down again, sweeping through the evidence of her pleasure as she continued her soft moans. Moans that were the sweetest music to my ears.

Her body trembled as she waited for my next move. Gripping both of her cheeks in my hands, I pulled them apart and leaned down, running my tongue from her clit to her entrance. The taste of her arousal filled my mouth, making me ravenous. I licked and sucked until Natalie's elbows gave out and her body shook with her release.

"Oh, god," she cried out with abandon. It made me want to beat my fists against my chest like Tarzan. Honestly, I didn't think I'd made Natalie moan like that before, and I realized how much I had been missing out in our sex life as well. The urge to make her come again took over, and I kept licking Nat through her release.

She squirmed forward, pulling her pussy away from my mouth, and I let her. I could bring her orgasms with my tongue again later. I just stashed that idea in the back of my mind with all the others living there.

I ran my hand along her back and leaned down to kiss the center. "That was only round one, love."

Her breathing still hadn't calmed, so I gave her a minute.

But only one.

The metal of my belt clinked as I unfastened it. I didn't bother passed pulling myself free before I ran the head of my dick through Natalie's slick core.

If I thought I had been hard before, that was nothing compared to how hard I throbbed when I felt the proof of just how turned on my wife was. I couldn't remember the last time Natalie had been this wet.

"Jesus, Nat," I murmured as I pushed in just the tip, reveling in the warmth.

Natalie let out what sounded like a mewl before whispering, "More, Matteo, more."

She asked; I delivered. I thrust in the rest of my length, groaning at how tightly her body gripped me. Like a fist. A hot, wet fist.

The walls of her core quaked around the invasion as she gasped. "Christ."

I pull back and shoved in again . . . and again. "God, love, you feel so good."

Nat pushed her hips into me and bowed her back. Her head snapped back, and she let out a loud cry. "I'm going to come."

And she did. She came so hard I was afraid my dick would snap with the force her body clamped on to mine. It had felt as if it had been forever since I felt her come like this.

"Yes," I cooed. "Please, love. Come on my cock."

I rode her hard as she climaxed. I gripped her hips tighter and rocked into her, waiting for her to finish. As soon as she did, I pulled out and flipped her onto her back. Hooking her legs over my forearms, I slid back in, missing her heat.

"I can't—I can't," she protested, but I didn't let up. Instead, I reached out and pinched one of her nipples between my fingers, twisting with a little more bite than I usually would.

"Yes, you can," I coaxed. "I'm not stopping until you come again."

I didn't mention that I felt like I would explode any second. I would do whatever I needed to make sure she came again, even if it meant thinking about anything other than how good she felt or how gorgeous her full breasts looked jiggling up and down with each pump.

"Matt—" She didn't get to finish crying out my name before her third orgasm of the night wrecked her body.

Her neck strained. Her fingernails clawed my arms. Her back arched off the bed, and her legs tightened around my hips.

I relished it all. Seeing Natalie go off like that was more than I needed to drive off the edge into the bliss of climax.

Chapter Five

NATALIE

A LIGHT TOUCH SKIRTED DOWN my arm, stirring me from sleep. Warmth surrounded me, pulling me to nestle into it. Wanting to claim just a few more moments of rest, I shifted my hips to try to get comfortable and a delicious ache emanated from my core. The naughtiness of the night before flashed in my mind like a smutty graphic novel.

The blindfold.

The authoritative commands.

The orgasms

Matteo's arm wrapped around my waist as he lowered his mouth to my ear, and his breath whispered over my jaw to my neck as he spoke, "Good morning, beautiful."

I shivered.

His arm tightened, pulling my body flush against his. His hand inched down to the apex of my thighs where my legs were still closed, curled up almost to my chest.

He tapped the side of my leg. "Open." His voice was gruff, but it wasn't still heavy with sleep like mine as if he had been awake for a while.

My legs begun unfurling on their own as if they took their orders directly from Matteo. A chill ghosted down my back as he shifted away from me. A moment later I was on my back and Matt was settled on top of me. His fingers played between my thighs, and his mouth lowered to my exposed nipple. He added pressure with his teeth and pulled the hard nub of flesh just the way he knew would make me moan.

"Matteo." His name was like a sigh, a plea. I didn't really know for what. More, perhaps. It felt as though it'd been a lifetime since our intimacy felt intimate, and I yearned for it. I craved this connection with him, even though I had no idea where and why it started. I was a junkie jonesing for her next fix.

His lips moved from my nipple down my belly to my core. "Natalie." His breath fanned over the sensitive skin between my folds as he spread them apart. Looking down my body, I sucked in a quick breath at the sight of Matteo and his tousled hair, black-rimmed glasses instead of his usual contacts staring at the center of my body as though it were the fountain of youth.

Our eyes locked for a moment and then his tongue was on my clit. The pads of his fingers were soft on my swollen flesh as he held me open, devouring me. I tried to remember the last time he had taken his time playing with me. Foreplay had become a means to an end, a step to check off on the instruction manual of sex. There was always just enough to get some juices flowing, but there was never an indulgence of it.

That wasn't the case last night nor at the moment. The juices were more like a broken faucet that wouldn't turn off. Everything was on overload.

My body was on fire as zaps and jolts coursed through me like lightening during a summer storm.

Matteo's goal seemed to be to elicit as much pleasure from my body with his fingers and mouth as he could. My back arched, my shoulder stiffening as he thrust his tongue into me. My hips ground on his mouth, relishing the feel of his assault as I trapped his head between my thighs.

Then, just as an orgasm started to coil inside me, my mind shifted from the onslaught of pleasure to why he was worshiping me the way he was. Where was this change in him coming from? This change that I loved, that my body hungered for. Was it wrong for me to love this side of Matteo? My mind had finally woken up and wouldn't stop thinking.

But the way his fingers dug into my hips, holding me to his mouth as I thrashed demanded and battled for my attention.

His voice vibrated against my core. "Stop thinking. Just feel."

The bite to his words had me obeying as if I had spent a lifetime being trained to react to it rather than just having heard it for the first time twelve hours ago. The knot at the base of my neck loosened first. My shoulders and back dropped back down to the mattress. The giant birds fluttering in my stomach calmed, and my legs release the hold on Matteo's head.

"There you go," Matteo cooed as he slid his fingers into me. "Turn it all off and let me make you feel good."

I blocked it all out and concentrated on his fingers and his tongue. He pinched my clit between his teeth and traced circles around it with the tip of his tongue over and over as his fingers got rougher and rougher. My hips moved as if I could suck his fingers deeper into me if I only tried hard enough. With my mind solely focused on what Matteo made me feel, I wanted it all.

Matteo gave me everything I wanted without even knowing it.

It only took a few swirls of his tongue to have me crying out his name as I came.

"Matteo," I chanted as he licked me through the last waves. Then he stood—a serious tent in his pants and sheen of moisture on his upper lip—and stared at me as if he were seeing me for the first time. It was disarming and erotic as hell.

He dropped his pants, and his erection bobbed with its freedom. It looked painfully hard as he climbed up the bed until we were face to face. His lips captured mine, and I opened. Our tongues explored every recess of the other's mouth. I could taste myself on him and while it usually grossed me out, I couldn't get enough of it.

Matteo poured his heart into that kiss while shoving his rock-hard erection against my pubic bone.

His hand snaked between us so he could gather the evidence of my orgasm, using it to coat himself. We watched together as he aligned his dick and pushed inside.

I gasped at the invasion. Matteo was of average size and a little on the thick side, but I swore it felt as though he shoved twelve inches deep inside me.

"Argh." He groaned, throwing his head back so I could see the muscle strain in his neck. "So tight, Nat."

My breath lodged in my throat as all the nerve endings in my lower body reignited.

He pulled back and rocked into me again. And again. Each thrust harder than the last. I couldn't catch my breath around the kisses and onslaught of sensations raging through my vagina. I was suffocating in pleasure. My walls quivered, trying to grip Matteo's length, but he kept pulling back out only to drive in again.

The bones of his hips slammed into the back of my thighs as the hairs from his legs tickled the delicate skin of mine in the most delicious way. He lifted himself up, his upper body looming over mine.

"Come on, Nat," Matteo demanded as his eyes bore into mine. His arms strained on either side of my shoulders. "I can feel it coming. Don't hold back. Let it all out."

He was right, knew I was closer to coming than I did. It all barreled into me at once as the pure ecstasy pillaged through me like Vikings on a village raid.

Our eyes locked as I screamed his name. It'd felt like I'd

rode the tallest roller coaster all the way to the top only to drop back down at one hundred miles an hour into a smooth release. My orgasm came from a place deep inside me and ravaged my body.

It took a moment for my breathing to return to normal, and as it did, I let loose a deep breath, feeling as if a lot was released during that moment. Almost as a catharsis. A tear slipped down my cheek.

"Holy shit," I cursed as Matteo kissed my face, my neck, and my shoulder. Good lord, I came so hard Matteo's orgasm didn't even register with me. "That was intense."

Matteo chuckled as he pulled his hips back, leaving my body. "I'm going to make us some coffee," he said, wiping the wetness of my lone tear away. "I'll give you a minute, and then we are going to talk about what just happened." He gave me a pointed look as he stood from the bed, his erection still strong as he pulled his pants back on. "We're going to talk about a lot, Natalie. No more secrets between us."

He was out of the room before my brain caught up with his words.

There was only one secret that I was keeping from him, and there was no way he could've known about it. I hadn't told a single soul.

As he made coffee in the kitchen, I glanced at the clock on the nightstand. Eight fifteen. Jackson's game was at eleven. I dragged my sex-tired body out of bed and hopped in the shower for a quick rinse while I tried to convince myself that Matteo wanted to discuss something else.

Maybe he was the one with a secret. Did he get a promotion at work? No, he wouldn't have hidden that. We would celebrate that—unless it involved us moving or something.

Did an investment of ours go south? I didn't handle our financial investments; that was Matteo's department.

But none of that would equate to us having the sex that we had.

I wasn't going to figure this out, so I dragged my ass from the shower.

When I exited the bathroom, Matteo was sitting on the bed, his back against the headboard, a steaming coffee mug in his hand. There was another mug on the dresser for me.

"What did you want to talk about?" I asked, going for casual as I walked into our closet to grab something to wear.

"I want to talk about why you've been faking your orgasms for the last few months."

His voice was calm and even, as if he'd practiced saying those words without any inflection, without giving me any indication as to how this conversation would go.

He knew. How could he know? There was no way.

My instinct was to deny. Deny. Deny. Deny.

There was no way he could prove that was true.

I grabbed a sundress off a hanger and went back into the bedroom.

"Matteo, I don't—"

He stood from the bed, cutting off my words. "If you finish that sentence and lie to me, I will be beyond angry. That will devastate me. Right now, I look at this as something you haven't figured out how to tell me. If you lie, then it becomes something else entirely. Don't do that. Not to me. Not to us."

The flush of embarrassment crept up from my toes. It burned as it radiated like acid through every part of my body.

He always smiled at me after sex, kissing me and telling me loved me. I was certain he couldn't tell the difference.

But . . . he clearly knew, so what was I supposed to tell him? That our sex wasn't doing it for me? That I'd been craving something more adventurous? Something more like last night and this morning? He seemed to have already figured that out.

"I . . ."

I didn't know what to say. My voice wasn't there. I couldn't tell him what I needed.

But he was the one who orchestrated this whole thing, Nat.

He seemed to be fine with it, but would my admitting to something he only assumed change how casual he seemed to be about it?

I didn't want to hurt his feelings. I didn't want him to feel inadequate because it was the opposite. He was everything. What if this changed things? What if he felt insulted? What if he never looked at me the same again? There was a reason I hadn't told him.

He ate up the space that separated us, deposited his coffee on the dresser, and grasped my face between his hands. His thumbs swiped under my eyes, and wetness smeared across my skin.

"Don't cry." His voice was soft and loving, which only made it worse. Sobs heaved from my chest as guilt took up residence in every molecule of my soul. I'd been deceiving my husband, the love of my life, the most amazing man in the whole world, and *he* was comforting *me*.

God, that ate me alive from inside out. Feasting hard and fast on my conscience as if it were a flesh-eating bacterium.

I couldn't keep this to myself any longer. There was no way. I had to tell him, but I didn't want to. I didn't want to see his brightness dim, not even a bit, and I certainly didn't want to be the reason for it.

Chapter Six

Matteo

Shit! Tears were not what I intended for when I started this. I wanted to make her feel comfortable. Show her that I could do this, be this person she wanted or needed. The plan was supposed to draw her out of her shell, not push her deeper into it. I hadn't been kidding about what I said, I didn't consider this a lie at the moment, but I could sense she was about to deny what I knew was true. That wasn't something I could settle for, no matter how much I loved my wife. Maybe I shouldn't have been so blunt with her. Maybe I was too aggressive.

"I . . ."

Indecision warred on her features. Her arms wrapped around her body protectively as if she were shielding herself from me of all people. She never needed to hide herself from me, which was the whole point of this entire exercise, but with the way her skin flushed pink all the way to her ears, it was clear she didn't feel the same way.

The tear sliding down her cheek might as well have been an arrow shot through my heart. I hated seeing Natalie upset, and it was a thousand times worse when I was part of the reason for her tears.

"Don't cry." I tried to sooth her frayed edges. I wasn't sure what Natalie was going through, but I felt the need to tread carefully moving forward. My strong, resilient wife reminded me of the runt of a litter of kittens left behind to sink or swim on her own, only she wasn't alone. She just needed to let me in so I could help her swim.

Deep sobs heaved from her body, ripping me apart as I pulled her into my arms, and she buried her face in my chest.

"Please don't cry, love." I stroked her wet hair as it soaked the T-shirt I'd thrown on while I waited for her to come out of the bathroom. "There's no need to cry."

Her fingers clung to my shirt as if were her life raft in the storm she waged in her mind. "I'm sorry," she murmured. "I'm so, so sorry."

"What are you sorry for?"

She looked up at me with so much emotions swimming in her brown eyes. "For this. For me. Because you are everything, and it's me. It's me. It isn't your fault."

Jesus! I had so many things to say to her, but she needed to explain first. I was running on assumptions and, eventually, that could turn into trouble.

"Nat, love, I need you to open up. You need to let me in for this to work. I need to know what's going on."

Her lips turned down into a frown. "I didn't want to hurt you."

"Seeing you like this," I explained, sweeping a chunk of wet hair off her face, "knowing something is bothering you and you not letting me fix it is hurting me."

She blinked as her eyes volleyed back and forth between mine. "Natalie, I promise you. It will all be okay. Once you finally get it out into the open, you'll see that."

She took a deep breath. Then another. Then another. Her lips parted as she let the words escape on a bated breath as if they were the worst betrayal of all. "I'm bored, Matteo."

It should have stung, and for some men, it would have, but not so much for me. All I wanted was a happy life with a happy wife. If that meant kinking up our sex life, I could take one for the team.

Fear and remorse swarmed her eyes. It was as if she was waiting for me to drop my arms and step back from her, as if I were going to shame her and walk away.

Instead, I smiled, letting her know that I wasn't hurt or mad or upset. "I know."

Her brows pinched together. The brown in her eyes swirled as her lips pouted. She opened them to say something but then closed them. She opened them again and repeated the pattern two more times before asking, "How?"

I kissed the tip of her nose before grasping her hand and leading her to the bed to sit. I grabbed our coffees off the dresser and handed over hers because we were still on a time limit and Natalie definitely needed to drink at least one full cup of coffee to function correctly. Maybe I should have had her drink that before we started this conversation.

"Because I know you, love." I smiled, standing in front of her while she sat. "I knew you were faking it from the first time."

She shook her head as if she could make that statement untrue.

"No," she muttered.

I nodded. "Yes."

"How?" she asked again. My revelation reduced her to one-word sentences.

"Simple," I replied before bringing my mug to my mouth. The coffee had no taste as I drank because my focus was on Natalie and only Natalie. "I know what you look like when you come. Your acting skills were commendable, but you forgot one thing."

Her fingers curled tighter around the mug cradled between her palms. "What's that?"

"You closed your eyes," I told her. "You never close your eyes."

"Okay, but how did that mean I was bored?"

"I didn't know you were bored. I just knew you were having to fake orgasms. I knew something was wrong, but you never said anything." I raised an eyebrow, but when she didn't offer up an explanation, I continued, "I waited and waited until I couldn't wait any longer, so I snooped through your iPad to see what I could find out."

There were no traces of anger on her face. Her shoulders didn't stiffen. She barely moved except to shake her head slightly as if the pieces still didn't fit together correctly. "But I never said anything to anyone, how could you have known?"

"Your search history was a big tell."

The pink returned to her cheeks but darkened to a deep rouge. She stammered over her words, tripping over her tongue, trying to find something to say as if she even needed to explain herself. "That was . . . I mean—you were never supposed to see that."

Taking the coffee from her hand, I put both of our mugs back on the dresser. I sat next to her and took her hand in mine and shook my head. "Why not? You don't have anything to be ashamed of. There isn't anything wrong with wanting a little spice, love. All you had to do was tell me."

Her eyes glistened. "It didn't start out that way. At first, it seemed more like I couldn't concentrate. My mind wouldn't stop thinking about the kids or work or laundry. We were always rushing. I had a hard time getting into it. Not all the time but often enough that I started faking. I didn't want to hurt your feelings. I didn't want you to think that you weren't enough for me or anything, but I couldn't stop imagining myself as those girls in the videos."

With a thumb, I wiped away a tear that hung from her lashes. "We're humans. We're supposed to grow and expand our horizons. Even in the bedroom. It's healthy. Keeping things from me is more hurtful than your honesty. I'd like very much for you to tell me what's been going on."

She seemed to have an internal battle for a few moments as she looked down to the hands wringing in her lap and back to my eyes. "What do you mean exactly?"

"Tell me what you fantasize about?" I clarify and let my lips tip up in a grin. "As you can see, I'm not opposed to the idea of playing them out. I just need to know what you're thinking about. What you want. There's no judgment from me, love. All I want to do is make you happy. Making you happy makes me happy. And, in case you were wondering, last night was absolutely amazing. I wasn't sure how I'd feel being in that role, but I liked it. A lot. It was hot. There are no other words to describe it."

"What role is that?"

"An Alpha," I said with a flick of my wrist. "Or whatever you call those guys from your books."

"My books?" She chuckled. "You read them?"

"Just a few," I admitted, trying to look chagrin. Reading her books was the slightly embarrassing truth of how far I'd go for my wife. "You and the girls always talk about how much you love the men in them. I figured that could give me some insight into what was going on in your head and what you were looking for."

"Wow, you really went all out on the research, huh?" I shrugged. "Why didn't you just ask me like you are now?"

"Because I wanted you to tell me." I paused and gave her a pointed look, letting my eyes convey some of my frustration with her and her secret. "And, when you didn't, I figured you were convincing yourself that you were the problem. I needed to show you—as well as see for myself—if this was something you wanted." I paused again. "Or if we were dealing with something else altogether different."

The unspoken question hung heavy and ominous between us. Did she want this or did she want someone else? I was steadfast in my confidence in our relationship, but having Natalie confirm it couldn't hurt the situation.

She picked up my question without the words and shook her head. "I love you. *You* are who I want. It's just I was stuck in my head, imagining all these different things. I kept thinking about what it would be like if you smacked my ass or pushed me down and just had your way with me or . . ."

"What if there was someone else filling you with me?" I gave her a cheeky smirk. I knew she favored that kind of porn, and one of the books she had recently read was about best friends who shared a woman.

She didn't return the smirk, clearly too stunned to form words, so I cut her a break.

"What?" I stood and pulled her up with me. "You seemed to like those videos best. And you had quite a few highlighted sections in that ménage book. It isn't a big deal. We have plenty of time to figure out if you really want it. What we don't have much time for, however, is getting to Jackson's game."

She shook her head, still slightly bewildered by the chain of events of the morning. It seemed to me that she was still a little uneasy with the whole situation. I didn't want that. I had some time to adjust to her wants, to embrace them. She needed some time to do the same. To understand that nothing was going to change in our relationship because of this. I pressed my lips to hers and then smiled, giving her the out I knew she needed at that moment. "You don't have to lay it all out now, Nat. We have time. But stop hiding it from me. Talk to me when you figure out how to put it into words."

Chapter Seven

NATALIE

WE PARKED IN THE SCHOOL parking lot and made our way over to the stands to grab a spot to watch the game. I watched Matteo's back as we walked—his step was a bit more upbeat than usual—and attempted to wrap my head around all that'd transpired since last night.

Matteo acted as though he hadn't dropped a huge bomb on me this morning. He explained some new assessment software the company rolled out at work yesterday as we pulled through the drive thru of my favorite coffee place. He ordered me another coffee and a chocolate croissant, passing it over with a smile. His thumbs tapped the steering wheel as he sang along with Cold Play as if he didn't just tell me that we had all the time in the world to figure out if I wanted to bring in another man for a threesome.

Did I wake up in the *Twilight Zone*?

Truthfully, I couldn't make heads or tails of anything. My brain was muddled with thoughts of my being with Matteo and another man at the same time. He didn't sound the slightest bit jealous when he threw the suggestion into the hat as if it were a restaurant we were considering eating at.

The cool late-March breeze blew as Matteo turned back,

looking over his shoulder for me. I had fallen a bit behind, unable to get any part of my body to work properly since we left the bedroom.

"Come on, slow poke."

I picked up the pace, and he grabbed my hand and pulled me into him. He kissed my temple. "Did I fuck you silly? You really seem out of it."

I gasped with mock indignation. Matteo was a well-spoken man who, even in his worst of moods, rarely swore. For him to say the mother of all bad words at the entrance of a crowded field where anyone could hear him was unthinkable.

Appearances mattered here, and Matteo asking if he fucked me silly was scandalous material.

A laugh bubbled from my lips. Apparently, I found this alternate universe amusing and continued rolling with Matteo's free spirit, listening ears be damned. "And you don't seem at all like a man who just offered his wife another man in the bedroom."

Matteo saw my laugh and upped the ante to a deep chuckle. "Of course, that's the part you choose to focus on, huh? One-track mind over here." He waggled his eyebrows, and I swatted his chest. "Seriously, though, I hope that isn't all you took away from that conversation." He bent and pressed his lips to mine in a quick kiss. "I just want to see you happy, love. If that's something you want to explore, I want to explore it with you. But, right now, I just want to cheer on our son and spend my Saturday with my family." A conspiratorial grin tipped his lips. "And maybe watch you squirm a little when you sit. I know you have to be a bit sore. We haven't gone at it like that since college."

I raised a brow. "Maybe not even then."

His laugh had me smiling as I walked away toward the blenchers.

"I'm not against spanking your ass for real," he cautioned with a bit of promise as he caught up to me. "We could find out just how much you like having my handprint on your behind. Last night was just a prelude to the main show, baby."

My eyes widened, stretching with my shock.

My mother-in-law's voice broke through my sexual haze like Miley on her wrecking ball. "Yoo hoo, Matteo. Natalie. Over here," Michelle called as she waved her hand to make sure we saw her.

Get your shit together, Nat. You're acting like a teenager who just got the attention of the most popular boy at school. This is your son's lacrosse game.

Matteo and I had a quick, silent conversation with our eyes.

His narrowed. *This isn't over.*

My brows rose. *I hope not.*

His head tilted. *You're going to get it.*

And then we were off to join his parents and Emma in the stands.

"Hello, darlings." Michelle kissed our cheeks as we sat. "Did you guys have a good night?"

I snickered as I bent to kiss the top of Emma's head. Matteo tossed me a wink before replying, "The best."

I swear my ovaries just fluttered with that wink. A freaking wink. And since when did Matteo wink at me?

This whole bizarre universe had me on edge. A very fine edge that resulted in my fawning over my husband, who had suddenly slipped into the shoes of a man I didn't know. I looked forward to finding out who this new man was. My whole being felt off kilter as if I had just gotten off one of those crazy spinning rides at the carnival where the floor drops out and you're suctioned to the wall.

I was in a daze when I sat on the cold, hard bleachers. So, it was more of a plop than a sit, which resulted in a jolt of tenderness whizzing through me. I sucked in a quick breath, and Emma turned her head. "You okay, Mom?"

Matteo cast me a knowing look over our daughter's head and smirked. "Yeah, you okay, Nat?"

I donned the biggest grin I could. "Peachy. I tried a new exercise routine yesterday. I'm a bit sore after using muscles I never have before."

Matt's eyes darkened and smoldered, and we picked up our silent conversation from before.

I shrugged. *What can I say?*

He sunk his teeth into his bottom lip. *You aren't going to be saying anything when I make you pay for that.*

I shrugged again. *I guess we'll see.*

Emma's eyes volleyed between the two of us, and she huffed in the way only an irritated teenager-in-the-making could. "What's going on with you guys? You're acting weird, and I have friends here. Please stop."

Matteo and I laughed at the same time. I was fairly certain it was in that moment that the stress of trying to figure out this new dynamic in our relationship lifted. Matteo smiled more vibrantly than he had in years, and I felt lighter than I had in months. It seemed that having this huge, weighted secret off my chest made me see my life and my husband in a new way. A new way I was content to enjoy.

Chapter Eight

Natalie

My nails bit into the flesh of my palm as I tried to keep my cool. I had this conversation with artists before, but it never got any less stressful or any less insulting. I was tired and cranky. It had been a long day, and I still had dinner to cook and laundry to wash.

Bastien was a madman at work. He was an artistic pain in the ass. The first whine of "Natalie!" came at ten o'clock this morning. His red wasn't the right shade. We needed to find a new supplier *immediately* because our current one couldn't tell the difference between wine and burgundy. Spoiler alert—he got the color he wanted. I checked the order form. Then he called me because his brushes weren't clean enough. Considering he was the only one who used them, cleaned them, or generally touched them, it was his fault they weren't to his satisfaction. Then his easel was wobbling. It was complaint after complaint. When Annetta arrived, it was more screaming—only in French.

That was what Bastien needed to spark his creativity. He needed to throw a fit and act like a spoiled child. He needed to yell at people to get his blood pumping and claimed it was how the magic happened. The man may have been an artistic genius, but he was hard to tolerate when he was in these moods. A cloud of tension filled the air like humidity—hot and sticky. We had the new gallery opening in Portland in four months and Bastien was behind schedule. Annetta kept on his ass all day about focusing on painting and not being a diva.

All afternoon, my shoulders were tense, bunched up around my ears as I tried to get through my day unscathed.

The last thing I wanted to do was argue with a client who wanted to complain about commission rates when the only thing I wanted to do was go inside, put my sweats on, and get started on dinner before the kids got home. Was it too much to ask to leave the stress of work at work?

So much factored into how successful a gallery was in attracting top-quality art and potential buyers. We maintained a website, created post cards publicity announcements, and bought advertising. We had employees and maintained the physical gallery. Any gallery worth a damn was doing all those things. Metro was worth a damn. I loved my job, and I cared about art. For artists not to want to pay for all my work to help their careers was a major hot button for me.

My button was already pushed before this call. The tension I thought I left at the gallery crept back into my shoulders as I resisted the urge to smack my head off the front door as I entered the house.

Nigel Beckman was a sculptor who made brilliant assembly sculptures. We had several of his bronze works on display—a pair of which sold just this morning—but he wanted to get mad about fees. "Nigel, whenever an artist complains about paying gallery commissions, I tell them the same thing: you're viewing the commissions as money we're taking out of your pockets. But that isn't how this is. You're paying Metro to market your art. You know to expect the fees when you agree to work with us."

He huffed and interrupted my speech. "Fifty percent is too high, and you know it. What are you doing besides allowing my sculpture to sit on a column in your building? Thirty is sufficient for that kind of service. It isn't like you held an event in my honor."

"We help your work stand out in a sea of beautiful art all over the world," I remind him as I hung my coat and bag in the hall closet and resisted the urge to slam it shut. I maintained my cool when what I really wanted to do was scream at the top of my lungs and punch Nigel Beckman in the throat. "If the gallery is selling your work for you, we earn our commission and you know it."

It costs money to market work, hold events, and get people in to buy pieces.

Every time I had this conversation with an artist, which was at least five to six times a year, my blood boiled. I respected and appreciated their work, but they didn't respect mine.

"I didn't say you didn't deserve to be paid." He scoffed indignantly. "I said fifty is robbery. You gave me the bare minimum of work so thirty is more than enough."

I yanked my scarf off and tossed it on my bed. Thirty percent to a gallery was the equivalent of leaving a server ten dollars on a hundred-dollar check. He was also forgetting that for every piece that didn't sell, we didn't profit either.

Do not snap at a client. Do not snap at a client. No matter how ignorant they are acting.

The front door closed, alerting me that someone was home. It was quiet, though.

He signed a contract with us to show his pieces. He could go elsewhere if he was no longer happy. I was done with this conversation "You are more than welcome to try a consignment gallery if you are unhappy with our agreement. Just keep in mind, sales are never easy and the tighter the economy gets, the more difficult it becomes. Let me know what you decide, Nigel. Have a good night."

I disconnect the call and grabbed a pillow from the head

of the bed. Smothering my face in it, I screamed in attempt to release some of the tension overtaking my body. I flopped down on the bed and screamed again.

A body brushed up against my bent-over ass, and his fingers gripped my hips. "What's wrong, love?" Matteo asked as his hands quickly abandoned their spot on my hips and drifted down to the apex of my thighs. "You seem stressed."

His voice was full of sarcastic mirth.

"You think?" I guffawed into the pillow. His finger stroked down and rubbed over my clit. I turned my head back to look at him.

God, he looked amazing.

His tie was loosened, hanging down. The top two buttons of his dress shirt were undone. The arms of his jacket seemed a bit snug, but it looked good on him. His eyes were mischievous and empathetic. He was sorry I was having a bad day, but he also wanted to play.

"Where are the kids?"

He massaged my mound with the pads of his fingers.

"Scotty's mom is dropping them off." He pulled his tie from his neck with his free hand. "She asked to switch days with me earlier. Tomorrow, she has an appointment. Emma is catching a ride from student council with them."

His ministrations were starting to draw all the stiff tension in my body toward my core. He dropped the tie on my back and grabbed one of my wrists. His fingers left my clit, and he grabbed the other arm. With scary quickness, Matt had my hands bound behind my back.

From what I could tell from over my shoulder, Matteo was just staring down at me. Probably enjoying the view of his handy work. Stepping back, he unbuttoned my slacks and yanked them down before his finger played between my lips, toying with me. "I can probably relieve some of this stress for you. At least twice if we hurry."

It was too hard to stay still. I squirmed, trying to get more from him. Excitement moved through me, and no matter how much I tried to temper the anticipation, it was as though my subconscious was bypassing my conscious. It wanted a break and Matteo was offering it.

"Please," I whimpered as he skirted around my entrance, rubbing up and down but never slipping a finger inside.

"Please what?"

"Please put your fingers inside me."

His pinky was resting on my nub, barely moving as his two fingers dipped into me. "Like this?"

My moan echoed off the walls in response.

"Have you been a good girl?" he asked, rubbing along my front wall. He yanked on the tie around my wrists as if he knew I would try to move them.

His thumb circled my back entrance at the same time as he squeezed in a third finger. My body stiffened as if a whole other part of it was activated for feeling. My pussy burned, and I tingled under his thumb. I hissed, but it was a sound dripping with approval. "Yes."

"You good?" he asked, curling his fingers inside me. My eyes rolled back as undiluted pleasure coursed through every single atom of my being at once as if someone just plugged me in.

"God, Matteo." The "o" in that word may have been a bit over enunciated as I came. Hard. And wet. I heard the squelching and felt something sliding down the inside of my thighs. Matteo dropped to his knees and licked up my leg to my slit as if I were a line of salt for a tequila shot. My body still shook with pleasure as Matteo grumbled something into my core about 'fucking beautiful.' After shocks kept buzzing through me as Matteo freed himself from his pants. His cock slid in like he owned my pussy, which I had no objection to. He thrust a few times and then used the leverage of my tied hands to pull me back into him.

"That was incredible, love," he murmured from behind

me. "I didn't know if I could make that happen. I should've known that you are perfect in every way. Next time, I want you to squirt on my face."

If it meant coming that hard again, sign me the hell up.

"God damn." His fingers dug into my waist as he tried to hold on. "You're gripping me like a vise."

I wasn't actually doing anything but laying there and absorbing everything Matteo was giving me.

All those sensations melded into one another, coming together for one big performance. And it was going to bring down the house.

Car doors shut in the driveway.

"You have about three seconds to come before the kids come barreling in here," he informed me as if I didn't understand that. "I'm not stopping until you do. So, I suggest you act fast."

I heard the kids thanking Scotty's mom in the driveway.

Slap.

"Focus, love," Matteo demanded.

The tip of his finger prodded my back hole. Matteo spit and as soon as it landed where his finger was, he used the added moisture to help him push inside.

It was too much but just enough.

The pillow and the sound the front door made as it slammed open muffled my scream. The kids' racket of coming in and dropping their shit hid my orgasm from their ears. It was intense but quick.

The ringing in my ears ebbed as I heard the kids calling out for us.

"Mom," Emma yelled.

"We're home," Jackson added.

Matteo smacked my butt and whispered, "Go clean up in the bathroom. I'll stall 'em." He made quick work of stuffing himself back into his pants.

I scurried across the room into the bathroom. I even

giggled a bit. My bad day had practically been erased by a quickie with my husband.

On the other side of the door, I heard Matteo chatting with the kids. I used the bathroom and fixed my hair.

"Mom will be right out," he said. "But clean up for dinner because it should be here soon."

The kids were gone by the time I opened the door, quirking a questioning brow at their father. "Dinner will be here soon?"

He smiled and nodded. "Yep. I ordered pizza while you agued with whomever. I heard consignment and figured you were having *the* talk with an artist. That means lots of wine and an episode or two of *Ozark* tonight. Maybe a little more dick. No cooking for you. Unwind, love." He dropped his voice, making it gravelly. "Tell Daddy . . . what happened?"

Saliva spit from my mouth as laughter burst out. "That's so gross." I practically gagged. "It's so creepy. Thank god I already came. I think my vagina ran and hid from 'Daddy'."

"Don't worry," he continued with the same tone, "after some wine, she'll be begging for Daddy."

I shook my head just as the doorbell rang. "So wrong. So wrong."

Chapter Nine

Natalie

The view of the sunset from Norah's back deck was stunning. Lately, I'd found more and more about life beautiful. It was amazing what a bit of good dick could do for a woman. I'd heard about those couple's sex challenges over the years. Claims that spending thirty straight days connecting with your partner through sex would strengthen your relationship.

Matteo and I made our own version of a deeper connection. We explored each other's minds and bodies. Our bond was strong before, but I felt closer to Matt, lighter and freer, than I ever had before. It was as though we had the new thread between us that made all the other threads brighter and more vibrant—like the sunset before me.

"I'm going to run to the bathroom," I told Penelope as she stood next me on the deck. "I'm going to grab another glass of wine. Do you want me to grab you one too?"

She glanced down at her watch. "Sure, why not? It's only seven. I've got time before I need to drive."

I smiled. "Coming right up."

We were celebrating Norah's birthday. About a month ago, Derek, Norah's husband, approached us and asked what we thought about him throwing Norah a big surprise party. He wanted to do her birthday up big but wanted to surprise her. Considering Norah loved being the center of attention, a big ass surprise in her honor would make her year.

I admired his dedication to "big". He was going all out. Their backyard had a great view of Lake Washington, and Derek hired people to put on a firework display for her. There had to be about fifty to sixty people milling around, completely unhindered by the unusually warm mid-May evening.

Glancing around the expansive yard, I spotted Matteo standing with Norah's husband and a few men. I had no doubts that he would leave the party with a new client. He always seemed to find one at every large party we went to. A minute later, I found Emma in the pool, which was heated to a warm ninety degrees, playing volleyball with some of the other kids. They were going to be a bit chilly when they got out of that water.

My eyes roamed through bodies until I found Jackson sitting at the end of the pool, his feet hung over the side and a pretty girl sitting next him. Hmm . . . that was interesting.

Turning my head back toward Matteo's direction, our eyes met and I pointedly glanced to where our son sat chatting with a girl. A proud-dad smile sprawled Matteo's lips, and when he looked back at me, I raised an eyebrow. He would be sitting Jackson down soon to have the girls talk before our son got too much bad information from his friends.

My heart hammered just thinking about how soon we would need to have the sex talk with our kids, though I didn't worry too much about Emma. She wasn't going to let boys hinder her path to perfection.

Shaking that parental nightmare from my mind, I remembered my need for the bathroom and another glass of Pinot Noir.

The hustle of the party filtered out as I slid the patio doors closed behind me. I savored the moment of quiet. Derek and his family owned one of the prominent legal firms in Seattle. Every event or get together they had was always top-notch. Caterers, cleaning crews, a pool crew that made sure it was clean and had enough floats and tubes all flittered around working their butts off.

There were three different bathrooms on this floor, and I chose the one off the beaten path. I slipped down the hall toward the guest bathroom near the garage. I hated the awkward "just a minute" you called out whenever someone knocked on the door while you were in there.

I flicked on the light and was just about to close the door when a hand gripped it and pushed it back. A frightened squeal pushed past my lips a second before I saw it was Matteo who squeezed past the door and close it behind him.

"You scared the hell out of me. What are you doing?" I glared at him and tried to calm my breathing.

His eyes sparkled with mischief. "You, in a second." He inched closer until I was backed up against the vanity. "I've been watching you flittering around the yard all afternoon in that cute little dress. Every now and again, I'll catch little glimpses of your creamy ass cheeks poking out of your bathing suit underneath." He caged me against the marble of the sink. "It's been driving me mad all day."

My core clenched at the thought of Matteo watching me all afternoon, at the thought of where all that watching had led his thoughts. "We're at a party, Matt." I tried—sort of—to push his hand away from my hip and the tie of my bathing suit. "I came in to grab wine and I have to bring one to Pen."

"Fuck the wine, Natalie. Penelope can grab her own." His voice was low and gritty. The same tone that he had learned would get him whatever he wanted from me. The same tone that made my nipples pucker like eager and needy beggars on the street corner looking for a dollar. His eyes dropped to them. "Seems like your body agrees."

The top of my dress was halter style, giving him the easiest access on the planet to my nipples and he took full advantage of it. His nimble fingers slid the material of my dress and bathing suit top down with ease, and his tongue swirled the distended peaks.

My head lulled back, savoring the zings of sensations shooting to my clit. Matteo had become the master of playing my body. We'd tried so many things I didn't even know I wanted to try. It didn't matter what it was, Matteo made sure to make me sing.

He knew every button, no matter how small, and he knew exactly how to press it.

He knew whether to go hard, soft, or barely touch me.

He knew just the right amount of breath to breathe in my ear to make my knees buckle.

I had become the puppet, and he the puppeteer

He fingered the tie of my suit bottom at my hip, pulling the bow free, allowing the material to slide down my legs and pool around my feet.

His finger had precision accuracy as he strummed my clit in an upward motion, ripping a low moan from my throat.

"Matteo—" I said, aiming to be a voice of reason. "Someone could hear us."

He pulled his mouth from my deliciously sore nipple and smirked as he plunged a finger into me. "Then I guess you better be quiet or embrace the fact that anyone who walks into the house in the next ten minutes is going to hear me fucking my wife over this sink until her pussy creams around my cock."

"Shit." I shivered, equal measures of thrill and trepidation filled me.

At first, the idea of someone hearing us embarrassed me. But then the thought of someone out there getting turned on by listening to us having sex made me want to fling open the door and let them watch.

Matteo ground the heel of his palm against my clit and growled in my ear. "Do you like the idea of people hearing you, darling? Is that why your pussy is drenching? What dirty thoughts were crossing your mind, Natalie?"

"I was thinking about opening that door and just letting them watch." I panted as Matteo vigorously rubbed the sweet spot on my front wall. "Wondering how hot it would be to see someone making themselves come while watching us."

"Jesus," he grumbled, grinding his very hard erection against my hip. "The things that run through your dirty mind are going to get you fucked so hard."

My orgasm hit crescendo as Matteo spoke low in my ear about me getting off seeing a stranger come while watching him fuck me, and it crashed down on me as he told me to imagine the cries of another woman coming, wishing she were me, wishing that it was her Matteo was bringing to climax. My shoulders slumped as I struggled to drag oxygen into my lungs.

Matteo withdrew his fingers from my body and licked them, clearly enjoying the taste of me on his tongue.

His hard-on was evident in his shorts, and he made fast work up freeing it. "Turn around, love."

When I braced my hands on the sink, he flipped my dress up over my ass, spread my ass cheeks, and plunged his cock into me.

"Oh god," I moaned without any inhibitions. Matteo savagely howled. "Yes."

It became apparent that neither of us cared about people hearing us in here. Matteo rutted into me, pumping and pumping. He wrapped my ponytail around his fist and pulled my head back.

"Eyes, love," he gritted. "Watch us in the mirror. I want to see them when you come all over my cock."

Our eyes met in the mirror, and my husband appeared beautifully untamed. His knuckles were white. His teeth were clenched. His biceps flexed. He was a skillful savage, making the most of every thrust.

I watched, transfixed as his body moved behind mine. He delivered each thrust with a precise intent—to make me scream.

"Let them hear you, love. Let them hear how hard I can make my wife come."

Every muscle in my lower body tightened. My nipples rubbed on the cold marble of the sink. My breathing became rugged, and my voice turned hoarse. Matteo's fingers gripped my waist, holding me to him as he circled his hips, grinding his dick inside me.

My eyes closed and I gave myself over, hungering for the bliss he was driving deeper inside me.

A sharp sting to my ass had them flying back open, finding a sight hot enough to have me flooding the bathroom floor. Matteo scowled, his eyes filled with a passion burning hotter than Hades and the underworld. "Look at me while I fuck you, Natalie."

Good god! I stared at Matteo in the mirror and wondered where this inner beast of his had been hiding. His neck corded as he slammed into me so hard my hip bones smashed against the vanity.

"Give it to me, Nat." He panted as he snaked a hand around and flicked my nub. Once, twice, and then I fell, over the cliff and down, down, down. Matteo ripped himself from my body and milked his dick to a finish, his hot cum spraying all over my ass. I was unable to tear my eyes from him as he watched each drop land, every one feeling like a brand on my skin. The fire burned hotter around Matteo's pupils, as if the idea of marking me brought him to a whole other level.

Then the bathroom was quiet except for the sound of our heavy breathing. The air was thick with sweat and the smell of sex. Matteo began opening drawers until he found a towel.

He cleaned off the mess he made on my backside and

smirked at me, his green eyes sparkling. "I figured it was better that way than you having to walk around with me dripping out of you at a party."

I giggled—yes, like a schoolgirl who just did something naughty she knew she shouldn't have done. "How considerate of you."

He tossed me his signature grin and knelt. "I'm romantic like that." He pulled the bottoms of my suit up, kissed the curve of my hip, and then tied it into place.

I spun, tossing my arms over his shoulders. "You're something." I smiled and pressed my lips to his. "We need to get back out to the party before Penelope or the kids come looking for us."

Matteo adjusted himself inside his shorts while I fixed my top. When we arrived in the kitchen to grab the good wine I knew Norah kept above the refrigerator, Norah was leaning against the center island, waiting for us with a knowing look on her face.

I could already feel the heat creeping up my chest. "What's the matter?"

"*What's the matter?*" She mocked and quirked one of her perfectly arched blonde eyebrows. "You were worried about Penelope and the kids but forgot about the lady who lives here." She snickered. "I want to be pissed that you just sexed up my bathroom, but at the same time, I can't begrudge you because that shit was so hot." Her eyes bounced between Matteo and me. "I didn't think you had an ounce of filthy in you, Matteo. And you, girlfriend"—her eyes cut to me, and she pinned me with a sharp look—"have been holding out on me. We need to have a discussion. Soon."

A deep chuckle emanated from Matteo. "On that note, I'm heading back out."

Bastard.

He left me with a best friend who had a mountain of questions in her eyes. "One of you is disinfecting my bathroom, and since Matt just skipped out . . . I guess you're it." She told me as Matteo slid the glass door open. His laugh filled the room before he closed the door behind him.

Double bastard!

That romp had been his idea, but I was the one who got stuck cleaning the bathroom? But damn was that orgasm worth it.

"Ugh," Norah groaned. "I can smell the sex on you and hear you reliving it in your mind."

I, at least, had the decency to pretend to appear embarrassed, but if I were honest with myself, I wasn't really embarrassed at all. That was something I was going to have to unpack later.

"I don't know what that was." She pointed down the hall back toward the bathroom. "In all the years I've known that man, I can count three times I've heard him curse. And when he did, it was nothing like *that*. Never once have you mentioned that your husband likes to bend you over in random bathrooms and demand you let them hear how hard he makes you come. You've been holding back from us."

"You're right." I couldn't lie when she heard it for herself. "I haven't told you or Penelope what's been going on with Matteo and me. It all just unfolded, and I've just been holding on for the ride. But I'll explain, I promise. Just not now, it's too long of a conversation to have here with everything going on."

She cocked her head, pursed her lips, and then sighed. "Damn, talk about a cliffhanger."

I patted her back and smiled. "In the meantime, let's go find those Oreo ball things I saw the caterers bring in earlier. Oh, and grab the bottle above the fridge."

Matteo gave me a conspiratorial wink as I joined him on the patio, one Oreo ball in one hand, wine in the other. "Looks like you got away unscathed."

"She still has a bathroom to sanitize," Norah corrected as she breezed by us.

Matteo's rich laugh wreaked havoc on the lower region of my body. Discovering these hidden versions of him gave me a heady rush. The Matteo who followed me into Norah's bathroom and screwed me with abandon and then laughed about it was not the same man who had been sleeping next to me a few months ago.

Was he just discovering these parts of himself or had they been there all along?

I guess he could be asking the same questions about me.

I knew I was asking them about myself

"What are you thinking about so hard?" he asked, nuzzling my neck.

I searched out the kids before answering. "I was just thinking about whether this is a new part of us that didn't exist before or if we are just uncovering another layer we didn't know was there all along," I replied after finding Jackson and Emma in a group with some other kids across the yard.

His brow furrowed. "Does it make a difference either way?" he asked, wrapping me in his arms and shifting me closer to his body. He rested his chin on my head and sighed contentedly. "As long as it's a journey we're taking together, I don't think it does, love."

His words turned over in my head for the rest of the night. During the fireworks, I glanced over at him and the kids sitting next to me on the lawn. The three of them looked up at the colors filling the sky while I looked at Matteo. His face radiated with joy. Emma squealed, "Look, Daddy!" as a red and purple firework exploded into a heart shape.

In that moment, I could almost see an image of her at five years old, saying the same thing to her dad at a different fireworks display. Then, just as suddenly, it was gone, and I had decided that Matteo was right. It didn't matter whether these new sexual beings were new parts of us or parts we just discovered, just so long as we experienced it together.

Chapter Ten

Matteo

My smile was bright and eager when Natalie left the bathroom wrapped in a towel. I made sure the kids were good. Emma was wrapping up a math project. Jackson just packed away his homework and was sitting down for his hour of video games for the night. The bedroom door was locked, and we were in the clear for some fun. "I bought you a present."

"Oh yeah?" she said over her shoulder as she padded across the room to her dresser. "What is it?"

Curious wasn't a strong enough word to describe my feelings about seeing Natalie's reaction to the gift. Intrigued. Excited even. I felt like a child on Christmas morning as I handed her the box.

"Lush?" She read, her eyes widening as she got to the smaller print. "A remote-controlled vibrator?"

I nodded, anxiously awaiting some sort of clue as to whether she was on the same page as I was about this.

This whole sexual exploration thing might have been Natalie's need, but it was quickly growing into something that I wanted too. I might've been nervous that first night I walked us onto this path, but since then, I felt a comfort in stepping into a side of me I didn't know existed. Natalie and I connected on a level so much deeper than either of us could've ever thought.

I spent a decent amount of time thinking about different nuances to add to this new avenue of our relationship. This . . . was *one* of them.

"I can make you come without ever touching you." I encroached into her space. "I've already downloaded the app on both our phones and iPads."

Her pupils dilated, and her breath hitched alerting me that the idea of this appealed to her in some way. "You want to explore your exhibitionist desires, and I figured we should start small before jumping into public performances."

There was one big secret—or surprise perhaps was a better word—I kept from Natalie. It would open a series of doors to endless possibilities for us, but I wasn't quite ready yet. This new side hadn't entirely taken over the old Matteo. I still had a lot of research to do on that surprise and I wasn't quite finished with that process yet. Plus, we needed to walk before we ran.

Her towel slipped down, exposing the tops of her breasts, nearly forgotten at the thought of something new to try. "What are we going to do with it?"

"First"—I ran my middle finger down the length of her arm and then dropped it to the apex of her thighs—"I'm going to play my fill with your little sweet spot. Then I'll slip that"—I tapped the box—"inside you. I'll sit in the chair I set up over there and watch you come in the middle of this bed with your legs wide open for me."

She panted lightly against my skin as she rested her forehead on my chest. Her nub swelled under the barest of touches, the promise for more hanging in the air. A moment later, the towel dropped to the floor, and Natalie reached for my erection. She stroked it up and down through my pants, gripping it firmly. "You'll come with my eyes staring at your pretty pussy. Seeing each clench of those walls as I add more and more until you can't take anymore."

She was so hot her heat was almost burning my fingers. "Jesus, Matt."

Her fingers squeezed my cock as she desperately wanted to come, so I pulled the box from her hand and popped the lid off. It was fully charged, I made sure earlier.

"Open," I instructed as I pulled the device free. Her lips parted, jaw slacked, and I slipped the hot pink oval over her tongue. "Get it wet, love."

She licked it as if it were my cock. I didn't miss the fire in her eyes as she stared at me. Her annoyance over not coming a moment ago flared as she ran her tongue around it, trying to temp me, to make me crazier for her. It only fueled my desire to sit back and watch her come from my hand without me even touching her.

I gave the tail of the toy a quick tug, and Natalie dropped it from her mouth. "Lift your leg onto the bed or turn around, your choice."

She turned and leaned down on the bed resting on her elbows. She glanced back over her shoulder with her desire practically throbbing through her veins. Her nipples were taut. Her skin flushed. Her chest rose and fell in rapid succession. A glisten sparkled from the apex of her thighs.

My dick throbbed.

Natalie shifted from foot to foot as I slid the soft silicone into her. I pulled it back and slipped it in again and again until I had the app up on my phone. I turned the vibration on. As the buzzing woke up Nat's nerve endings once more, I pushed the toy in deep and stood back to admire the view.

"Climb onto the bed, love." My voice was hoarse. All the blood had rushed down to my steel-hard length.

She followed instructions and crept slowly to the center of the bed, giving me a prolonged look at the swollen flesh between her legs. I stepped back until my legs hit the chair in the corner of our bedroom. I sat; my focus still glued to the center of Natalie.

Tapping the screen on my phone, I changed the steady vibration to a patterned wavelength. Natalie jumped in reaction and then her arms weakened a tad as her head lulled down.

"Lie on your back and spread your legs for me, love," I told her as I freed my straining dick from my pants. "Get comfortable."

She did as I asked, and when she centered herself in the middle of all the pillows on our bed, I saw she was approaching another level of arousal. One thing I quickly learned during this whole new foray was that it wasn't necessarily what we were doing that turned Natalie on, it was that I was the one doing it to her.

We'd been dabbling in this spiced-up life for a little while, but on the nights we just had plain old sex, Natalie still came all the same. I worried that regular missionary style sex would never get my wife off again, but I was wrong. It was as if, just by my being more in tune with what she wanted, she was free.

I stroked myself up and down to the sight of her wetness. "Tell me what you feel, sweetheart."

She caught sight of my straining erection, swollen and veiny in my hand and she was transfixed, my command forgotten. So, I upped the intensity of the toy.

"Argh." Her body spasmed slightly. "I feel full and a lot of pressure on my g-spot."

My hand dipped down to cup my balls. "You're supposed to feel it there."

She moaned my name as though it were her salvation.

I tapped my finger to the screen, and she moaned again. "Does that feel good?" I asked but didn't wait for an answer. "Let me see you strum your sweet little clit, love. I can see it begging for attention."

She complied, and as she circled her finger around it, I

fisted my length again and stroked, no intention of stopping until we were both satisfied. "You look beautiful. I could only imagine what someone would think watching you enjoy yourself like I am now. And a man sitting here, watching it all unfold and wishing he could suck one of those rosy tips between your fingers into his mouth."

Her breathing sped up as if it were in the last lap of the Daytona 500. Her back curved slightly as she arched off the bed, and her fingers moved faster and faster.

"Do you know what the best part would be, Nat?" She was so lost in the fantasy, seconds from coming, she couldn't answer. "When he growls as your sweet little cunt"—the vulgarity of that statement set her off as her orgasm barreled through her body—"clamps down on my fingers. When you come for me, jealousy flares in his eyes for all to see. He wanted to feel everything I felt. He wanted your heat, but it's mine. It's all for me, and I don't want to share that with him. He should be happy I let him see the beauty of you coming at all. You're a fucking goddess."

Her attention focused solely on me as she lifted her fingers from her clit and licked them, mewling. A few tugs later, I was coming onto my stomach as Natalie slowly pulled the toy from her body, putting on a show just for me.

A half hour later, curled up in bed together with Natalie's breath ghosting through my chest hair I asked, "Did you like that tonight?"

In the past, I'd never thought to ask about what Natalie liked and didn't like in the bedroom. I wouldn't make that mistake again. I never wanted her to sneak off to the shower to achieve her orgasm again.

She nodded. "It was different. Something I never would have thought of. I didn't even know they made remote controlled things like that."

I chuckled. "I can't wait to see how you react when we use it in public."

She picked her head up and looked at me. "I just need you to remember something, this is all new and exciting and fun, but it was you who made that hot for me. It's exploring these things with you that's the turn on, eo. Don't ever forget that. I don't want this with anyone but you."

My arms banded around her tighter. I already knew this, but it was still good to hear it from her.

"Also," she continued, "that little scene you described? Good god, my heart almost beat out of my chest thinking about how damn hot it was. Don't be surprised if I ask you to recreate that in the future."

Chapter Eleven

Natalie

The restaurant was alive with noise when I arrived fifteen minutes late for our seven o'clock dinner plans. "Sorry, babes." I smiled at Norah and Penelope. "Thank you for waiting."

I kissed both of them hello, and the hostess brought us through the dining room to our table. "Enjoy your meals, ladies."

"I needed an evening with you guys after my day today," I told them as we shuffled into the booth.

We'd been doing this since UW, meeting up to discuss our days. We did it almost every day at college and as we grew older, the frequency became less and less but we always tried to meet at least once a month for a sit-down dinner. We met in the Greek Life at the University of Washington. The three of us all pledged the same sorority. It was history from there.

Norah snatched the iPad used for ordering and started tapping on the screen. "I have been craving their bacon cheddar burger all day. I'm getting hangry ladies so let's order quick, please."

Norah passed the tablet around the table so we could add what we wanted. Beside the incredible food, the other thing we loved about this restaurant was that you ordered everything from iPads, and it was all brought over when it was ready. It made it so that we could catch up without any interruptions.

Norah was tapping her foot under the table and drumming her fingers on top. "You seem anxious," I commented, my gaze on the beat her fingers were tapping out.

She shrugged and pulled her hand down to her lap. "I could use a drink, and I'm starving. You know how I get when I'm hungry."

"Mmm hmm," I murmured. She did get cranky when she hadn't eaten, but I had a feeling she was waiting to pounce on me about that incident in her bathroom. We still hadn't had the conversation I promised her two weeks ago. Norah wasn't the most patient person, so I knew it was only a er of time before she brought it up.

"So, did you have a bad day or something?" Pen asked as we waited for our drinks to arrive.

"Not bad." I shook my head. "Just so much unnecessary stress. Bastien is almost unbearable some days. He was in another one of his moods."

The server arrived with our drinks and I took a generous sip of my Long Island Iced Tea the moment she placed it down.

"I swear that man has all of my upper back and shoulder muscles in a permanent knot lately. I feel like a giant ball of tension. This new gallery and showing may turn all my hair gray by the time it opens." I continued.

Norah's eyes glittered with mischief. "I'm sure Matteo could help relieve some stress. He probably has plenty of ideas of how you can *give it to him.*"

I groaned. I knew she was waiting for the perfect segue.

Norah cackled like the evil step-monster in a Disney film. "Did you really think that I wouldn't bring it up first chance I got? You're lucky I let it go this long."

I hung my head and groaned, then quickly snatched the iPad to order myself another drink. Thank god I'd taken an Uber so I didn't have to drive home because a decent amount of alcohol would be needed to handle Norah and Pen throughout this conversation.

Penelope glanced between the two of us, looking out of the loop. "What are you talking about? And give what to Matteo?"

Norah's smile stretched her entire face as she turned to Penelope. "Her orgasms. Seems Natalie here has been holding out on us. You should have heard them in the bathroom at my party."

My cheeks were definitely reddening. I cut my gaze to Norah. "No one told you to stand at the door and listen."

She raised her brows. "No one told you to defile my bathroom and moan loud enough for the whole first floor to hear you."

Touché.

Penelope huffed. "Can you please fill me in?"

Norah was more than happy to oblige. "Well, during my party, I went inside to grab a sweater, and imagine my shock when I heard hot sex happening in the half bath across the hall from the laundry room."

Penelope's eyes bugged, and she looked over at me. "You and Matteo?"

"Oh my god, Pen." Norah gushed. "I wish I had my phone to record it. Matteo was all, 'Let them hear you scream,' and Nat was moaning like a porn star. Then Matt was like, 'Give it to me.' It was so weird to hear. I honestly didn't know he had it in him."

Norah fanned herself and made goo-goo eyes as if the Hemsworth brothers were standing in front of us. She had a shit-eating grin on her face. "They were completely shameless."

Penelope's shock had faded, but her curiosity had been

flamed. "You had sex in Norah's bathroom? You little hussy!" She laughed with no judgment in her voice. "I can't believe you didn't care who caught you. What if it was Emma or Jackson who came inside and heard you? What in the world brought that on?"

"One day, Jackson and Emma will understand that you take good sex whenever and wherever you can get it." I shrugged. "Until then, I'm sure we could find them a good therapist."

Norah smacked her hand down on the table. "You owe us some juicy gossip, Miss Not-So-Goody-Two-Shoes. How did sex in my bathroom come about?"

I took a generous sip of my drink before admitting, "Things got a bit boring, and we've been spicing it up."

Our appetizers arrived, and my stomach growled. I wasted no time pulling a potato skin onto my dish. I felt their eyes burning holes into the top of my head as I focused on my food, but I was in no rush to spill all the beans just yet. I was hungry and wanted to stuff my face a bit first.

Penelope huffed her annoyance with my lack of verbal vomit first. "No way," she protested. "You aren't just going to give me that. I don't have a sex life. I live vicariously through you two. I need details. It isn't fair Norah got the live action version, and I can't even get a decent recap. Start spilling, woman."

Penelope's been divorced for two years and still hadn't stepped back into the dating pool. Her ex-hubby moved on before they were even officially divorced. He found love in a twenty-five-year-old blonde model, and Penelope has felt inferior ever since.

I rolled my eyes as I cut into the potato. "Dramatic much. Things had become dull between us. Although, I guess I can't really say that since we had been doing the same stuff we'd been doing for years. It just wasn't working for me. Matteo figured out I was . . . disinterested, and then we started this bucket list of things, I suppose, that we want to try, and we've been checking them off."

Pen seemed a bit mystified. "Doing it in Norah's bathroom was on your sex bucket list?"

Norah looked skeptical. "What do you mean by disinterested?" She made air quotes around *disinterested* as if it were a code I was using.

"No, it wasn't. It was spur of the moment," I answered Penelope before addressing Norah, "I'm almost embarrassed to admit." I sighed as I thought back to the morning Matteo flat out told me not to lie to him. "He said I wasn't as good at pretending as I thought I was."

Pen gasped as if she were watching a telenovela.

"Don't take this the wrong way," Norah said, which meant she was going to say something kind of bitchy, "but you kind of sounded like someone who was faking it from what I heard. Like Meg Ryan in *When Harry Met Sally*. How was he able to know the difference?"

"Could you keep your voice down?" I snapped and leaned in closer. "The whole restaurant doesn't need to know my business."

She shrugged unapologetically and raised her brow in anticipation of my answer.

"He said I was closing my eyes and that was how he knew. Apparently, I don't close my eyes when I come."

Penelope scoffed. "You mean to tell me that Matteo could tell you were faking it because you closed your eyes? That's insane. No dude pays that close of attention to his wife's come face."

I hadn't wanted to point out she didn't have the best frame of reference, so I answered simply. "Matteo has always been an attention-to-detail kind of guy. After he figured it out, he waited for me to tell him about what was going on, and when I didn't, he took things into his own hands."

A few servers arrived a moment later with our food, and

we fell into a comfortable silence as we ate. I could see the girls' minds swirling. My last comment was pretty vague, and I knew they had follow-up questions, so I laid out the rest of the story.

"He snooped through my iPad, looking for clues. He thought maybe I was discussing why I couldn't . . . umm . . . finish with you guys or someone else."

"But you never said a word to us," Penelope cut in.

"Yeah, why didn't you tell us about this?" Norah added.

My eyes were glued to my alfredo as if it was Van Gough's *Starry Night*. "It was kind of embarrassing," I finally admitted. "Matt's great, and it felt wrong to say that I was bored. Guilt weighed heavy on me. As if I was betraying him or something."

Norah nodded as if she understood. "Then what happened?"

"When he didn't find anything in text or email"—I lowered my voice—"he checked my browser history."

Both girls' eyes widened with surprise. "No . . ."

"Weren't you pissed?" Norah asked, her fork paused mid-air.

"No." I shook my head. "Matteo wasn't snooping because he was trying to find me doing something wrong. He wanted to help me fix the problem. I'm actually glad he did because it took the uncertainty and guilt out of it for me, and I was finally able to tell him what I was feeling."

"I don't know," Norah disagreed. "I think I'd be super pissed."

That was an understandable response, and it was how most people would probably feel. The fact that I didn't wasn't wrong; it just wasn't the standard. Each person's situation was different. "I think that if he had been accusatory when he asked me about it, I probably would have gotten defensive. But he didn't. He planned an entire night to show me that he could be who I needed. He even read a few of our books for tips and ideas."

A sly grin spilt Norah's lips. "That explains all that dirty talk."

Penelope chuckled. "I guess that's kind of sweet."

The way he understood me and accepted me was more than sweet. It was everything. God, I loved that man. "I'm glad that it happened this way. I love that he went so far to show me what I mean to him. It's really been freeing to explore this with him, hence the sex in Norah's bathroom. We couldn't help ourselves."

We laughed and then remembered our food. The sauce on the pasta was buttery and rich, and I almost choked on it when Penelope turned to Norah and asked, "So, is dominant Matteo hot? I keep trying to imagine it, and I can't. I just can't place Matteo and dirty together."

Norah nodded her agreement with the sentiment as she chewed and swallowed her burger. "Right? If I hadn't heard it, I wouldn't have been able to picture it either. But he has this whole Clark Kent vibe. Like he has this bad-ass persona only Natalie is allowed to see. Although after I caught them, he had an I-don't-give-a-shit-that-you-just-heard-us bounce in his step."

"Hello?" I attempted to cut in. "That's my husband you're talking about."

They ignored me. "On a scale of one to ten, how hot is Matteo's sex voice?"

"Since that was the only time I'd heard it, I don't know how he sounded before all this, but hearing him tell Nat to let everyone hear her come, I almost creamed my panties. I was worried I might've gotten pregnant just listening. It was low and deep and controlled. Definite seven for me since he isn't my type. If Derek spoke to me with that same voice, my ovaries would explode."

She emphasized her point with hand explosions. "Good to know." I snorted.

Penelope's gaze flew back to me. "What other crazy stuff have you done?"

We spent the next twenty minutes discussing the adventures of Natalie and Matteo. I was almost ashamed to admit that seeing the excitement in their eyes made me want to tell them more. This wasn't just a story; this was my amazing husband and me. I was proud of us.

Chapter Twelve

MATTEO

Nerves rattled in my gut. Dessert had just been served, and it was time to move onto my after-dinner plans. Plans that Natalie had no idea of.

I'd spent weeks planning and researching and thinking about all the details. I'd hired a babysitter, made reservations, and vetted everything I could about where I was taking Natalie.

It was time to share the part two of the night with her.

Nat dug into the slice of triple-chocolate fudge lava cake and moaned around her fork. "This is so good. I really love that you did all this. Date night was a really good idea."

Last week, we had our first Date night. We hired the neighbor's daughter to come hang out with the kids for a few hours one night a week. During those hours, Natalie and I could do whatever we liked.

"This is only the first half."

She paused, licking the fudge from the fork. "What else are we doing?"

"I have a surprise for you, and it requires an open-mind."

She considered things for a moment then asked, "Are we going to a strip club?"

The waiter chose that moment to come by with the bill. He smirked and said, "Have a great night."

I pulled enough bills from my wallet to cover the check and tip and tucked them into the billfold. "Nope," I told her, stealing the last bite of the chocolate cake before she could eat the whole thing.

She eyed me wearily. "Where are we going?"

My tongue darted to the corner of my mouth and licked the bit of fudge there. "Do you know what surprise means, love?" I questioned.

She grumbled the entire way to the car.

"Some women would kill for surprises and date nights, you know?" I reminded her as I pressed the unlock button on the key fob.

She sighed as she sat inside and closed the door. "You're right. It's just you know how impatient I am."

"Trust me," I told her, starting the car. "You'll see in fifteen minutes."

Immersion was a private club a few blocks over from the city's sports complex. I called every reference the owner gave me. I asked Derek to have his firm look over the NDA with a fine-tooth comb. He also was able to get his PI to dig into it to see if there were any legal issues, police reports, or complaints. Their record was clean, and the NDA was the real deal and enforceable by law.

That was what I wanted to know most of all. I wanted to make sure that no one would be able to reveal any personal information about the members. If I was going to take my wife to a fetish club, I wanted to make sure that if we saw anyone there, they couldn't tell everyone about it without risking a lawsuit.

Immersion wasn't a publicly known club. There was no listing for it in the yellow pages. There was no website. No Facebook or Instagram page. It was strictly a word-of-mouth club. I only learned of it because it came across my desk as part of a client's portfolio. One of the owners was a client of my firm and I was the one who ran the numbers for adding it to his insurance policy.

The building was nondescript and looked like a regular factory on the outside. It was a production plant back in the day, but it had been renovated into a sex club.

"Is the surprise an empty building?" Natalie chuckled. "Where are you taking me?"

You couldn't tell it was a club from the front. In the back of the building, there was an underground parking deck where the valet parked members' cars. It helped keep identities more secure. Since members of the upper echelon of society came here and their cars were easy to tie to them, it was an extra layer of security.

"Ready to keep that open mind?" I asked pulling the car to a stop in front of the door as directed in my membership contract.

She nodded.

"The name of the place is Immersion," I started, wanting to see if it rang any bells.

Natalie wasn't familiar with it. "Okay, what is it?"

"A sex club," I confessed. "Or a fetish club—I mean . . . I guess it's the same thing either way. But this is a place where people come to explore their sexual fantasies and desires."

It was a risk to have done this as a surprise, but I was anxious to see her reaction. Natalie *could* freak out, but I didn't think she would.

If she didn't want to do this, I would be totally okay with it.

"Wow, really?" Natalie asked, gazing up at the average, red-bricked building with amazement. "I didn't even know we had one of these close by."

"That's the idea." I smiled. "I'm pretty sure they're all over, but in order to know where, you have to know the right people."

She quirked a brow. "And how do we know the right people?"

I laughed. "It was chance." I explained how I came to know about this place. "But don't worry, I had Derek look over the paperwork and check to see if there was anything nefarious attached to the club ."

She gasped. "Derek knows?"

"He's a prominent criminal defense attorney, love. Do you really think this is going to skew his view of us? People he's known for a decade? Besides, I'm sure Norah has told him some of whatever you've told her."

She nibbled on the corner of her thumbnail. "True."

"Are you ready to go in?" I asked. "We are supposed to have our tour tonight."

As we exited the car and waited at the door, I took Natalie's hand and explained what we were doing for the evening. "One of the owners will give us a tour of the facilities and explain how the club operates."

Immersion was owned by three men. Cole Masterson, Leo Hughes, and Max de La Cruz. Part of the membership process was meeting with each man. Cole Masterson called me after vetting my application. He asked a few questions including if I was planning to bring any guests, and then after adding Natalie's information to the guest list, said I'd hear from one of his associates. Leo Hughes called to inform me my application was approved for probationary membership. I was assuming I'd be meeting Mr. de La Cruz today for the tour. He would go over how things operated, explain the rules, and so on.

The door opened and a large man in a black suit greeted us. "Mr. and Mrs. Collins, welcome. Mr. de La Cruz is expecting you."

My assumptions were correct.

Nat gripped my hand as we went inside. The entryway was dark, but I saw the blinking red light of a camera in the corner by the ceiling. The large entry space housed three doors, and the man directed us to the one off to the left. "The door ahead is the exit. The door the right is the security room. Please follow me this way."

Natalie's hold on my hand tightened as we walked into what looked like a waiting room area. A sofa and two chairs sat around a table in the middle of the room. There were a few more doors, one of which opened and man in a navy suit exited. He extended his hand and smiled. "Natalie, Matteo, thank you so much for joining us here at Immersion. I'm Max de La Cruz."

I took his hand in my free one. "It's a pleasure."

He winked as he moved onto Natalie. "I sure hope it will be." Her cheeks pinked a bit, and she tucked her hair behind her ear.

"If you're ready"—Max turned and walked toward one of the doors—"let me take you inside."

There were two wings off the waiting area. One led to Max and his associates' offices and a small clinic-like area for emergencies. The other led to the club itself.

My attention was focused more on Natalie's reactions than seeing it all for myself.

On the other side of the door there was a vast lounge area. A bar was set to the left and took up a major portion of one corner of the room. In the far corner opposite the bar, sofas lined the wall, and groups of over-stuffed chairs sat around tables. A handful of people were already drinking and chatting, but most of them were watching the show that was happening on the platform stage in the middle of the room. A woman was bent over a bench of some kind, and a man smacked her ass with what I thought was a flogger.

"This is the main room," Max explained. "This is the only bar, and we only allow alcohol consumption in this room. There is usually one demonstration a night. We like to think of it as a tutorial for some of the less experienced members or those interested in trying something new."

Natalie's eyes were bouncing all over the room as if she didn't know where to look.

"We ask that no sexual acts, other than those on the stage, be performed here. Consider it almost like the landing zone, a place for people to relax and have a drink before and after visiting the other rooms."

Max gestured at the hallway off to our right. "The layout is basically a figure eight with this room as the middle. There are two halls on both sides of this area, each one leads to a different section of the club and they connect on the other side. Let's take a looksee, shall we?"

We followed him down a corridor lined with numbered doors. Some were open; others were closed. "These are regular rooms available for sex. The front sections are empty rooms you can use for play. We have some standard items available in all the rooms throughout the club." He checked the items off on his fingers as he went. "Condoms. Lube. Wipes. Towels. Water."

We continued walking. "These rooms are glory hole rooms, and what is and isn't allowed is always marked on the whiteboards." He pointed to one. "This is a straight female who allows vaginal penetration only." He pointed to another. "This one is a gay man available for anal penetration."

We reached the end of the hall and Max guided us around the corner. "This hall connects to the other on this side," he explained as we followed him around. "In this section, we have the exhibition and voyeur rooms." The walls were mostly glass. Some rooms had curtains drawn. Others had them open. There was currently a man licking a woman from behind in one. "The walls can be retracted to open the rooms to doubles if you'd like. These rooms work well for group play as well since they are larger. The specialty rooms have a variety of toys and apparatuses you can use. Paddles, floggers, and spreaders are the cabinet in the corner. Just make sure that you deposit whatever you used in the sanitation bins and please press the green button near the door on your way out. We clean the room between uses. We have dildos, anal plugs/beads, vibrators, and the such as well. Those are charged to your account and are yours to take with you when you are done."

We walked down the hallway back toward the main room. "In this room"—he pointed to a door—"there's a stripper pole. And the two across the way have sex swings in them."

Natalie snickered, and when I glanced over at her, she winked and waggled her eyebrows.

"Sounds like something has someone's interest," Max jested.

I smiled at Natalie's playfulness. "Seems like we know where we're going to start."

When we reentered the main room in the center, Max continued, "We have a dress code. No jeans. No sneakers. No hoods. Business casual to any degree of formal you'd like. Every new member starts off with a three-month probation period. If we see any type of behavior we do not condone or misconduct of any type, you will be removed from the club and your membership terminated. There are cameras in all areas of the club and every room, except the bathrooms. The recordings are kept on an isolated server and are automatically erased at the end of each day so long as nothing illegal has occurred, which has never happened. In the event something like that happening, the injured party may request a copy for legal purposes. We pride ourselves on being a safe establishment. We are membership only and have the best cyber security money can buy."

Another one of the big selling points for me.

He clapped his hands and stopped in front of the third passageway. "This side has a much more sinful taste." We started down the hall and most of the doors were open. "We have a suspension room. A punishment room complete with stocks." Each room looked like a different version of the Red Room in the *Fifty Shades of Grey* movies I watched before talking to Natalie. "These have various devices such as a whipping table, spanking bench, and Saint Andrew cross."

We rounded the corner as we did on the opposite side. "Down this hall, we have the theater rooms. There's a wide variety of porn on demand in there. You can masturbate, have sex, or just watch." He holds a hand off to the right as we get about halfway down. "We have a sauna room, a wet room for anything that gets messy, and the showers and lockers are down here. That pretty much rounds up the tour."

Max walked us back to the bar. "Do you have any questions?"

Yes and no. I had a ton of questions but not for Max. I was more interested in Natalie and what she wanted to do. "Not at the moment, but I will definitely reach out if any arise."

"Wonderful." He clapped me on the shoulder. "It was great to meet you, and I hope you enjoy yourself while you are here."

As he walked, a few people stopped him and there was small talk but none of that interested me. I turned back to Natalie. "So, what do you think?"

"It's . . ." She trailed as if she were waiting for the words to come. "I can't believe you set all this up. It's unbelievable."

"Unbelievable bad or unbelievable good?"

"Good." She smiled. "Undeniably good."

It was the answer I was hoping for, and my lips pulled into a wide smile. "Want to try that sex swing out?"

Her eyes lit up, and she nodded eagerly. "Absolutely."

Chapter Thirteen

Natalie

For two days, my time at Immersion stayed prominent in my mind. It was there, and it wanted to be acknowledged with all the other things happening in my life.

Really, all I wanted to do was call my two best friends and tell them all about it. One thing I learned about exciting things happening in your life was that a major part of the fun was sharing that excitement with loved ones. When it came to my sex life, Norah and Pen were the only ones who would share in my excitement.

Except, I had to fly out that morning to meet with a few people about the gallery location crew in Portland. We opened in two months and details needed to be finalized before the major work could be started. I spent yesterday finishing some last-minute things at the Seattle gallery and then had to prepare everything for two days away from home that I hadn't had time to call or see either of them.

At lunch, I texted them that we *needed* to have a FaceTime call because I had something to tell them. As soon as I finished up my meeting and returned to my room, I ordered room service and jumped into the shower. Half an hour later, I was wrapped in a plush robe, as I munched on the bread that came with my dinner and sipped a glass of Pinot Noir.

The sound of my ringing phone filled the room as I waited for the call to connect. Norah and Penelope's face joined mine on the screen.

My voice was sing-song-y as I smiled at them. "Hey!"

"Don't you look comfy," Pen lifted her glass up in "cheers".

I snugged farther into the robe *and* the super soft chair as I nodded my agreement. " I am. This thing is so thick. It's unbelievable."

Derek popped in the screen for a moment as he brough Norah a glass of wine. "Hi, ladies," he called out as he kissed Norah's cheek.

"Now that I've got the essentials," she said before she paused and took a sip from her glass. "What's got you demanding a meeting?"

Pen's head bobbed. "Yeah, what's up?"

I bit my lips between my teeth and try to contain my smirk that wanted to creep out. Tapping my finger on my chin, I pretended to think about what I wanted to tell them. "There's so much to tell." I giggled, knowing that what I was about to tell them would really knock their socks off.

"Tell us, bitch." Norah laughed. "You know you're dying to say whatever it is so do it."

She was absolutely correct. The words burst from my mouth. "Matteo joined a sex club."

Penelope squeaked. "What?"

Norah gasped. "No way! Did you go yet? What's it like?"

I nodded a bit enthusiastically as the wine sloshed in my glass. "It's hard to put into words. It's a combination of a bar, dance club, and motel. I'm not allowed to tell you much, but it was amazing."

"What did you *see* go on there? I can't imagine how much shit you saw." They asked a bunch of questions about things that happened there, and I answered what I felt I could; things like were people just having orgies all over and did people crawl around on leashes. Respectfully, neither of them asked which club or who I'd seen there.

"So, what have *you* done there?" Penelope asked as she popped a couple of grapes into her mouth.

"We've only been there the one time so far," I told them. "We didn't see too much, but we did try out the sex swing. I think going there should become a regular part of date night."

Norah leaned in, intrigue coloring her face. "Did the swing live up to all the hype?"

The ache in my core could still be felt when I moved in certain ways. I relished it. "It was a great time."

Great wasn't the most accurate word to describe using that swing. Maybe something along the lines of spectacular would have been better. If I closed my eyes, I could easily picture the way Matteo's fingers clung to the straps holding me in as he used them to swing me on and off his dick.

A pensive look overtook Penelope's features. "What else is on your list? We never asked that during our last conversation."

"We don't have an actual list, you know?" I chuckled and took a drink of my wine.

Norah scoffed and lifted her brows. "Yeah, you do. Maybe not a physical one, but you definitely have a mental one."

"Come on, tell us," Pen encouraged, excitement livening her tone.

"Well, we've talked about a few things we want to do . . ." I paused, wondering for a moment if my friends were going to think about me any differently after we had this discussion. Rational thinking flew back in, and I remembered that these women would love me if I shaved my head and took up a career as a mime.

Penelope looked as if she were a kid arriving at the gates of Disney World for the first time as she placed her phone against something to prop it up across from her. She crossed her legs and cupped her wine glass between her palms. "Start with the big stuff first. Like what's number one on your list."

I didn't have to think about that much. "A threesome."

"Oooh," Pen murmured as she placed her lips against her glass.

Norah cocked her head to the side. "With another guy or with another girl?"

"My fantasy is with another guy," I said. "I'm sure Matteo wouldn't mind another girl, though." I hitched my shoulder. "He hasn't mentioned it yet."

The thought had crossed my mind. If Matteo was willing to have a threesome with a guy, I had to consider the possibility of him wanting one with a woman. We were playing things by ear here, but I also wanted to make sure Matt was getting his fantasies too. This was a two-way street.

"You guys are seriously considering a ménage with another dude?" Penelope asked. "Who? When? Where?"

She was like a two-year-old who just discovered questions.

I shrugged. We hadn't finalized any plans or anything, so I didn't have the answers to her other questions. "We have other things we need to do before we get there."

"Like what?" Norah asked.

"Well, anal for starters." You couldn't have a threesome like I wanted if you weren't comfortable with anal. "We've only played with toys and fingers. We haven't gotten to the actual sex part yet."

They both looked at me a little funny. "What?"

"You've been together for this long and haven't tried anal?" Norah asked with shock in her voice.

I shook my head. "I didn't think it would be something I liked—"

"Yet, double penetration is number one on your bucket list?" Penelope asked incredulously. "What are you going to do if you don't like it?"

"I mean I've liked everything relating to it so far, so I don't see why I wouldn't like the real thing." I considered things for a moment and asked, "Both of you have already done it?"

They nodded. "When?"

Norah laughed. "I was still in high school the first time. Not the time to try anal, FYI. But I did it in college a few times and throughout the years. It isn't bad. I'm just too impatient to work into it. I want my dick hard and fast. Anal takes time."

"Hence why we haven't gotten to it yet." I changed the direction of the conversation. "I really want to try public sex, too."

The girls shared a glance, and then Norah raised her brow at me over her wine. "Didn't you already cross that off at my party?"

"Still a bit salty that I missed the show," Pen chimed in.

"Depending on your definition of public sex, then I guess you could say that," I explained, tracing the brim of my glass with my finger. "I want to have sex while people watch, not sex in a public place."

Norah crossed her arms over her chest and gave me an impressed grin. "It seems that Matteo isn't the only one who has some increased confidence around here, huh?"

The blush spread through my cheeks like wildfire, but I didn't care. "What can I say? Matt's been taking me to places I've never been before."

Penelope choked on a grape. "Who is he, Aladdin with his magic carpet?"

"Magic cock, Pen," Norah corrected with a snicker.

"Magic everything, girls." I waggled my eyebrows, and we broke into a fit of giggles.

Chapter Fourteen

Natalie

"It's going to be fine, Mom," Emma reassured me with a hug. I swished her not-so-little body a bit harder than usual. "We've been doing this for years. You'll see us in two weeks."

It didn't matter that we'd been sending them off to this camp for three years, I was saying my good-byes to my babies. My heart was sad. It already missed them, and they hadn't even left my sight yet.

The first year they went to Oakville Sleepaway Camp it was for the four-week program. The second, they begged us to stay for six weeks. And then a few months ago, the dreaded request for increased camp time hit us. They wanted to stay the full eight weeks.

All the campers started at the same time, but they left in staggered groups, and Emma whined that they missed so much when they left early.

So, we agreed to the whole summer. They were twelve, going on thirteen, but at the same time, they were still four to me.

Jackson came up and wrapped his arm around my shoulders. As if I wasn't feeling they were slipping through my fingers as it was, my son had to come stand next to me, reminding me that he was an inch taller than my five-two. "She's right, Mom. The first parents' weekend is just around the coroner."

Two weeks wasn't "just around the corner," but I refused to be "that" mom who was a mess at drop-off. The last thing I wanted was to embarrass the kids. Taking a breath, I sucked it up and smiled.

"I know. I'm just going to miss you, that's all."

Jackson kissed my cheek. "We'll miss you too, Mom. But we'll be fine and having fun. That means that you and Dad should go have fun. You're always doing everything for us, enjoy some time to yourselves."

My sweet little boy. He was just like his father, and nothing could make me prouder. "You're a good boy, Jackson."

We stood at the end of the sidewalk leading to the cabins. The kids were itching to get to their friends. We'd already helped carry their bags up, and they wanted to go see who they were bunking with this year.

Matteo reached for my hand, pulling me out from under Jackson's arm and against his body. "I'll keep your mom distracted so she doesn't miss you guys too much." He nodded toward their cabins. "Go on, have fun."

Smiles lit up their faces as kisses and rushed good-byes fluttered all around us. Then they were gone, running out to where all the other kids were grouping.

"How do you plan to keep Mom distracted?" I asked, bumping my shoulder into Matteo's arm as we headed back up the path toward the parking lot.

Matteo smirked as the rocks of the parking lot crunched under our feet. "Well, you heard the boy. You're supposed to have fun and do things for yourself." He clicked the button, unlocked the car, and opened the door. After I sat, he peaked his head in. "We did join a sex club a few weeks ago. There are plenty of ways we can have fun while the kids are away."

I hadn't thought about how much more we could explore with the kids not home. We were about to have eight weeks of living the no-kids life again and a new hobby. Things were about the get interesting.

Matteo got into the car, and his aura might as well have been the sun. "We're meeting Adam for dinner, and then we're going to the club."

The squirm of my butt was involuntary. It was a new conditioned response already. The club meant pleasure. It meant another delicious evening, to join a handful of others, where Matteo made my body sing new notes. "What's on the agenda for today?"

His eyes smoldered. A lightning storm crashed in their depths. "I think it's time my cock becomes acquainted with your ass, no?"

A shiver danced down my back and fluttered deep in my womb.

Well, that was certainly one way to keep my mind off the kids.

Before we made our way to the club, we stopped to have dinner at one of the guys' favorite bars and had a quick beer and burger.

Adam, Matteo's best friend, told us about a structure fire his station put out last week while Matteo attempted to inch his fingertips under the skirt of my dress, trying to start a small blaze of his own. Adam seemed oblivious to me smacking away Matteo's hand. Either that or he was too busy checking out the waitresses' asses.

I'd known Adam as long as I'd known Matteo. He was one of Matteo's two roommates when we started dating. Trevor, who lived in Napa Valley with his wife and two young daughters, was the other guy. Those two were there when we found out we were going to have the twins. Trevor joked that he always thought it would be Adam who knocked someone up, not Matteo. Adam was the clichéd ladies' man of the group.

He was friendly and had a healthy appetite for women. Adam wasn't ready to settle down, and he was enjoying his life as it came. I couldn't fault him for that. Especially since he was good-looking, single, and a firefighter, who was definitely calendar worthy. I understood the appeal. That also meant that his attention wasn't solely focused on us which allowed Matteo to rub my clit through my panties under the table on several occasions.

Then we were on the way to the club where Matteo wanted to have anal sex.

I was impatient and nervy at the same time. We had only gone to the club a handful of times since we joined last month. Date night was our fun "sexy" time.

On those nights, and a few at home, we'd worked on making our way to anal. Just like I told the girls, so far, I'd liked everything. The fingers. The beads. The plugs.

Even still, the idea of a dick in my ass made me edgy.

Matteo broke the thick cone of silent anticipation. His voice was amused. "You seem a bit antsy over there, love?"

There was no point in lying. "I am."

"Good thing we're here." His tone spoke of promises to come.

We headed straight for the bar as soon as we were inside. Matteo ordered a jack and coke for him and a long island for me.

I needed some alcohol to loosen me up. My neck felt coiled so tight it could snap.

We floated away from the bar, looking around until Matteo guided me toward the front of the room. "Let's see what's happening on the stage."

We stood for a few minutes, watching the flogging session, but it wasn't something Matteo or I were into. It didn't get my juices flowing the same as watching a couple—or group—just go at it. It was their fervor and passion that made me wet, made me wanton. I wanted to feel the same bliss she was feeling.

Which was how we found ourselves finishing our drinks and heading down the exhibition hallway. It was a collection of rooms that left you exposed. There were doors, of course, but they were French style and typically left opened for people to see and or enter. Floor-to-ceiling glass panels framed the doors. A thick velvet curtain hung across the top. There was a button that slid them open. People could come in and sit in the chairs in the corners or on the sofa if they wanted to be up close. Or stand in the hall and watch from afar.

We checked it out on our second visit. I was mesmerized the whole time. Some couples allowed viewers to touch during the scenes. Some invited people in. I was turned on by it all.

A beautiful woman with curves I was entirely envious of was pressed between the chests of two men. Their hands were everywhere, her breasts, her pussy, her ass. She pulled her lips from the one man and laid her head back on the other as she moaned under their touch.

I stopped in front of the window and watched with fascination.

My core tightened. It was as though someone pulled my favorite porn genre out and brought it to life.

Matteo stepped up behind me. His fingers slipped under my skirt, making their way to my center. "Tell me what you'd feel if you were her?"

My breath hitched as he rolled my clit between his fingers. "I'd feel their touch. I'd feel their hands. Their mouths. Their breath ghosting across my skin. I'd hear their sounds and how much they want me. How much they enjoy my body."

Matteo licked the shell of my ear and whispered, "What else?"

My knees buckled a bit, but I kept telling him my fantasy

as he played with my body. "I'd feel the energy buzzing between them. I'd feel how hard their cocks are for me."

He rubbed my clit with his thumb and sank two fingers into me. "How hard are they?"

"Like stone." I panted, silently urging Matteo to moved faster, harder. I wanted to come. "I'd feel them everywhere. On my skin . . . in my pussy . . . in my mouth . . . in my ass."

The men guided the woman to the bed in the middle of the room. One man lay in the center, and she climbed over him. He held his cock up, and she sank down on it, riding him. The other man nudged her down, and he licked her ass.

Matteo's voice was thick with desire. "Does she like when he licks her ass?"

I nodded as the tempo of my slowly building orgasm increased. Matteo was finger fucking me while I imagined what it would be like to be the woman being double penetrated.

"Damn, love," Matteo crooned as my orgasm broke and ran through my body. Watching that man slip into the woman's ass and the ecstasy on her face shoved me right over the edge.

Matteo kept rubbing his fingers along the length of my slit. "Do you want to go into one of these rooms? Or the private ones?"

There were a few people hanging around watching. Another couple and a single man were down the hall a bit. There was another woman watching the threesome from inside the room. For a moment, I wondered if they were two couples and she was waiting for her turn. A pang of jealousy hit me for a quick second.

The room behind us was empty and I had no idea what was going on in the other rooms. All I knew was that I wanted to be watched. The idea of these people watching Matteo and me, us making them feel as heated as I did in that moment, made me feel powerful.

"Let's go in the room behind us," I told him as I tore my eyes away from the scene in front of me.

MATTEO MADE ME COME WITH HIS MOUTH BEFORE HE brought me back to the edge with his cock. I stood, bent over the bed, my ass on full display for those watching. He pushed in and out of me slowly as his fingers toyed with my tight hole, stretching it, driving me crazy.

He unsheathed his length from my pussy and licked me from bottom to top. His fingers scissored in my ass as he looked down at me and asked, "You ready?"

"Yes," I practically begged. My voice was high-pitched and needy. He grabbed the lube and spread a healthy amount where he needed it.

As our eyes met again, the green of his eyes vanished. His pupils fully dilated, so all I could see was black. Over my shoulder, I watched as he lined himself up. His tip felt huge and hot at my entrance. I hissed as he pushed in just a bit.

"You okay?" He stopped his forward progress and spoke through gritted teeth as if he were experiencing the same discomfort I was.

It would only last until he fully entered me.

"Go," I encouraged him. "Don't stop unless I say so."

It was the longest ten seconds of my life, but they were so damn worth it as he was finally in all the way. It was a different full feeling and a deeper pleasure. Matteo rubbed my clit with his thumb and slinked his middle finger back into my pussy.

He rocked into me, and my back arched, my eyes rolled, and I moaned. I heard a muttered, "Shit," from the corner and glanced over to see a man jerking off on the couch.

Matteo noticed him too, and I felt the possessiveness in his motions kick up. His hips slammed a bit harder. His finger shoved a bit deeper, and his thumb moved a bit more forcefully.

"Yes, Matt. Yesss." I purred as I hit the trifecta of orgasmic bliss. My clit, my pussy, and my ass all sang a beautiful melody together, taking my body to church as it worshiped at Matteo's alter.

He chased his own release. He roared as he ripped his cock from me and turned me over just before he came. Hot jets of cum landed on my pussy, my stomach, and some even reached my tits.

Matteo bent over me, sank his hand into my hair, and yanked me toward him. His lips crashed onto mine. He was savage—consuming me as if I were the last morsel left on Earth.

"God, I fucking love you." He growled into the kiss as he smeared his cum all over my pussy like a marking, which reminded me that we had voyeurs in the room.

When Matteo let me up for air, I glanced over at the sofa, only to find it empty. Over Matteo's shoulder, I saw a man watching from outside. He raised an eyebrow and smirked at me before heading off.

A half hour later, I smiled at my husband as we waited for the valet to bring our car up. "That was one hell of a distraction."

He kissed the top of my head. "And I've eight more weeks of distractions to deliver. Think of the other ways we could have fun now."

Chapter Fifteen

Natalie

THE ONE THING THAT CONTINUALLY shocked me about my husband, was that through this whole exploration of sexual discovery he was so okay with doing whatever I wanted. It didn't matter what or how insane it may sound to some. My husband was willing to try out anything I wanted while also adding his own little twists. Like tonight for instance. We didn't come to the club with any one thing in mind. We came just wanting to try something new. But Matteo knew I wanted to explore having an audience and informed me he had something he wanted to do with me. That was it.

"Are you ready, Natalie?" Matteo asked. "I have big plans for you tonight, but we can do them without the audience if you've changed your mind."

Last time we were down here, Matteo made my body sing under his touch. He commanded, and it obeyed. My pussy tightened just remembering it. Public sex added another layer to these club experiences for me. I could feel the difference in Matteo when we were in front of people. He became deeper and darker. That was the only way I could describe it. He was like a caveman claiming his woman. I loved it.

Matteo's khakis look a tad tight in the crotch area. "Are you thinking about last time we were down here too?"

His gaze incinerated the remaining tension in my upper body as he looked over at me. "I don't think I've stopped thinking about it all week." Something flared in his eyes. "You were so damn sexy."

As soon as we entered the room, Matteo went right for the cabinet in the corner where all the club toys were kept.

He took out the metal ankle bar and satin ties. "Strip," he'd told me as he tied the straps to the bed. When I was down to just my bra and panties, he ordered, "Hop up, darling."

He tied my wrists to the wrought iron headboard. Then he buckled the cuffs around one ankle and moved to the next. My nipples were standing at attention as I thought about how skilled Matteo seemed with all this stuff. It was as if he committed to learning as much about everything he could.

My heart hammered in my chest as my straitlaced subconscious was telling me I shouldn't be shaking from pent-up excitement, but rather from fear. People were going to be able to see me naked. To see my most intimate parts. To see Matteo do whatever it is that he wanted to those parts. And, I couldn't freaking wait.

Matteo walked to the door and pressed the red circle next to it. When the curtains slid opened, I felt more like we were on a Broadway stage as the next performance rather than in a sex club exhibition room. The anticipation in my belly ramped up a notch when Matteo opened the door, signaling that anyone could walk in and have a seat. As he stalked back to me, his eyes roamed all over my exposed body. His gaze felt like a laser beam warming wherever he looked.

When he reached the bed again, he leaned down and sealed his lips over mine and plucked my nipples through the lace as he spoke. "I want you to turn your mind off, love. Just focus on feeling. Feel me and feel what I'm doing to your body.

I want you to hang on as long as you can. Just trust me, I promise it will be worth it." His fingers danced across my belly down to the top of my panties. A shadow caught my eye in the doorway as Matteo teased my clit. A saw a few faces looking in through the window. My core throbbed with a bit more intensity than before.

Matteo reached his whole hand inside my panties, slinked two fingers into me, and stroked them in and out, arousing my senses before he stepped away to the table where our bag of toys and the remaining piece of ribbon sat. He grabbed the satin and slipped it through the binding around my wrists.

A smirk played on his lips as he angled me toward the edge of the bed. His fingers curled around the metal bar between my ankles, and he lifted it, pushing my legs toward my chest and up.

Thank god for all those yoga and spin classes Norah had dragged us to for years.

"You okay?" he asked as he tied the ribbon attached to my wrists to the bar. I nodded, and he replied, "Hold on to the bar."

There I sat, tied to a bed with my legs tied to my hands. Matteo's eyes burned with an intense passion. I had no clue what he had planned, but whatever it was, I knew it promised pleasure.

He snatched a pair of scissors from the table, and before I could try to imagine what he was going to do, he snipped off my panties, letting the cool air from the room bathe my warm flesh.

My pussy was on full display for all to see. The thought had my walls clenching.

Matteo looked back over his shoulder and chuckled as he ran a finger through my open slit. "Everyone can see how excited you are, darling."

I moaned as he rubbed from my clit down to my ass. Up and down. Up and down.

"How many times do you think I can make you come, love?" Matteo's voice was full of hunger. He licked his lips as though he was ready to chow down at his favorite buffet. "I think I can pull at least three out of you, maybe four if you'll let me."

Matteo wanted to see how far he could push the boundaries.

It sounded fun and scary all at the same time.

I knew that after two orgasms I was spent. After four? I'd probably have to be carried home.

"All this added excitement should make it really easy," he added as he dipped two fingers back into my entrance. "Are you ready to see, sweetheart?"

I nodded. How could I not be?

He growled in response and then bent and licked my clit. He had two fingers massaging the front wall of my pussy, and his pinky was teasing my back hole. It was pleasure overload, and my first release of the night came quickly and with minimal effort on Matteo's part. Igniting my body seemed to have become child's play for him.

"Matt," I whimpered as he continued licking me.

My eyes drifted to the door as a man moved into the room closer and took a seat on the sofa. When he reached down to adjust his crotch, a deep feeling of being desired washed over me. There were two more people in the hall and another leaning against the wall just inside the door, which only added to that feeling.

Matteo stepped back to the table, giving the man on the sofa a front-row seat to my still pulsing core. I felt his eyes probing my center almost like a forbidden caress. Matteo returned with a silver toy shaped kind of spade-like. I knew instantly what it was. We'd spent some time looking into a new one—a bigger one.

He dipped it in a smaller container I knew was coconut oil

and traced my rim with the tip. "Your eyes are begging for it, love."

"Yes."

He added some force. "Then you shall have it."

The cool metal slipped in easily and created the best kind of burn. Matteo was moving it inside me, but I couldn't tell exactly what he was doing. Not that I cared because it felt incredible.

He leaned down and traced my opening with his tongue. "How do you feel?" he asked before licking his way back to my clit.

"On edge," I replied, and he sucked hard on me. Watching the way he ate me—consumed me—was erotic as hell. I relished every flick of his naughty tongue.

Matteo stood, and I missed his mouth instantly. He ran his hand between my folds again and again, only briefly glancing back to the man on the couch, who had taken his dick out and was pumping it up and down.

"Do you see how he's looking at you, love?" Matteo asked, inserting his fingers back into my pussy. His thumb pressed my clit as he curled his fingers forward finding the spot he was looking for. The pulsing ache for more began to take over, and without the use of my arms or legs, I just had to take it all.

My gaze shifted to the side, and the man was jerking his length hard. He looked almost familiar, which should've had me worried considering my pussy was on display, but I couldn't quite place him while Matteo manipulated my body. The man's cock looked angry, but that wasn't my problem.

I was no match for Matt's touch as I lay there absorbing it all. The beginning of a new blast sparked. An earthquake of pure bliss shook me down to my center as it radiated outward from deep in my core. Matteo twisted the plug in my ass and set off a chain of mini fireworks. But they were only a prelude to the main event. A supernova detonated in every cell of my body, but I could still hear Matteo's voice through the noise.

"Feel it," he coached. "Don't stop there. You can go again."

Could I? I probably could, but at the same time, it felt like my body couldn't. I was too sensitive, and my body was ready to shut down.

Matteo's hand began moving more forcefully. He applied a ton of pressure deep inside me with his fingers. He leaned on my lower belly with his other hand. "You're almost there, sweetheart. Embrace it."

I didn't have a choice. I had to embrace whatever he gave. I was at Matteo's mercy, and he had plans of taking me as high and far as he could. We were hurdling into the unknown, and there was no stopping it.

My chest rose and fell rapidly as I panted. It was all I could do in response to the bomb about to blow and turn me to mush.

A familiar tingle and burn scorched through my limbs, and I cried out. My mind finally gave control over to my body. Matteo was quick to cover me with his mouth. He licked and sucked and savored that orgasm as my tied-in-half body convulsed under his attentions. It felt as though it lasted a full minute. I just kept coming, and Matteo knew how to extend it. I felt like a leaky faucet he was turning on and off.

He wiped his mouth with his hand as he pierced me with his glowing green stare. He looked savage, and his stare never left mine as he pulled out his dick. I tried to calm my body, but at that point, it was if my brain was floating beyond me. I got to feel and watch from above as Matteo extorted my body below.

The head of his dick felt enormous as he surged forward, slow and sure. Between the plug and the swelling from the last three orgasms, I couldn't imagine how he was going to get in there. But he did—inch by delicious inch.

When he was fully seated, he leaned down, smashing his lips against mine. "God, I love you," he murmured. "I need you so bad right now," he confessed. "Can you take it? Can you give me more?"

Every ounce of everything was drained from my body, but I would give it my all. "I can try."

A cocky smirk flashed across his pouty lips. "How about I do all the work? Trust me?"

Without a doubt. "Always."

His tone flicked to serious as he began moving in shallow thrusts. "If it's too much, just say stop."

This exploration was just as much for Matteo as it was for me. He seemed to be coming into his own and looking at it as something more than just trying to spice things up for my benefit. He was fulfilling some of his own story ideas here. I loved that. I knew he wouldn't take it too far. He knew what he wanted to accomplish and how to do it. I was just along for the ride. "I trust you."

He dragged out of me and shoved back into me. He was gentle and powerful at the same time. Each jerk of his hips had a target deep inside me. His balls slapped the plug each time he sank deep, bringing my ass back to life. The pads of his fingers circled my overstimulated clit. It was too much yet not enough.

As if he had a gateway into my mind, Matteo bent and closed his mouth around my nipple. His teeth grazed up the sides of it, and a storm began simmering in my womb. The force growing in me picked up speed, and I clasped the bar as tight as I could. I felt like a tight rope pulled taut, and any moment, someone was going to step on me, and I'd snap.

That snap came a few beats later when Matteo slammed into me so hard he hit me so deep that it hurt in the most extraordinary way. His free hand crept down and pulled the plug. It stretched me back open, and I was done for.

My head lulled to the side, and my eyes focused on the man coming on the couch for a second. It was like the calm before the storm.

Then it happened.

I screamed.

I screamed so loud I didn't recognize my voice. Matteo was kissing my face as tears ran down it. A blinding force tore me apart, atom from atom and then let me piece back together slowly.

Matteo whispered sweet words in my ear as I came down. "You are beautiful." Kiss. "That was unbelievable." Kiss. "I love you."

He untied the bar first, letting my legs back down. He uncuffed my ankles, and my legs immediately curled up. My hands were freed next, and then Matt closed the room back off. He returned to the bed and gathered me into his arms, holding me like a precious treasure.

I didn't have much energy, but I had one question I needed answered. "Where the hell did you learn to do all that?"

His chuckle was rich and smooth and the perfect balm to my sore body. "I can only do what you let me, love. That was all you, not me."

I snorted. "I've had this body for thirty-five years and was never able to make it do that."

He bit the bottom of my ear playfully. "I can't wait to make it do that again."

"Easy, tiger." I stopped him with a limp hand on his chest. "I still can't feel my legs, so let's not get ready for more just yet."

Chapter Sixteen

Matteo

The muscles in my biceps burned as I pushed through the last rep. I heaved a harsh breath as the metal bar clinked into the metal hooks and I was able to drop my hold.

Adam cast me a side-glance as I sat up. "Back in college, I couldn't blackmail, beg, or bribe you to hit the gym with me, but now you're coming three times a week. What's changed?"

He was absolutely correct. Back then, if he wasn't in the dorms or at the house or in some co-ed's bed, he was at the pool or the gym. He tried to get me on the workout kick, but it wasn't really my thing. I'd always preferred going for a run over lifting weights at the gym.

Until recently.

In all the books of Natalie's that I read, the men had sinewy muscles. They had bulging biceps and impeccable pecs.

I had been rocking a dad bod. I wasn't over-weight or even really out of shape, I was just soft and dull where I could've been hard and cut.

"Nothing has changed." I stood and grabbed my towel, wiping the sweat from my forehead. "We're getting older. It can't hurt to make sure I stay in shape."

Adam's skepticism painted across his face as brightly as the graffiti mural on the corner building of Hillshire and West Ave.

"One"—he held up a finger—"we're only thirty-five. Two"—he added a second finger—"most people take up running or biking for some baseline calisthenics and toning." He shook his head. "Not a three-day-a week intense muscle packing program. I mean if you don't want to tell me what's up, that's cool. But I'm not buying that shit lie at all, buddy."

It wasn't that I didn't want to tell him what was going on. Hell, I'd have killed for a guy to discuss this stuff with, but I also felt that maybe it was a bit too personal to tell him. It was my sex life with Natalie after all.

But, then again, Nat discussed these things with her friends. Why couldn't I do the same? Norah caught us and had no shame over listening. Plus, this whole thing had been hard to navigate on my own.

"If I tell you"— I looked over at him as he sat on the bench I just vacated—"you cannot say shit in front of Natalie—"

He vehemently shook his head. "Dude, no. If you're about to tell me you're having an affair . . . I don't want to know about it. I like Natalie. I respect her, and I don't want to be complicit in your shit."

"That isn't—"

His neck started turning red as his anger rose. "You have kids, man. How can you treat their mother like that?"

I opened my mouth to try to correct his assumption, but he just kept going, clearly enraged over the idea of my cheating on Natalie. As if that would ever happen. "I stood next to you at your wedding. How could you do this?"

"Hey, dickhead." I smacked the back of his head to get his focus. "I'm not having an affair with anyone other than my wife. But it's nice to know that, despite your desire to screw anything in a skirt, you respect the sanctity of marriage."

"How do you have an affair with your wife?" He looked utterly confused. "And cheating is for cowards. Either work on your problems or end the relationship. Cheating does no one any good."

Adam is a child of divorce, which was brought on by his father's multiple affairs with women he worked with and with one of his mother's friends. His mother was crushed, and his father, well, he wised up too late. His wife wouldn't take him back, and it took a while for her to move on. She remarried about five years ago while his father wound up spending too many evenings with one-night stands and a ton of booze. It all had a great effect on Adam's impressionable teenage mind. He vowed to love all the ladies until there was one who made him only want to love her.

We were still waiting for her to arrive and knock him on his ass.

Taking a deep breath, I started trying to put into words the things happening between Natalie and me. "Natalie was bored. She wanted to spice things up. Have the kind of sex she reads about or watches in porn."

Shock colored his face. His voice was filled with awe as he asked, "Sweet little Natalie? No way." He pondered something for a moment before a serious look darkened his features. "What the hell kind of porn is she watching that's more than a dick sliding into some pussy? Or butt. Is it that dark-ass stuff? I fell down that rabbit hole watching video after video once, and I felt like I needed therapy and a hug by the time it ended."

"Nah," I shook my head. "She's—"

Adam cut me off, his imagination clearly having overtaken his logical side. "She isn't into that snuff shit, right? That's a whole other level of insane shit."

"Jesus, man." I hung my head. "I'm not entirely convinced you don't need therapy. Natalie is not into snuff films or gangbangs or being hung from the ceiling in latex. No kinky doctor fetishes or anything else your head is conjuring. She just wants a little domination, some spanking, hair pulling, dirty talk, that kind of thing."

His brow furrowed as the confusion returned. He was dumbfounded. "What were you doing before if that's what she's calling spicing it up? I mean that isn't anything too over the top. It's all fairly normal stuff."

Damn, if that didn't make something twist in my gut. I guess our sex life really had been boring before. "Normal sex. Nothing was wrong until about six months ago. Then she started faking it."

"No..."

I nodded. "And when I finally got her to talk about it, the whole list of things she wanted to try and the way she wanted to be handled in the bedroom was a big eye opener."

"So, like role-playing type stuff? You pretended to be the plumber or pizza guy or gardener, and she can't pay so she has to *pay* type of thing?"

"That was an oddly specific example, but no, not really. It's more like instead of stopping in fifth gear, I shoved it into sixth. Faster. Harder. More Passion. At first, I didn't think I could do it. That I couldn't be assertive in the way she wanted, but when I saw her reaction to it? It was like I couldn't get enough and pushed her further. See what else we could discover, you know?"

"Wow," he says sincerely before busting out in a fit of laughter. "You just waxed poetically about getting Natalie off. Are you sure you're as assertive as she needs?"

I flipped him the finger. "Fuck off."

"He curses now too." A shit-eating grin plastered across his mouth. "Now all the gym time makes sense. You're trying to get Natalie's attention again. Be all sexy and shit. Ladies always go gaga over some nice muscles."

"That's part of it."

"What's the other part?"

Tossing my towel over my shoulder, I brought it around my neck to the other side and held on to both ends, watching Adam's face for his reaction. "Well, Nat wants a threesome, and I can't be rocking my dad bod for that. Need to make sure I look as good as, if not better than, the other guy."

Adam's facial expression reminded me of one of those cartoon dogs who saw a bone or hot girl dog. His eyes widened as his jaw dropped. He stared at me for a good long moment before he choked out, "You're going to have a threesome with your wife and another dude? Are you insane?"

I doubted many men would be down for something like that, but not everyone had the type of relationship I had with Natalie. I wasn't worried about her falling for someone else. That wasn't what she was looking for.

"I have nothing to be worried about," I explained. "It's just something that she wants to experience, and I'm willing to give it to her."

Adam's voice was incredulous. "You just finished telling me that your wife has been faking it in bed and that she wants a threesome, and you aren't worried?"

My gaze turned hard. "Do you honestly think that Natalie would leave me for a man she met during a threesome?"

He shrugged. "It's possible."

I shook my head. "It isn't. Natalie and I have a strong relationship, which is why we've been able to add this to our lives. I trust her, and she trusts me. The only hard decision is trying to find some third party to trust my wife with."

That was the one thing that was proving to be a thorn in my side about it all. How did I go about finding a suitable third person to be intimate with Natalie? I supposed I could ask someone from Immersion, but I didn't want to have it at the club. That was something too personal, too intimate for the club. I didn't want to do it in the same room where hundreds, if not thousands, of other people did kinky shit. This was an experience that was just for us.

"You aren't . . . like . . . putting an ad out on Craigslist or some shit, are you?" Adam looked truly worried. "I don't want to read about how the two of you were hacked to pieces inside some seedy motel room."

He was starting to stress me out. "Can you be serious for a minute?" I asked. "You asked. I'm telling you. Now, either be supportive and help me think through this or shut up and do your reps."

His silence lasted about thirty seconds before he settled back on the bench, positioning himself under the bar. "I was being supportive. I don't want to see anything bad—physically or emotionally—happen to you and Natalie. Walk me through this while you spot me, please?"

I waited until he had the bar in the air and had started his set. "When I realized that this was something Nat was interested in, I let her know that it was a definite option. She hadn't brought it up again. But last week after we watched a threesome, I saw how much she wanted it, so I've started working on planning one for her."

"Where did you watch this threesome?" he asked as he lowered the bar to his chest.

"I joined a club."

"Which club?" Adam asked, heaving out a harsh breath.

"I joined Immersion a little over a month ago. We've been going there once or twice a week since. Two weeks ago, there was one going down in the exhibition room. We stopped to watch, and the discussion grew from there."

"Okay." Adam blew out. "And?"

"The way Nat explained it to me is this: in her mind, this experience is all about focusing on her. She wants to be brought to heights I could never bring her to on my own. She said it's about feeling two sets of hands, two mouths, two dicks. It's about being in a room with two other people who are wholly focused on her. Something about feeling owned and taken on the ride while only having to feel."

Adam finished his reps and placed the bar back into place. He glanced around, taking in the people within earshot as he sat up. "I can't believe you joined a fetish club and didn't tell me. But that aside, how will this work?" He lowered his voice before asking, "Are you going to let this man actually have sex with Nat or will it be an oral-only type of thing? I mean there are so many ways to pull off a threesome."

"I haven't figured out the details yet," I answered. Truthfully, I didn't know exactly how this was all going to play out. "But she wants double penetration."

"Have you guys already worked up to regular anal?"

I nodded. "We have. I thought it'd be more of a bucket-list type of thing. Something she wanted to experience so she could tell herself she tried it, but we've done it a couple of times. Enough to where I think she can handle this."

His features hardened. His shoulders stiffened, and his voice was stern when he asked, "Will *you* be able to handle it? Are you going to be all right with some other man touching Natalie? Being inside her?"

If I thought there was even a slight chance of my not being able to handle it, this conversation would never be happening because the idea would have been vetoed. He should know me better than that. "It isn't about another man being inside Natalie; it's about working together to bring Natalie to a level of pleasure she's never felt before. That's the goal. That's what gets me going. I can't explain it. Just thinking about seeing Nat go off like that makes me hard. When we tried out the exhibition room at the club, I came so hard, man. Seeing the looks on people's faces as they watched."

"Having some guys watch Natalie come and having some man make Natalie come are two different things," Adam countered. "Listen, I'm not trying to talk you out of anything. I'm just playing devil's advocate here. I'm all about threesomes and hot sex"—he shrugged—"but I'm also single."

"Have you done this kind of threesome before?" I wasn't sure where I was going to go with this, but I decided to water the idea and see what grew. I knew that Adam lived life to the fullest. He was a good-looking guy with a friendly personality. He had a good job, was easy-going, and I trusted him implicitly.

"Two men and a woman?"

I nodded.

"Yeah, I've had two. One in college and one about five or so years ago. I prefer two ladies."

Interesting. "Tell me about them." I wasn't the type to ask about his bedroom escapades. This was probably the one and only time we spoke in detail about this kind of thing. I was married in college and had kids. Adam wasn't and didn't. I knew he got around.

"In college, it was a party that I went to with the swim team, and the other one was when I was asked to be the third by a couple in a night club."

He filled me in on the details about too much drinking with his team at a victory party and then about dancing with a woman whose boyfriend was watching from across the room. They asked if he'd be willing to join them for a party at their place.

We headed toward the locker room. Our workout was clearly over as we dove headfirst into the land of threesomes.

The way he described his reaction to the couple from the bar asking him to join them made it seem as if it was just another night for him. "I didn't have anything else going on that night, so I figured, why not?"

The seed was growing. I wasn't sure how Adam would react, but I was sure that I wouldn't take offense to his answer either way. We stopped at the lockers, and I glanced over to him. "And if I were to ask you if you were interested in being our third person, would you feel the same?"

His entire body froze. His brows shot into his hairline. His mouth fell open a bit. It was as if he had been pushed out onto a stage to perform a solo but didn't know the song. "I'm . . . I'm not sure I follow exactly. Feel the same about what?"

I couldn't believe I was asking one of my longtime buddies if he'd be interested in sleeping with my wife and me, but at the same time . . . it made sense. "As in would you say, 'why not.' I mean this is something big for us, and I was struggling to figure out how I'd find someone who I could trust implicitly. I doubt that will be possible with some man I just met. But with you, I know you respect Natalie. I know you respect me. You aren't going to do anything to hurt her. It might be a bit awkward seeing your junk, but I'm sure I'd get over it."

"You're serious?" He sat on the bench and ran a hand through his hair. "You're really asking me if I want to be a part of this experience you're putting together for Nat? Would she even like that idea?"

It was a good question. "I'd have to find out whether or not she wants to know the other person. We haven't discussed all the details. There's still a lot to work out. I'm not asking you to come home with us right now, I'm just asking if you'd be willing to fill the role if I asked. No hard feelings either way."

He stood and gave me a curt nod. "If you trust me enough to be with your wife, and she's comfortable with that, I'd be honored. It's kind of weird because as beautiful as Nat is, she kind of feels like my little sister." He let out a gruff chuckle. "I'll have to get over that."

Adam seemed a bit over the top, as if I was giving him some kind of award, but it was cool. This was why having Adam would be perfect.

I just had to find out if Natalie would be willing to know the third party?

Chapter Seventeen

Natalie

My palms were wet with a mixture of sweat and condensation from my drink. I'd crossed and uncrossed my legs about twenty times since I sat, as if the more I fidgeted, the faster time would pass. I knew this was coming, Matteo told me he made the arrangements, but that didn't suppress the anticipation. We were having a threesome. Tonight. My heart pounded in my chest just thinking about it.

"Excuse me, Miss?" A tap on the shoulder had me turning to find a handsome gentleman looking down at me. "My friend and I haven't been able the take our eyes off you all evening."

Channeling my energy, I smiled. "Then you and your friend have impeccable taste."

"Nothing is more intoxicating than a confident woman." He tipped his square jaw at my almost empty martini glass. "May I buy you another?"

My gaze shifted, looking for his friend, but there were a few men standing in the lounge and most of them had their backs to me. I reverted my attention back to him and asked, "Won't your friend get lonely?"

He shook his head. A hint of lust flared in his eyes, and a

dirty promise snaked through his smirk. "He knows when it's worth the wait. Plus, he doesn't mind anonymity."

I hummed my interest as Jumanji-sized butterflies rose in my belly. "A man of mystery."

The bartender slipped back down the bar, and the man was quick to order me another round.

"Matteo." He stuck out his hand and introduced himself.

I took his hand and smiled. "Natalie."

In true Matteo fashion, we had discussed and planned for this night over the course of a week. Did I want a stranger, or did I want someone we knew? Was there a man in particular I wanted? Was there a certain way I wanted the night to go? We discussed rules and boundaries endlessly until Matteo knew everything I wanted and didn't want. We had talked about it a few times before, but this last week, it was clear Matteo was putting things into motion.

We decided that Matteo could be the one to decide on the guy, but I asked that it be someone we both knew and trusted. I had the option to know who it was before, but if I was going to do this, I was going to do it all the way.

So, I had suggested the blindfold.

The creativity of it was left up to him.

I was just to simply follow his lead, which seemed to be a strangers-in-a-bar theme. Matteo wanted to set up the room and asked me to meet him here. I wasn't sure what to expect and the anticipation had been eating me alive in the best possible way.

He took a seat next to me and nodded toward two people sitting at the end of the bar. "See them?" he asked.

"Yes."

He jutted his chin at them. "What do you think their story is? Are they work colleagues or here on a blind date?"

They were sitting close enough that they could have been on a date or just familiar with each other. They weren't touching at all yet seemed content in each other's company.

"Maybe they're work colleagues who secretly want to date but can't."

He tilted his head and took a good look at them for a moment. While he looked at them, I looked at him. I could see his pulse point on his neck. It throbbed steadily. His chest rose and fell with calm breaths. He hadn't seemed the least bit uneasy.

"And why can't they?"

I ran my finger along the rim of my glass and smirked. "Oh, she desperately wants to accept, but he's her boss and that could lead to a scandal at work. He knows how hard she worked to get to where she is, and he doesn't want anyone to think she got there by spreading her legs."

He drummed his fingers on the bar top and looked at me lasciviously. "Or maybe she's the love of his life and he was finally able to take her out for nice night at a fancy hotel. And she got all dress up, and he is barely containing his desire to slam her on top of the bar and have his way with her."

I shook my head and turn my gaze to a couple sitting at a high-top table behind us. "Now, those two seem to barely be able to keep from jumping over the table and mauling each other."

He shifted in his seat and angled his body so he could see the couple I was referring to without being obvious. "He looks ready to eat her alive. Can you feel the sexual tension pouring off him?"

My eyes flitted between the two of them as I observed their interactions. Her brows her draw in and her jaw seemed to be clench. Her eyes, though, seemed to scream out for his touch. "She looks ready to slap him then kiss him. As if she can't make up her mind whether she wants to fuck him or kill him."

A fire blazed in Matteo's eyes. I didn't know what he was thinking. He didn't add anything to the conversation as he took them in.

"Maybe they're star-crossed lovers meeting in the night." I winked. My voice dropped to sultry rasp as I said, "What a sexy concept."

It seemed our little game of people watching was over as Matteo's attention focused on my thighs as I shifted in my seat, uncrossing and crossing my legs. My core tingled as he took in the intricate lace pattern of my garters. "You're the most beautiful woman in the room. Like a fine piece of art: alluring and exquisite."

His praise had me sitting straighter in my seat. "It's funny you say that." I stirred the little plastic straw around the ice in my glass. "I happen to truly appreciate art. It's one of my true loves."

The corner of his mouth tipped up on one side. "You don't say?"

My lips closed over the straw and I nodded, sipping my drink. "What about you? Have any true loves?"

My eyes roved over his body as I waited for his answer. His button-up fit him flawlessly. Sun-kissed skin peaked out from behind the top two buttons left undone.

He pierced me with his gaze as my focus hit his face. "You could say that." His forearms flexed under the cotton of his shirt as he leaned an elbow on the bar and asked, "What about any other true loves? How's a pretty lady like yourself sitting at a bar all by herself?"

I pursed my lips and tilted my head. "I'm waiting for a handsome man like you to come and sweep me off my feet."

A devious grin played on his lips. "Off your feet, huh? And what are we doing with your feet off the ground?"

A buzz of exhilaration pulsed through me as the background din faded. He made everything else us die out leaving me emersed in this cat and mouse game. I was looking forward to finally being caught. I sipped the last of my drink, letting my muscles relax. My nerves seemed to take a hike, leaving me ready for the night of my life. "I'm sure we could think of a few things."

He winked as he stood and reached into his pocket. He picked a bill out of a stack and slapped it down on the bar. "I've already thought of several."

His skin scorched under my palm the instant I laid my hand on his arm. "Will your friend still be joining us?"

His eyes flamed with desire as he leaned forward and spoke into my ear. His warm breath ghosting across the shell and down my neck. "He's already upstairs waiting."

My breath caught in my throat.

The noise of the bar died out again.

The lights dimmed.

He was already upstairs waiting for us.

We were doing this.

There was another man waiting upstairs to have sex with Matteo and me.

Holy shit.

"Ready?" he asked, holding a hand for me to take.

Glancing down, I saw that my nipples had stiffened into hard peaks under the purple satin of my cocktail dress. I was more than ready.

This was happening.

Matteo helped me from the high bar stool and placed his hand on the small of my back as he guided me toward the elevator. We exited on the third floor and strode down the hall, stopping in front of room three fourteen.

"Take a deep breath," Matteo said as he fished something out of his pocket. It was a black silk sleep mask. "I'm going to slip this over your eyes now. You can choose if or when it comes off. Just know that you are in good hands. I trust him and you do too." I had to force myself not to ask who was waiting for us again. "Remember, you can stop this at any point if you don't like it or you feel uncomfortable. I may have planned it, but you're in charge, okay, love?"

I nodded, swallowing the fresh bout of nerves trying to claw their way up from my stomach. The material of the mask was a gentle caress as Matteo slid it into place over my eyes. "Do you remember your safe word?"

Even though we weren't dipping a toe into the depth of the BDSM world, Matteo wanted me to choose a safe word that couldn't be ignored or confused or misconstrued. I had glanced around the room and picked the first thing I saw that wouldn't ever be used when having sex was. "Banana."

Matteo's body shifted and then there was a soft *beep* followed by a *click* and I knew he had just slipped the keycard into the slot on the door.

Having my sight taken from me enhanced all my other senses. The sounds of our footsteps on the carpet echoed like claps of thunder. The inhale and exhale count ramped up with the third person in the vicinity. The air was thick with lust. My body temperature rose with the extra burst of pheromones and adrenaline.

Someone came to a stop behind me, warming my exposed back. "You look so sexy," Matteo told me before placing a kiss on my neck. "Doesn't she look sexy?"

Something cracked open inside me at his acknowledgment of the other person in the room. A heady bout of arousal mixed with hunger surged through me, swirling like a tropical storm in my lower belly.

The other man mumbled a quiet, "Uh-huh," before the tips of slightly calloused fingers ran down my left forearm as slightly softer fingertips ran down my right one.

Goose bumps danced across both arms and shimmied down my back.

The strap of my dress was slid down one arm and then the other strap followed.

We were jumping right in.

The bodice of the dress sat at my waist; my breasts exposed to the too-cool air of the room.

The other man hummed a pleased tune as Matteo wrapped his arms around me and cupped my heavy breasts before lifting them to our friend.

An offering, if you will.

"She loves when you play with them," he told the man, who wasted no time pulling one of my nipples into his mouth. The difference in his touch versus Matt's was there. He was a bit hesitant, not as steadfast but also eager and greedy as his fingers dug into my hips.

His fingers relaxed quickly, and he began running them up and down my side and along the skin just under where my dress had settled. "Take it off," Matteo ordered him. I missed the warmth of his mouth as the other man pulled away. Matteo's hands left my breasts and guided my chin back toward him so he could capture my lips with his. My dress slipped down my legs, and the material caressed my skin all the way until it laid soft around my ankles.

One at a time, the man lifted each of my high-heeled feet, and my dress was no more. Pads of his fingers trailed up the outside of my legs as Matteo deepened the kiss, silently asserting his dominance in the situation. The other man was touching me, but Matteo was consuming me.

Matteo broke the kiss, leaving me dizzy and breathless. "Lean your head back on my shoulder."

I complied with zero hesitation.

A few moments later, sensation overloaded my body. My skin was hot and cold as two sets of lips kissed me, and two sets of hands touched me. Matteo's touch was easily identifiable because of his position behind me and by how it seemed to direct the other.

The man's fingers toyed with my nipples while Matteo's touch drifted lower. His expert finger slid right between my folds. Back and forth.

"You're so wet, my love," he cooed in my ear as the other man's mouth returned to my breasts. "You feel like fire. Do you like all this raw male attention focused solely on you? Do you like making our dicks hard with your little moans and the smell of your arousal?"

I whimpered as he pinched my clit. "You're very swollen, darling."

When Matteo stepped back and the other man followed suit, I almost stumbled at the sudden lack of sensation. Being left to stand in the middle of a strange room, naked save for my garters, a pair of heels and a blindfold while two men watched me, was a feeling I wanted to cling to.

I tracked their movements, listening to the different sounds coming from different areas of the room, but it was nothing I could make heads or tails of.

"Open." Matteo's command was followed by immediate compliance. Something metal sat at my lips, but I couldn't make out what it was until it was pushed fully into my mouth. It was the shape of a butt plug. "Suck."

The lust-thick, one-word orders fanned the flames flickering in my core. Matteo had an extra bite to his voice, and I couldn't help but believe that he liked asserting himself over me in front of our guest. Matteo wasn't very alpha, and he was on board with this threesome, but that didn't mean he didn't have the baser, carnal need to mark his territory.

God, it was so damn sexy.

"Do you know what this is, love?"

I nodded.

"What is it?" he asked as he pulled it back.

I licked my lips. "A butt plug."

"Very good." Matteo's voice was rich and full of deviant intent. "Why did you get it wet?"

The answer was pretty self-explanatory, but I gave it nonetheless. "Because you're going to put it in me."

"Why am I putting it in you?"

Ah, I saw where this was going.

"Because there is going to be a cock in it soon."

I heard the groan in Matteo's voice. He had become a big fan of anal sex since we started to expand our horizons. We'd had it a few times over the last month, and Matteo was like a barely controlled madman every time he slipped his dick into that back entrance.

"Where else is there going to be a cock, love?"

I shivered just thinking about it. "In my pussy."

A hot, wet tongue licked up the side of my neck to my ear. "That's right. My dirty girl gets two cocks today. You're going to be so full you won't be able to move. You're just going to lay there while we fill you over and over until you cream all over both our dicks. Isn't that right, love?"

"Shit," the other man cursed under his breath. If dirty talking your wife were an Olympic sport, Matteo would be going for gold. He was pulling out all the stops.

"Matt . . ." I whimpered—or begged, which seemed more apropos.

Fingers tickled the top of my slit before gliding through it. "You need it bad, don't you, Natalie?"

I had no shame. "God, yes, please."

My lower lips were spread, and a tongue teased my nub. A myriad of sensations pulled at me. Being held open allowed the chilled air to mix with the heat of his mouth and the two temperatures battled each other with each lick.

The other man's mouth left my aching core, only to be replaced with the coolness of the metal of the plug at my entrance. My body was overly ready to reap the first of its rewards. The plug slid easily into me, feeling colder than I'd expected considering it had just been in my mouth. Matteo glided the plug in and out of my pussy. I could only imagine how shiny it was with all the evidence of my excitement.

"Ready?" Matteo asked as he positioned the tip at my butt.

I was so ready. "Yes."

The man, who I could still feel kneeling in front of me,

tossed my leg over his shoulder, supporting me as the sting of the plug zipped through me. "Mmm." I moaned as the wide part stretched me to a sweet burn. The man's tongue was at my clit again. He was masterful as he circled it. Clearly, the man knew how to work his way around a pussy.

My core clenched.

"Don't you dare come yet, love," Matteo demanded, pulling his hand from my lips to pinch my nipple just hard enough to draw me from the edge. As soon as the plug was seated inside me, two of Matteo's fingers found their way into my other hole. "I need to feel your pussy gush with the first. It's going to be a big one, isn't it? I can feel it. You're so fucking swollen, love." He wiggled his fingers. "These barely fit in here. How are you going to fit two cocks, sweetheart?"

The vibration from the man's mouth tipped the scales, and I was dangling at the edge, waiting to be thrown over into a free fall of bliss. Matt kept talking—more dirty words most likely, but I couldn't make any sense of them. All I could focus on was the impending orgasm. Only the first of many that would ravage my body before I couldn't take anymore.

I crashed around Matteo's fingers. The other man's tongue lapped and until there wasn't any more to lap. As he stood and my body slumped back into Matteo, I contemplated taking off my mask. I wanted to know who the man with the talented tongue was.

Chapter Eighteen

Natalie

My fingers unconsciously drifted up to the mask covering my eyes.

"Are you sure?" Matteo asked. "We still have some much left to do."

He was right. Even though I really wanted to know who else was here, I was also sure I didn't want to know yet. I didn't want to run the risk of messing up this cocktail of excellence. There was the perfect amount of mystery and comfort and lust.

I dropped my hand, and Matteo kissed my mouth. His fingers gripped my chin and guided my jaw to the side. A set of hot lips met mine, and the taste of my own arousal filled my mouth. "Do you taste good from his mouth, love?"

My core spasmed. Whether it was an aftershock or a precursor, I couldn't tell.

Ripping my lips away from one set, I slammed them onto the other. "Why don't you tell me?" I panted as I pulled away from Matteo's mouth long enough to speak.

He groaned and bit my bottom lip. "I need to be in your pussy."

He stepped away from me, and the sound of rustling

clothing filled the room. My body hummed despite the intense release I just had.

A hand slipped into mine. "This way." Matteo led me to the bed. "Climb up."

The bedding was soft under my knees as I crept forward. "Don't go too far." A hand rested on my hip, holding me at the edge of the bed.

The echo of Matteo spitting into my slit bounced off the walls a second before the head of his cock slipped through it and slid into me. The fullness felt like a prayer I hadn't prayed being answered.

Matteo moaned, and it sent shivers up my spine.

Soft fingertips skated up the curve of my ass to my hip then across my ribs and down my arm. The bed dipped, and seconds later, our friend knelt in front of me. A hand lifted my chin, and the velvet-smoothness of a cock rubbed over my lips. They parted, and he slipped inside. He was thick and smelled of citrus and sandalwood body wash. He was long and hard and so hot.

Matt's balls slapped against my clit with each thrust making it throb with need.

Behind me, I felt Matteo's hunger. His movements were possessive. His grip was punishingly tight. His pace quick, harsh, and deep, and his desire heavy in every one of his exhales. He wanted to come all over me, mark me like he did when we were being watched at the club.

At my head, I felt something different. Something cautious. This man didn't know me sexually, and I felt the exploration in the way he threaded his fingers in my hair, pushing it off my face. His thigh tightened against my shoulder as his thumb caressed my cheek, and I couldn't resist moaning.

My orgasm brewed at the rate of an express train. Fast and with force. My fingers itched to rub myself. I needed to touch my clit.

"Do you want to come, Natalie?"

My mouth was filled with cock, so I moaned my plea. Matteo tapped the plug, and it lit me up. The orgasm flooded my core, and release was only a light breeze away. I wanted to beg him to touch my clit, but since I couldn't speak, I reached down myself.

The barest skim of my finger had me ready to erupt, but Matteo slapped my hand away. "Not yet," he chided.

I growled at him and was rewarded with a deep groan from the other man.

So, I did it again.

And again.

"Does her mouth feel good?"

"God, yes," he answered. I recognized his voice but couldn't concentrate long enough to place it.

His admission combined with Matteo pinching my clit had me coming. There was no stopping it as I moaned and thrashed. I couldn't hold myself up a second longer. When I opened my mouth to cry out, he pulled himself from me and my upper body dropped to the bed.

"Matteo!"

My husband slowed but didn't stop, dragging as much as he could from me. My ass tingled. My core clenched. My clit pulsed.

When a finger skirted around the delicate skin of my neck and collarbone, it warred with the demand of the hands gripping my hips.

Then, as the orgasm ebbed, Matteo slipped the plug from my behind.

My heart skipped a beat when I thought about what was next.

The man at my head left the bed, and new sounds entered the room.

The click of something opening.

The squelch of lube being rubbed on a dick.

Fingers were at my butt, which was still high in the air, covering it with a cold liquid.

Hands pulled me from the bed. My feet hit the floor, and I was guided across the room.

"Ready, love?" Matteo asked, letting me know he was the one acting as my eyes.

Exhilaration careened through my body, and I shuttered. "Yes."

Hands on my shoulders turned me and guided me back until my legs met what I thought was a sofa or chaise of some kind. Scratchy hair greeted the outside of my calves and thighs. The other man settled his hands on my hips and steadied me, helping Matteo move me over his lap and guided me down.

"Do you feel him?" Matteo asked just before I felt it. The head of his cock prodded my hole. Matt's voice was calm but thick with desire as his fingers toyed with my overly sensitive bundle of nerves.

My reply was more like a whimper. "Mmm."

"She's so tight." His voice was strained, but I was fairly certain I had identified the person behind me. "It's incredible."

I hissed as he pushed in. Matteo rubbed a bit harder. "Relax," Matteo said kissing the hallow of my neck. I really wanted to see him. I wanted to look into his eyes as we experienced this. So, I ripped the mask off and focused on Matteo's smile. He captured my lips with his and poured every emotion he felt into this one kiss. It was consuming, breathtaking, and absolutely perfect.

The sensations demanded control, and my eyes rolled back as Adam continued pushing into me. "Does he feel good, love?"

I nodded and moaned simultaneously, making sure to let them both know I knew who he was. "Damn, Adam."

He froze for a moment, and before I could tell him to keep

going, he pulled my hips down hard and seated himself into me fully.

Adam pressed his chest to my back and then shifted so I was lying on top of him—my back to his front and his hard length deep inside me. His hands went to the insides of my thighs, and he guided my legs wider so he could hook his arms under my knees and expose me fully to my husband.

Matteo stepped between them, looking possessed as he gazed down at me, watching as Adam slowly drew out and then pushed back in. I felt like a little lamb being offered up as a sacrifice, but instead of death or dismemberment, I'd be rewarded with pleasure. Lots and lots of pleasure.

Matteo licked two fingers and sank them into me. He wasted no time hooking them up seeking his favorite button to push. I knew exactly what he was going to do, and my walls were already starting to clamp down around him. "You know what's coming, don't you, darling?"

"Please," I begged shamelessly.

"Want to see what I can make her do, Adam?" he asked with a smirk. And, shit if that didn't make this all that much hotter.

Adam's dick swelled in my ass. His thrusts were easy and short, but when he throbbed like that, it felt like an earthquake. "If you're going to make her squirt, hell yes, I want to see it."

"Let's show him, Natalie," he coaxed as he added more force into the tips if his fingers. The pressure built, and I squirmed. Matt placed his hand on my lower belly and held me in place. The fingers inside me pressed up. His other hand pressed down. It stung and burned until I felt the burst. Matteo tore his digits from inside me and rubbed feverishly at my clit. Hot liquid sprayed from my body as Matteo smiled victoriously.

Adam groaned in my ear. "That is so damn sexy."

My body felt like mush as Matteo rested his hard dick at my entrance. "Ready, sweetheart?"

Each and every molecule of Matteo screamed "barely controlled" as his neck muscles corded and teeth gnashed while he pushed into me inch my inch. His thumb rubbed at my clit, electrifying the dying spark of my last release. "Let me in, love," he coached. I was trying, but with my flesh swollen and a dick stretching my ass, there wasn't much room. Matteo's thumb swirled, and I moaned. "There you go, sweetheart."

Matteo pushed forward slowly, not stopping until his pelvis was flush against mine.

The urge to circle my hips took over. I tried to move, but Adam's hands squeezed my waist, holding me still.

"Don't, babe," he murmured in my ear as he caressed my soft skin. "Let us take care of you."

They moved in tandem. In. Out. In. Out.

I felt full. Consumed. Cherished.

This was everything.

Adam played with my nipples, adding more fuel to the fire, as Matteo's thumb became firmer. Everything built. Higher and higher. Tighter and tighter. Until it all snapped

My body just went numb with orgasm. It exploded from every corner of my brain. White-hot fire ripped through me wild and reckless like a bullet hitting me from close range.

I cried out Matteo's name and held on to Adam's hands, which were still cupping my breasts. My nails dug into his skin as I screamed and cursed. My orgasm became violent. The bullet slashed through everything inside me as the pleasure and burning mixed into one.

Adam cursed first. "Holy shit, I'm not going to last much longer."

The struggle for control in his voice called to me like it was heroine and I was an addict. I wanted—no, *needed* him to let it go. "Come in my ass, Adam."

His fingers grasped my breasts harder. I was definitely leaving with some bruises as souvenirs. His thrusts became frantic as he chased his own release. He gave one final, hard drive, and then pulsed his orgasm into me as his teeth bit, not too savagely, onto my shoulder

Then Matteo was pulling me up to him by my hair. His lips smashed onto mine, and he slammed into me one last time before he pumped me full of his cum. Our mouths never parted as Matteo rode out his orgasm.

Our chests were heaving as we broke apart and my body felt spent.

Matteo laid me back against Adam and then slowly unsheathed himself from my body.

His warm, sticky cum slipped out of me, and I giggled, picturing it running down Adam's balls.

"What's so funny?" Matteo asked.

Adam's groggy voice filled the air. "Hundred bucks says she's laughing about your cum running down my balls." There was a bite of annoyance in his words at the end, but I laughed harder.

"Yup." I popped the 'P' with no shame.

Matteo's laugh mingled with mine as he gently lifted me off Adam's lap and dick. Adam's cum dripped from me, mixing with Matteo's.

He laid me on the bed as Adam strode across the room. I couldn't help but watch the way his firm ass muscles flexed as he walked. The sound of water running filled the air, and Adam returned a moment later, giving me a glorious view of his naked body as he handed a damp towel to Matteo. "Thank you," I said as my eyes zeroed in on the divots of his V muscle that lead to a very nice package. I tried to take in as much as I could before he headed back into the bathroom for a second time. No wonder the female population of Seattle loved him so much.

"Did you enjoy it?" Matteo asked as he skimmed the towel across my skin, wiping away the mess they made.

I closed my eyes and smiled. "I loved it."

He pulled a robe off the chair in the corner and helped me slip it on before he stepped into a pair of pants. His hands were warm as he leaned down and cupped my face between his palms. "You were so amazing." He kissed my lips. "So sexy." Kiss. "So beautiful." Kiss. "Thank you."

I chuckled against his lips. "I should be thanking you."

"Are you weirded out about Adam?" he asked sincerely.

The answer was quick and easy. I shook my head. "Not at all. I can see why you thought he would be the right one."

Adam strode back into the room. His hair was wet as if he just stole a quick shower, and he held a duffle bag in his hand. He walked over to us and kissed my forehead. "Thank you for letting me be a part of this with you guys." He smiled affectionately at me and then Matt. "It was something amazing. I think it's time for me to head out, though."

He shook hands with Matteo and smiled back at me as he grabbed a pile of clothing from the chair. "I'll see you guys soon."

Then he was out the door as if he hadn't just been having mind-blowing sex with me moments before.

"We have the room for the night," Matteo said. "Why don't we stay here."

I could definitely enjoy a night away from home. "Sounds wonderful. Besides, I don't think I could stand if I tried."

My husband's rich laugh resonated off the walls as he pulled the blankets back, and we crawled in for the night.

Chapter Nineteen

Matteo

"It's always so hard to leave them." Natalie was pouting in the passenger seat as we turned back onto the highway to head back to Seattle.

We'd just left the camp after visiting the kids for parents' weekend, and we would see them again in two weeks, but Natalie was right, it never got easier for her to leave them.

She sighed. "When did they get so big? As much as they keep us running all over, it still feels like they were born last week."

"It sure does," I agreed, but Natalie was in her head, thinking about something as she stared out the window.

The car was silent for a moment before she shocked the shit out of me. "Do you ever wish we had more children? I mean . . . I know that we have two, but with them going through everything together at the same time, do you feel like we missed out on more? We're both still young, we could have another."

It took a herculean effort not to crash the car into the side of the bridge. We've had this conversation in the past, granted we haven't had it in almost a decade, but we had decided that we were good with Jackson and Emma.

"We've talked about this, love," I reminded her. "We decided that we had all we needed in Jackson and Emma. Do you really want another baby or do you feel as though the kids are growing up and we can't stop it?"

She rested her elbow on the ledge of the car door and laid her head in her hand. "No, I don't really want another one, but I'd be lying if I said that the idea of it wasn't appealing. We were so young and scared and stressed back then. Having one now would be a different story. Mostly, I feel like I'm losing my babies to the big bad world, and I want to keep them little for as long as possible. There about to be teenagers, and my heart can't handle it."

Reaching over the center console, I gripped her hand. "That's what happens, sweetheart. They get bigger and grow up. It will happen with every child we have."

She sighed again. "I know."

"We can still spend all the time you'd like pretending to make them."

She chuckled and squeezed my hand. "Oh yeah? What else have you cooked up in that mind of yours? The last thing you planned out was a phenomenal experience."

It had been a week since our night with Adam. We talked about it the morning after, but we didn't discuss the possibility of more of them. "I'm not currently planning anything. I feel like we've crossed a lot of things off our bucket list." Blindfolds. Toys. Binding. Anal. Threesomes. We'd done a lot to expand our horizons in just a few months. "But let me ask you this . . . that night with Adam . . . was that something you want to do often or was it just a one-time thing?"

"As in with Adam again or with someone else?"

"Either or," I replied. "Although, we'd have to have a serious discussion about who we would bring in. It was stressful for me when I was trying to figure things out."

She considered things for a couple of moments. "It was something I wanted to experience, but I don't know if I would want that all the time. I'm not sure if I would've enjoyed myself with someone other than Adam, but if we keep inviting Adam to have sex with us, I worry how that would change the dynamic of our friendship with him, yours especially."

I'd seen Adam three times since the night with Natalie. The first time, he strolled into the locker room of the gym and greeted me with a fist bump and, "What's up" as usual, but I had expected that.

Before Natalie arrived at the hotel, Adam and I had a conversation about how the aftermath of it would be. We decided that, unless something went terribly wrong, we'd act the same as always.

"I agree," I nodded then chuckled. "It isn't as if we are trying to be a throuple. Although, I promised Adam we'd have dinner soon. He's concerned that if you guys don't see each other soon, things will get weird."

My eyes drifted to the side quickly to try to catch her expression while also keeping my eyes on the road. She didn't seem to show any signs of unease at the idea of hanging out with Adam. Not that I thought she was going to, but it was still nice to have conformation that she was okay with Adam. "Sounds good. Let me know when."

"I will." We needed to finish our discussion. "Back to the threesomes—"

Natalie answered before I could finish the question. "I say we play by ear. If we find ourselves in a situation where the opportunity arises and we feel comfortable, we can go for it. I don't think we need to worry about it so much." When she turned to face me, she had a bright smile on her lips. "I know how much you love to plan stuff, and everything you've put together along the ride has been amazing, but we don't have to have all the plans all the time. Sometimes it's sexy to be spontaneous."

My smile mirrored hers as I merged into the right-hand lane.

"Spontaneous can be sexy, huh?" I asked, flicking the turn signal and breaking to take the off ramp.

Natalie pursed her lips and she looked at me expectantly. Her tone dripped with devilishness and curiosity. "What're you doing?"

"Being spontaneous."

She fidgeted in her seat and glanced at the sign for the rest area as we passed it. I pulled the car into a spot at the far end of the parking lot where there were no other cars, put it in park, and then moved my seat as far back as it would go.

"Hitch that dress up and come ride my cock," I told her, freeing my dick from my pants. "You should probably hurry too. Never know when someone could pull up next to us."

We hastily shuffled to put everything back into place when a police car pulled into the parking lot and started driving around, patrolling.

Thank god, we had already finished.

"Man, I had forgot how fun doing it in the car was."

Natalie snorted. "Funny, because I had forgot how awkward and uncomfortable it was. My head might possibly have a few bumps tomorrow."

Her head kept hitting the roof, and when I accidentally pressed the horn and startled her, she hit the window too.

I shrugged. "That's the price of spontaneity."

As we neared home, Natalie suggested meeting with Adam tonight. "See if he wants to come for some barbeque and beers. Is there a Mariner's game on tonight?"

"Yeah, there is. Text him."

She had his number. I didn't want anything to be weird

between them. I wanted their interactions to be business as usual. Before having sex with him, Natalie would've asked him herself, so there was no reason to change that expectation.

Adam arrived two hours later, and as he was climbing from his car, the delivery guy pulled into the driveway.

"I thought we we're grilling?" he asked, hitching a thumb over his shoulder. That had been the plan, but as soon as we had gotten home, Natalie decided she just wanted to veg on the couch.

"Someone gave me a concussion this afternoon, so I didn't want to cook or clean anything," Natalie called from the living room. "Pizza is better for the soul anyway."

He rushed into the living room and looked Natalie over. "How'd you get a concussion?" His concern was genuine, which made Nat an ass for joking like that.

"She doesn't have a concussion," I yelled back as I grabbed the pizza from the delivery guy and handed him a tip. "Thanks."

"I could have," Nat continued.

Dropping the pizza off in the kitchen, I rounded the corner and glared. "I didn't hear you complaining at the time."

Adam chuckled and shook his head. "Jeez, you guys. What'd you get into this time?"

Natalie smiled. "The car."

"What are you, sixteen?" Adam laughed. "And car sex kind of sucks. It's cramped and you never have enough room to move. Now, a nice BJ in the car, on the other hand, is awesome."

Nat nodded and stood to hug Adam. "That's what I said. I wouldn't say it sucked, but it's so awkward and confined."

A look passed between them as they greeted one another. He looked into Natalie's eyes as he asked, "Are we good?"

She smiled and nodded, not a trace of lie or hesitation in

her expression. "Of course. I'm glad it was you, and I'm glad you know how to use your tongue so damn well."

He smirked, but I swore his cheeks turned a bit pink. "You and the rest of the Seattle women."

I stifled my laugh with a slice of pizza and joined them in the living room.

Chapter Twenty

NATALIE

THE AIR WAS THICKER THAN I'd expected it to be, and the inside was covered completely in cedar planks. It was like being in a log cabin, surrounded by humid mist. It felt strange to enjoy the feeling of it on my face. Normally, I hated being encased in hot sticky air, but in this way, it made sense.

It relaxed me a bit as we sat next to each other on the built-in benches. We scooted into the corner. My legs tossed over Matteo's as I lay across the seat. There weren't many people in the sauna, so I could get away with it.

Matt's fingers drifted over my calves, sending goose bumps up my body. He rubbed in little circles. It felt wonderful. "People are going to think I'm rubbing a different part of your body."

"You *should* rub a different part of my body," I purred. His touch felt hot and left a blaze of sensation in its wake. "That actually sounds like a perfect idea. Let's do that."

His ministrations moved farther up my thigh. My core clenched, wanting some kind of contact *bad*.

"Patience, love." He cooed as he kneaded the bottom of my heel. It was also as if he forgot that he teased me all day. It started in the car to see the kids, and he dropped hot little promises in my ear at every turn while we were at the camp. "I've reserved one of the swing rooms for tonight. The wait will be worth it. I researched some ways to have fun with the sex swing." Whatever he was thinking about, it promised me pleasure. I couldn't be more interested. "There's one thing in particular that I want to try." The pads of his fingers rubbed circles into the arch of my foot. "Your hands are wound in, your feet are right next to them, and your pussy is exposed to me as you hang there, completely at my mercy. Just like with the spreader only I'll be able to fuck you deep and hard."

He was painting a hot vision and tempting me with lofty promises. Those had been some of my best orgasms I'd ever had, so if he wants to try to top them, I wouldn't protest.

I sat up and nodded enthusiastically. "Yes. A hundred times yes."

He chuckled. "Aren't you eager, naughty girl?" The desire in his voice whispered up my arms. "We've got time. Let's relax first. I know you need a few minutes to decompress."

He was referring to my whiplashing of emotions after seeing the kids. Two weeks was a long time to go without seeing your kids in person. We FaceTimed regularly, but it wasn't nearly the same as holding and hugging my babies.

He had switched feet and was massaging my right one. I loved how he anticipated all my needs. He knew the toll of these visits on my emotions. It was getting worse as they grew. I knew they'd be leaving the nest for good in the blink of an eye and I wanted to hold them close. Never let them go. My heart didn't care that the kids were fine and happy. It missed their sweet faces. It was hard to leave them.

"The kids looked so much more grown up." I'd sworn they had aged five years in the last fourteen days.

Matteo nodded his agreement and crept his fingers up the side of my calf. "Jackson seemed to be an inch taller."

He definitely did. "And do you see the lip-gloss on Emma? She looked like a little lady in her stage makeup."

"It always amazes me how great she is up on stage." Matt smiled fondly. Emma played Glenda the Good Witch in today's performance of the *Wizard of Oz*.

A moan slipped from my lips when Matt dragged his nails down the back of my leg.

I tried to concentrate. "Jackson almost had a bull's-eye." He looked like a pro with that bow today. He was almost there and should be proud.

Matt's fingers drifted higher and higher up my leg until he reached the apex of my thighs. A finger glided through my folds to my nub. He rubbed. "I found the bull's-eye."

My legs fell open in invitation. I wanted to come so bad. My vagina had become super greedy. It wanted Matteo—all the time. It was a feat to make it through the day without seeking out my husband for sex. We'd definitely opened the door to a whole new world where we were entirely different people.

"You need it bad, don't you?" I could practically hear the smile in Matteo's voice. It dripped with all that male rawness he seemed to exude at all times these days.

It took a thumb, two fingers, and less than three minutes to have me spasming around his digits and crying out his name.

Matt licked his fingers as I caught my breath. "That should tide you over for a few, my greedy girl."

He stood and guided me up from the bench. "Come on. Let's go see if our room is ready."

As we walked toward the locker room, I felt eyes on me. Glancing back, I saw a man who I'd seen quite a few times before. He'd been in the expo rooms watching us one time, and another time, he was sitting on the couch jerking himself off as Matt pulled orgasm after orgasm from my body. This time, he was in the far corner of the sauna, his eyes tracking us as we exited.

He didn't shrink away from my attention or turn away as if ashamed that I'd caught him staring. It must be part of his kink, so I tried not to think about him and focused on the fun about to come.

We dressed quickly, anxious to get to the swing room. The red light was on above the door. "Damn it," I swore, grumpy that I had to wait when I was already revved and itching to go.

Matteo wrapped an arm around my shoulders and pulled me into him. "Relax, love." His voice was laced with laughter. "Let's go get a drink or two at the bar and wait. I'm still going to trestle you up and have my way with your pretty little pussy."

I sucked in a breath. "Promise?"

His chest rumbled with his happiness. "I think we've created a monster."

My brows rose, and my lips tipped into a smirk. "Maybe you have."

We turned back toward the lounge, and I grabbed a seat on one of the empty sofas. Matteo made his way over to the bar, and I watched as he ordered our drinks before turning his attention to where I was sitting.

He caressed me with his eyes, letting them roam up my legs to my chest. He drank his fill of me, stroking the fire from across the room, until a man I hadn't seen before broke into our haze.

Matteo greeted him, and they spoke as if they were old friends.

"That's Cole Masterson." A deep voice wafted over me. "He's one of the owners."

I looked back over my shoulder and found the watcher from the sauna. I shouldn't have referred to him as *the watcher*. It wasn't nice since, without people who liked to watch, people to be watched couldn't get off as hard.

He sat in the space next to me. Not too close but close enough to carry on a conversation. "You looked as if you were trying to figure out who your husband was speaking with or how you could murder him for holding up your big plans. I figured I'd help you with one of those."

The level of attention he must have been paying to me to notice those things was unsettling, but I tried to remember that he people-watched and was probably good at reading a situation.

"Gerard." He extended a hand, and I accepted. He had no five o'clock shadow on his pale skin. His hair was thinning a bit, and his eyes were dark and slightly too small for his features.

"Natalie."

He scrubbed a hand across his chin. "I figured that, if we're going to keep running into each other, I should at least introduce myself."

No one had really approached us in our time here. For the most part, we came, explored, and then left. Our goal wasn't to make friends. I wasn't sure what the proper etiquette was for a situation like this, so I stuck with polite but not inviting as I turned my eyes back to my husband. This man had been listening to us in the sauna, had seen me naked, and had gotten off while watching Matteo and me.

I almost wished that I could telepathically call Matteo back over to where I sat. Something about the way Gerard watched me was disconcerting. I didn't feel it while in the midst of sex with Matt, but without the sex, I didn't enjoy the way his attention made me feel.

"The two of you put on a good show," he commented as he looked Matteo over. A shiver ran down my spine when his focus shifted back to me. "Did you know your eyes melt like chocolate when you climax? You looked deep into me the last time I watched you come, and it was a gift. Thank you."

What the hell was I supposed to say to that? I didn't look deep into shit with this man.

I struggled to find a response, and after the silence had

stretched well into the uncomfortable zone, Gerard shook his head and held up his hands innocently.

"I'm sorry. I bet that sounded really unnerving. I didn't mean to upset you. I truly only meant that as a compliment. I enjoy watching the two of you and wanted to at least introduce myself. I shouldn't have approached you without your husband."

My shoulders relaxed. His interest was just mere curiosity. He didn't want to peel off my skin and wear me as a dress. Or, at least, I didn't think he did because he seemed sincere. He stood and tipped his head. "It was nice to meet you, Natalie. I'm so sorry I unsettled you. I hope that you won't hold it against me."

When he finally backed away, my shoulders dropped just a bit, and I waved off his apology. "It's all right. No harm. No foul. It was nice to meet you, Gerard."

He slipped away, turning down one of the halls, and I returned my attention to Matteo, who had finally retrieved our drinks from the bar. He handed over my Long Island and sipped his bourbon.

"Who was that?"

I sucked down a healthy gulp of my drink. "His name is Gerard. He's watched us a few times and felt the need to introduce himself."

Matteo's scoff was filled with teasing. "I leave you alone for five minutes, and you have suitors coming to try to win your affections."

"Suitors? Affections?" I laughed, almost spitting my drink across the velvety fabric of the tufted sofa. "What is this, the nineteenth century?"

He shrugged unapologetic for his nerdy humor. I loved that he was who he was and owned it. I also loved that he had situated himself so that he could keep an eye on the hallway housing the swing room. He was just as ready for it as I was.

This turned out to be the best kind of foreplay as we sat

and daydreamed about what we were waiting to do. The images I was conjuring of being tied up in the swing might as well have been flicks of my clit with Matteo's fingers.

I was swollen and wet.

Matteo turned his dark gaze to me. "I can smell how badly you need my cock, love."

I rubbed my thighs together, wishing I could create enough friction to take the edge off. It was almost as if the orgasm I had in the sauna never happened.

He snickered as he shook his head. "I've definitely created a monster. What are you going to do when the kids come back and you can't have cock every time you want it?"

"I guess you have a month to fuck as much of it out of me as you can." The tip of my tongue traced my lower lip. "Hopefully, tonight will be enough to hold me over until at least tomorrow afternoon."

A deep noise rumbled from Matt's throat, as if he accepted the challenge. His focus flicked over my shoulder and then back. He spun me around in time to see two people exiting one of the rooms we were waiting for. "As soon as that room is cleaned, you're going to see how much you can take. I may have to carry you out to the car when we're done."

Two hours later, I did walk out. My legs felt like jelly, my vagina was swollen, and every molecule of my body was too warm, but . . . I walked out.

Chapter Twenty-One

Natalie

Cheers, hoots, and hollers along with the smell of sweat and beer filled the thick air as District 12 finished playing our favorite song. Matt managed to get tickets to the show they were playing at one of the bars in Tacoma. The place had a huge outside deck area they used for outdoor concerts. Lights were strung up everywhere under the wooden overhang that covered the deck, which gave off a rustic barn feel. Bodies melded together like the beat of the music.

Matteo and I discovered this band back in college, and after the first time we heard them play, we were hooked. Their sound was a cross between No Doubt and The Chainsmokers, heavier on the Chainsmokers side, and we hadn't seen them play in probably ten years.

We danced, sang, and drank as though we were in college again—pre-knocked-up status, of course. I enjoyed the feel all of Matteo's new gym muscles under the thin material of his T-shirt as we moved together. I tossed my arms around his neck, admiring his handsome face under the bright lights—his soft full lips, his sharp squared jaw, and the light scuff enhancing it—as he rolled his hips against mine.

We'd already had a couple of beers, and even though I

was having a great time, I was ready for more. I was craving some sexy time with Matteo. It had been a busy week at work prepping for the Portland opening and dealing with Bastien's up-tight butt. I needed some destressing.

The song finished, and Matteo leaned into my ear. "I'm going to get us another round."

Sounded good to me. I nodded and focused my attention back to the band as they fell into the intro of one of their more upbeat songs.

Despite the loudness of the crowd, it was a more intimate performance. Maybe only about forty people. A new group joined the party on the dance floor as the song changed. The rather small space was packed and hot.

A sticky arm bumped into mine. A petite blonde woman looked genuinely apologetic as she said, "I'm sorry."

She had big blue eyes that reminded me of a Disney princess. "It's okay." I smiled. My hand involuntarily went to her shoulder as I spoke. "I'm Natalie."

She looked over at my hand and smiled back. "Natalie, I'm Brooke." She danced next to me, bumping me with her hip and encouraging me to dance along with her. "I love this song. It reminds me of my college days at UW."

"*You* went to UW?" I pointed at her and then to myself before squealing like a drunken college girl. "*I* went to UW. And I listened to them there too."

The alcohol, music, and small talk with the stranger had my smile so wide my cheeks hurt.

Matteo returned with our drinks. A beer for him and Long Island for me. He looked at Brooke, who hadn't noticed him yet because she was swaying to the music, which had switched over to top-forty hits while the band took a quick break.

"Who's your friend?" he asked.

A rush of excitement bubbled up inside me as I tugged Brook closer to my side.

"Matteo . . . this is Brooke. We just met and have a ton in

common." He smiled and nodded at her. "Brooke, this is my husband Matteo."

"It's nice to meet you." She ran her tongue across her bottom lip, clearly enjoying the view of my husband, and I giggled. Yeah, he looked delicious tonight. His jeans hugged his ass and thighs, and his T-shirt looked shrink-wrapped around him. I couldn't wait to get him naked later.

The band returned, and as they took the stage again, they announced they were debuting a few new songs. The first one was sultry with a smooth tempo. Matteo sidled up behind me, pressing his front along my back as the lead singer crooned. Energy radiated from his pores as he started moving his hips again.

After the band played their four new songs, their show ended, and the DJ pumped upbeat dance songs into the air.

"Do you want to stay and dance?" Matteo asked.

I was having way too much fun to call it a night, so I nodded, and Matteo hitched his thumb toward the bar. "I'll go get us another round, okay?"

Even though I agreed, I told myself it would be my last one. If I wanted to have phenomenal sex with my husband, I needed not to pass out before we got home.

Brooke was still dancing right alongside me. I wondered if she had friends here somewhere, but figured she was a big girl. Brooke inched closer to my front. She leaned in and whispered, "You're a lucky woman."

Following her line of sight, I saw she was watching Matt at the bar.

"I am."

She started to dance, without stepping back. Our bodies were a mere inch apart as she placed her hands on my bare shoulders. Goose bumps pranced across my skin. Brooke's close proximity did strange things to my body. Her fingers swept up from my shoulder to my neck as she caressed my skin.

Matteo's heated stare burned from across the floor. My gaze locked with his as he watched intently. Something in the air shifted as Brooke closed what little space had been left between us. My focus never left Matteo as her soft lips pressed against mine.

My eyes closed as Brooke's tongue swept along my bottom lip before she delved deeper, tasting my mouth. Her hands cradled my face. When I opened my eyes again, I saw Matteo adjusting his crotch.

He was hard watching me kiss another woman.

She sucked on my tongue, and I moaned into her mouth.

When Matteo returned with our drinks, his hard-on was visible, and that made me happy. Brooke pulled back, ending the kiss. Her smile was bright, and her eyes were hooded as she looked at me.

A surrealness washed over me as I accepted my drink from Matteo and took a long pull on the straw. I had just kissed another woman for the first time. I liked it. My nipples were at attention. Matteo was hard. Brooke looked turned on.

Brooke danced in front of me, and Matteo danced behind me. We moved together in a cohesive current until long after my drink was gone. I gave myself over to all the heady sensations of feeling Matteo and Brooke sandwiching me. I felt sexy and confident—like I owned the room.

Brooke grabbed my hand and placed it on her hip, inviting me to touch her. Matteo had his hands on my hips, but dropped one, allowing me to follow Brooke's lead.

She inched her finger under the soft material of my top. Matteo's erection pressed into my ass as he watched everything unfold.

Maybe it was time to take care of some of Matteo's fantasies. He hadn't flat out said he wanted a threesome with another woman, but he was a man, and what man didn't want to see two women together?

Neither my body nor my mind seemed to have any qualms with Brooke's touch.

The charge in the air seemed to grow more electrified with each passing song, and finally, I couldn't take it any longer.

"Do you want to take this somewhere private?" I asked Brooke.

I looked back over my shoulder at Matteo and found no objection.

Brooke looked transfixed as she nodded and her eyes slide down my body, pausing on my cleavage before zeroing in on Matt's hand on my hip. Then she was taking in my husband, her eyes glinting with interest.

Brooke and I held hands and laughed together about nothing really as we waited on the corner for our Uber to arrive.

Excitement brewed in my chest as I caught the heated stares Matteo kept tossing my way. He was loving the dynamic between Brooke and me.

There was a moment of panic over the thought of having sex with another woman. I'd never done it before. I'd never kissed a woman, let alone gone down on one. Recently, I'd done a lot of things I'd never done before and there were few, if any, that I didn't embrace with enthusiasm. So, I wasn't sure why this caused a spike of panic, but it did.

Matteo almost choked on air and Brooke giggled. "It isn't as hard as you think," she said matter-of-factly. "Just do to me what you like done to you."

Matteo laughed again before leaning down and whispering, "You were thinking out loud, love."

Oops.

Our car pulled up, and we all piled into the back seat. Touching and light kissing filled the twenty-minute ride to the house. None of us paid attention to the driver, who was a middle-aged man who clearly got more than he bargained for.

Brooke pressed her lips to mine. Then I dragged mine from hers to Matteo's.

We arrived at the house, and as we exited, the driver called out, "Have a good night."

The flutters wormed their way back into my tummy as we entered the house, but as soon as the door closed, they were gone because Matteo shoved me against the solid wood, kissing the shit out of me in a way that was definitely not suitable for public.

Chapter Twenty-Two

Matteo

Watching Natalie touch and kiss Brooke had me teetering on the edge. My wife was fucking hot as hell. I tried not to get too excited because I wasn't sure where things were going. Natalie was the one who wanted to let things play out on their own, so I followed her lead with this. It was her show. She invited this woman here for a reason.

But at the end of the day, I was still a guy. One who wanted to watch two women together.

My cock ached at the thought.

I slammed Nat into the door as soon as it closed behind us. I needed to feel her heat.

"The two of you are straight fire together," Brooke commented as she watched us without shame. She was a tiny thing with short blonde hair and big blue eyes. Her chest rose and fell in quick breaths. Her nipples were hard under her almost see-through tank top.

Natalie snaked a hand out and grabbed Brooke's, bringing her closer to us. She leaned away from me and pressed her lips against the other woman's. Natalie licked into Brooke's mouth, making her moan and grip Nat's hip.

She pulled back and then grasped Brooke's jaw, guiding her mouth to mine. "Taste him."

Brooke's lips were wet and pillow-y. They were bigger than Natalie's, and for a moment, it felt weird kissing someone who wasn't my wife. Then Nat's hand was cupping my rock-hard dick and stroking me over my clothing. My mouth opened on a groan, and Brooke took full advantage, consuming my mouth.

Natalie leaned forward and pressed her lips into ours. Three tongues tangled together, and hands started roaming. Brooke ran her hand up Natalie's back as Nat slipped her hand under my shirt and traced the dips and rises of my abs.

I pulled back from the kiss first. Natalie and Brooke remained kissing for a moment before separating. Since Natalie was in charge of this endeavor, we waited for her next move.

She yanked her top over her head, dropping it in the entryway. She sauntered into the living room, heading toward the hallway with a little extra sway in her hips. She pulled different articles of clothing off as she went. Brooke followed her like an obedient puppy, leaving me as the caboose as the two of them stripped on their way to the bedroom.

The two girls hopped onto the bed as I entered the bedroom. Brooke leaned in and kissed Natalie as she guided her back. Her lips trailed from Nat's mouth down to her shoulder then her breast. I slowly removed my clothing as I watched them with rapt attention. As soon as my dick was free, I stroked my length.

Natalie's head was close enough to the edge of the mattress that she could easily take my cock while Brooke toyed with her nipples. I wanted her mouth on me.

Nat's eyes locked on mine, and she could clearly read my need.

Her voice was filled with lust as she spoke. "Let me suck you."

The head of my cock slipped passed her lips. She ran her tongue around the crest as Brooke shifted again, moving her attention down my wife's body.

Natalie moaned around my cock as Brooke's tongue found her clit. The sound tugged on my balls.

Watching this woman go down on Natalie was incredible. I wanted to watch her make Nat fall apart. "Make her come," I ordered because I couldn't help myself.

Brooke looked up; her eyes zeroed in on the way Nat licked the underside of my dick. Her hands caressed Natalie's torso and over her stomach until she reached her pussy. Her gaze was still firmly planted on my cock in Nat's mouth. Fingers danced over Nat's mound before they disappeared inside her.

Nat's mouth opened, moans spilling out and vibrating my cock in the back of her throat.

"You like having her eat your pussy, love?"

She nodded.

"Doesn't she taste good, Brooke?"

Brooke angled her head so I could see her tongue lick a long line from bottom to top before she said, "Delicious. I want to taste your cum, Natalie."

She squirmed as Brooke's lips sealed over her clit, and she sucked hard. Natalie's back arched up off the bed.

It wouldn't take much more for me to come either. My senses were on overload. I pulled my length from Natalie's mouth and bent to ravage her lips, swallowing her cries of pleasure as Brooke ate her through the orgasm.

"I need to be buried deep inside you, Natalie," I told her. "What do you think about taking care of Brooke while I make you come on my cock?"

I thought she might balk at the idea, considering what she said at the concert, but she nodded, almost eagerly. Her lips tipped up at Brooke, and they switched positions.

Brooke lying across the bed with Nat kneeling between her

legs with her ass in the air was not only porn worthy but also put my wife at the perfect height for my cock.

Before anything else, I *needed* to see what Nat looked like between Brooke's legs. She moved tentatively at first, clearly unsure of what to expect. It only took a few seconds for her to find a groove.

"Do you like eating her pussy, love?" I asked as I watched Brooke squirmed under my wife's touch. "Because I love watching you do it."

My hand fisted my cock hard as I stepped up behind her. Natalie glanced back at me over her shoulder, her eyes hooded and her cheeks pink. "She tastes sweet and salty."

My cock wept, and I couldn't wait any longer. I thrust into Natalie's pussy hard, and in one long stroke.

Natalie's cries were muffled by Brooke's pussy, but Brooke's were sultry and full of need. Nat began to explore her core with more vigor. Brooke squirmed on the bed as she tweaked her dusty pink nipples.

My hips moved fast, pumping in and out of Nat's warm pussy.

"Right there," Brooke directed as she twined her fingers into Natalie's hair and held her in place against her core.

The walls of Natalie's pussy clenched my cock as she licked Brooke higher and higher. It looked like Brooke was about to come as Natalie pulled her mouth away and screamed as she came, falling apart around me.

"Matteo," she shrieked as her legs wobbled, struggling to stay up as I thrust a few more times.

"It's too much," she protested as she sank to the floor in a heap of sweat and other bodily fluids. Brooke and her orgasm forgotten.

I scooped my wife into my arms and deposited her on the bed. Brooke turned her head to Nat, her skin was covered in a thin sheen of sweat. Her breathing was heavy, and her cheeks flush. She reached down, finding her clit as she waited for the next move. "Did that feel as good as it looked?"

Natalie rolled onto her side and nodded. "It was incredible." Her voice was dreamy and far off, but she somehow found the energy to play with one of Brooke's nipples. "I can't feel the lower half of my body."

I stroked my cock, keeping my orgasm on the horizon. Brooke's eye zeroed in on my hardness. She watched my hand work up and down as she swirled her fingers around her clit. "Looks like we could both use a bit of help, huh?"

There was no objection from Natalie as I stepped between Brooke's legs. Brooke continued strumming herself as I slid inside her.

Natalie leaned in drawing one of Brooke's nipples into her mouth. She licked a circle and then scraped her teeth up it. The urge to come drove me, and I fucked the woman writhing under me like a mad man. My balls tingled as Brooke mewled, her body beginning to spasm.

A roar ripped from deep in my gut as I tossed my head back and came. The blood whooshing through my ears drowned out Brooke's moans.

As I stepped back, my body felt wired from all the adrenaline and alcohol mixed together, and I made my way to the bathroom to clean up. When I returned to the bedroom, Natalie was out and Brooke was cuddled next her, a few blinks from sleep.

Chapter Twenty-Three

Natalie

My head pounded, and the scent of the bacon, which would normally smell good, made my stomach toss. Ugh, god I felt like I'd been hit by a truck and then it reversed over me again just for fun.

My arm might as well have been lead as I tried to roll over. Matteo snored softly next me, and he grunted when my arm landed on him.

If Matteo was in here with me, then who the hell was making bacon?

My brain was sluggish as I tried to recall last night.

I remembered District 12.

The concert.

The dancing.

The singing.

The drinking.

The other woman.

I sucked in a quick breath and then was out of bed too quick for someone who was hung over and felt like death.

"What's the matter?" Matteo asked, sitting up. His voice was garbled, and his speech was slow, as if his tongue was stuck to his mouth.

I yanked my robe on and cinched the sash tight around my waist. "She's in the kitchen. Making bacon."

"Who?" He rubbed sleep from his eyes, letting the blankets pool around his hips.

How much of his naked body did she see this morning?

"The woman from last night," I hissed.

"Brooke?"

He stood from the bed, his morning wood on display. Something about him standing there naked, saying another woman's name—a woman who was in our kitchen using it as if were her own—ticked me off.

"Yes, *Brooke*." I spat her name as if it were acid on my tongue. "Put some clothes on. I'm going to tell her it's time to leave."

Everything was wrong. The air was thick with memories that flashed in my mind as I trekked down the hall. Women's clothing littered the gleaming hardwood floors. Some of it was mine. Some of it was hers. I wanted to crawl out of my skin.

I had pulled my clothing off as I beelined for the bedroom, feminine giggling echoing behind me the whole way.

Why did I invite this woman into my bed?

Nauseousness rocked my stomach as if I was on a boat in the middle of an ocean while in a hurricane. As I reached the living room, the kids' school pictures hanging on the wall stared back at me filled with judgment and disgrace.

I brought this woman into my house. What if the kids were coming home this morning? Or worse were home last night?

Clanking and scraping from the kitchen filled the air as I neared closer and closer.

What the hell was I going to say to this woman?

I didn't remember every word we spoke last night, but I certainly remembered her mouth on me and mine on hers.

OMG! I had my mouth on a vagina last night!

I let another woman eat mine. While Matteo watched.

Matteo fuc—

Shut that shit down right now, Nat.

I needed to get this woman out of my house.

Brooke stood at the kitchen counter in a pair of panties and a shirt. I didn't recognize either of them, so I guessed they were hers either from last night or she had them in her bag.

Toast popped up from the toaster and startled me. I squeaked, which drew Brooke's attention to me. Her smile was bright.

"Good morning," she greeted. "I thought I'd make you breakfast as a thanks for last night and for letting me crash here."

Great, she was nice and thoughtful.

There went my whole be-a-bitch idea to get her to leave. Matteo joined us a moment later. Brooke's eyes trailed over his shirtless chest—why the hell wasn't he wearing a shirt?—and my hackles went up. I didn't like the way she looked over his body as if she knew what he felt like inside her.

My blood pressure rose. My heart beat faster. Unjustified anger filled me at warped speed.

Calm down, Natalie.

This woman didn't do anything I didn't let her or invite her to do.

"Morning, Matteo." Her voice was sultry and smooth like Sophia Bush's, and it was enough to make me want to scream. I knew she was remembering how he fucked her last night. Her moans of pleasure assaulted my memory as she smiled at him.

"Morning," Matteo said, taking a quick stock of the situation. I was five seconds from a freak out. He put his hands on my shoulders as he spoke to Brooke, and all I wanted to do was shrug them off. How could he touch me and speak to her as if everything was fine? Nothing was fine. It wasn't okay. I was ready to go out of my mind.

What had we done?

I couldn't even stand the thought of Matt's hands on me at the moment.

"It was nice of you to make breakfast, Brooke," he told her as I counted backward from ten in my head as a way to distract myself from the situation. "This isn't something we normally do. Truthfully, I don't know if we'd have done it without all the alcohol, and we need some time to come to terms with everything."

"Oh . . . all right. I'll just grab my things." Brooke looked startled and a little embarrassed as she left the kitchen, but I couldn't give two shits. I felt as if my life was imploding. All I could think about was how we allowed this woman into our home, into our bed, into our private sanctuary from the world.

Matteo had sex with her.

My husband had sex with another woman while I watched. The face he made as he came last night invaded my head as if it was being spotlighted in a museum. The memory was vivid, technicolor almost. He looked possessed, as if he were on another plane he'd never reached before sexually. I couldn't remember him ever making that face while he fucked me. And he fucked her last night. Hard.

And . . .

And he came inside her.

We didn't have condoms, and I didn't remember anyone stopping to even look for one before he slid into her.

Anger, hurt, and straight up fear festered in my gut like a Molotov cocktail shattering against bricks.

"You didn't wear a condom, and you came in her," I snarled at Matteo, lashing out at the closest thing to me. Him. "You better go figure out if we have anything to worry about."

His face dropped, and fear etched all over every inch. I wanted to die.

How could this have happened to us?

I couldn't look at his face as everything came smacking

into us. My chest felt as if it were on fire as I darted out of the kitchen and into the kids' bathroom.

Sinking to my knees, I dry heaved into the toilet. If there had been anything in my stomach to come up, it would have.

What if Matteo knocked her up last night?

I had the implant in my arm, so we didn't have to worry about condoms.

How could we be so stupid?

What if she had some kind of STI? Oh, dear god!

Sweat poured out of every possible place it could. I needed a shower. I needed to wash this all away.

This was a nightmare. All I wanted to do was wake up.

Wake up, damn it!

The hot water from the shower didn't help me feel any less dirty as I jumped in and let it pour over my head. We brought some strange woman into our home. What if she'd been an axe murderer or a con artist who was waiting to clean house as soon as we fell asleep? What if she was leaving a window unlocked somewhere so she could sneak back in? She had been up first. She was chipper too. I doubted she was hung over. I questioned if she had even been drunk last night at all.

When I exited the bathroom, Matteo had pulled on a shirt and was sitting on the couch, waiting for me.

Sure, he put on a shirt after she was gone.

The first thing I saw when I looked at him was that damn face again. The wave of nausea surged back up. Fuck, would I be able to see anything but?

Things were not right between us. The difference was so evident in the air that it could have been tangible. I pulled my robe tighter, almost warding off the chill the distance between us was throwing at me.

Matteo's eyes were rimmed with red—from the hang over or emotion, I didn't know. While I felt ready to explode, it seemed Matteo was ready to fall apart. His voice cracked when he spoke. "She said she's on the pill but will stop and grab a morning after pill on the way home. She offered to come back here and take it in front of us, but I didn't think that was the best idea. She'll send video confirmation when she's taken it. We exchanged phone numbers to follow up. She also said she's clean, but we should get tested anyway."

A torrent of fury radiated up my body. "So, now she has our address *and* your phone number."

"It was necessary, and once we know we are in the clear, I can block her," he said, leveling me with a hard stare. "I don't have any intention of contacting her outside of making sure she doesn't wind up pregnant."

A sob ripped from my chest as he said it aloud, casually putting the idea into the universe as if it didn't have the potential to destroy our lives. Matteo was off the couch in a heartbeat, but I still couldn't tolerate his touch. When he wrapped his arms around me, it felt tainted.

"Don't, please," I cried, stepping away from the man who could usually fix all my problems.

He fell apart a little more. "What's happening here, Natalie? I get that I screwed up with the protection last night, but why does it feel like you're acting as though you feel like I cheated on you? I followed your lead last night. You were there the whole time."

"I know that," I choked out, knowing he was right, but my feelings were raw and nonsensical. "But that doesn't seem to matter." Anger rose in my voice, taking over. "I can't stop seeing your face when you came in her. You never make that face with me. You've never looked so far gone before."

His eyes widened then narrowed. "Natalie." His voice had bite and sadness to it. "I don't know what face I made last night, but whatever face I made was because my wife just had sex with another woman and it was one of the hottest things I've ever seen. It had nothing to do with Brooke and everything to do with you and what we were experiencing together. Brooke could've been anyone."

Everything started to spiral.

The gravity of all that had transpired was too heavy, too suffocating. I knew I was about to break, and I didn't want to break in front of Matteo. I felt too vulnerable for that.

I couldn't look Matteo in the eyes. I really felt as if he cheated on me, but it was more than that or the face he made while he came inside another woman.

It was that there was a chance he could have a child with that woman. I didn't care how big or small the chance.

Even the smallest fraction of a percent was too much for me.

Everything felt soiled. Everywhere I looked, I saw some part of last night. The idea of heading into my bedroom sounded as welcoming as being water boarded.

I didn't know how I'd ever feel comfortable in our room again. How would I walk in there and not compare the blue of our walls to the blue of that woman's eyes? Every time I climbed onto the bed, would I think about her all over it?

The tricks a distraught woman's mind could play on her rational one were endless. Emotions were running the ship, and those bitches were steering straight toward the iceberg.

"Natalie . . ." The sound of his voice sliced me open wide, but I couldn't reassure him. I just needed to get out of there.

As I shook my head, I saw the tears tip over Matt's lower lids. Each one added a crack to my heart, but what were a few more when there were already thousands of fresh fractures? It didn't seem to matter how much I loved my husband. We crossed a line, and there was no uncrossing it. "I need some time. Away from here." It would have been easier to rip my own heart out than it was to say the next two words. "And you."

Chapter Twenty-Four

Natalie

My hand ached with a fierceness as I banged on Penelope's door unnecessarily hard. It was barely ten in the morning, and I was wearing an old, ratty T-shirt and leggings with bleach stains on them. Her neighbors must have thought I was a homeless woman lost in their neighborhood. Not that it mattered what anyone thought.

The ache in my heart outweighed any judgement from her neighbors.

The lock of the door disengaged, and then Pen was there, standing on the other side in her cute skinny jeans and billowy tank top. Her auburn hair was piled up on the top of her head in a messy knot and she held a cup of coffee.

The smell hit my nose and for some reason the fact I didn't have coffee with Matteo that morning, like we'd been doing for the last few weeks it'd been just us, made the tears well up on my lower lids.

I rushed inside, snatching her coffee cup as I passed.

"What the hell?" she screeched at my back. "You pound on my door like the DEA on a raid, you look like something the cat dragged in, and you steal my coffee? All without saying a word? You could've called, you know?"

The coffee barely had any taste as I drank it down, but I didn't care. "My phone is dead." My voice cracked as I answered. Everything was bubbling up and ready to spill over. The tears started first. They slipped down my cheek without permission.

I was numb on the drive over and hadn't considered the simple action of plugging it in.

I didn't want it to ring.

I didn't want to hear Matteo ask me to come home.

My shoulders shook as I tried my hardest to contain everything festering inside me.

"Natalie?" Pen asked, her voice bathed in concern. "What's going on?"

She approached and assessed the situation quickly. My hands gripped the mug as if it were my only lifeline. Tears streamed down my face, and I seemed to be rooted to the middle of her living room floor.

"Sweetie," she cooed, and the dam burst, sobs ripped from my chest as I crumbled to the floor.

Luckily for me, and Pen's rug, she grabbed the mug just before it spilled everywhere. She discarded it on the end table, sank down next to me on the floor, and pulled me in a half hug.

"What can I do? Where is Matteo? Should I call him?"

His name on her lips was gut-twisting. Matteo has always had this way of making things all okay for me. Not this time. He wouldn't be the one to make this all better. At least not with how hurt I felt.

My voice was buried underneath my sorrow so I only managed to shake my head.

"No?" She was understandingly surprised. "Okay, should I call Norah? This definitely sounds like a crisis of some kind."

I nodded, and in the next moment, she unwrapped her arms from around me and stood to head to the kitchen.

A minute later, she returned with a mug of coffee for me

and her cell to her ear. "Code Red. My house. Natalie is here, and it doesn't look good."

"Oh, girl." Norah rubbed my back. "I am so sorry."

Putting everything that happened from last night to this morning into words was a monumental feat. By the end, I felt as if I were in a fog bubble, and my life was just some tragic train wreck that I couldn't look away from. We were that couple who broke what wasn't broken by trying to fix it.

I cut my narrowed gaze to the side table, to where my phone vibrated like crazy. Even though I'd asked her not to, Penelope had plugged it in while we waited for Norah to arrive. It was filled with text messages and missed calls from Matteo.

"Aren't you going to answer it?" Penelope asked. I knew she has been dying to ask that for a bit but was holding back. "You guys should probably talk."

Scooping up the phone, I flipped the button on the side that would silence the ringer and dropped it on my lap. "I can't." I was too stuck in a pit of despair, unable to move passed the very real fact my husband, the love of my life, the father of my children, could potentially have a baby with a total stranger.

The texts started popping up on the screen.

> **Matteo:** Natalie, please come home.

> **Matteo:** Please, I need you.

> **Matteo:** Just please tell me you're ok.

Norah was sitting flush against me, so we saw the messages at the same time. She cursed under her breath.

"What?" Pen asked.

Norah squeezed my leg and gave me a sad smile. "This feels like an impossible situation. Matt wants her to come home. I can feel the desperation in his texts, and I want to tell her to go home. But"—she turned her attention to me—"I don't know if I'd be able to be around Derek in a moment like this either."

I wanted to go to Matt, but I couldn't soothe him when I felt the most exposed and vulnerable I'd ever felt in my life. His arms around me would only rub my wounds raw.

What would everyone say if this baby was our reality?

How the hell would we explain this to the kids? To my parents?

All I kept seeing was a movie playing in my head of Matt sliding in Brooke. His face when he came. Her face when he walked into the kitchen shirtless this morning. Her with a big pregnant belly. The two of them holding a little baby they shared. Him leaving me for her. It was like watching some TV drama characters fall in love.

Penelope's voice interrupted my day-mare. "This is Matteo we're talking about here. He would never do anything to hurt you, Natalie. I get that this sucks, but you aren't going to actually leave him over this, are you?"

The image of him smiling down at a baby . . . over Brooke's shoulder had another sob barreling up from my chest. "How am I supposed to stand around as he has a child with another woman?"

"You don't know anything yet," Norah stated as she rubbed her hand on my leg. "Don't start planning for the worst."

That was easy for her to say. I wiped snot from my nose with the back of my hand and didn't think twice about it. "How can I not? He came inside her, Norah. He fucking came in another woman without wearing a damn condom."

Pen moved from the smaller sofa to our larger one and

pressed against my other side, leaving me sandwiched between the two of them. "She said she was on the pill. Let's all just pray that everything is fine, and in a few weeks, you can put this all behind you."

It didn't seem as simple as she made it out to be.

Chapter Twenty-Five

Matteo

The hours ticked by with an unnatural slowness. Days felt more like weeks as I sat around alone, dealing with one of the biggest things that had ever happened to me.

I was confused and hurt and angry about the way Natalie was handling all of this.

I'd thought our love was unconditional. That there wasn't anything that could tear us apart. Turned out I was wrong. One simple oversight—one that I wished with all my being I could go back and change—was all it took to burn it all down around us.

Things went too far.

Lines were crossed that couldn't be uncrossed.

We had to find a way to fix this divide between us. There wasn't another option. Living without Natalie was something I would never accept. Even with as angry as I was, two days without her felt more like an eternity. She'd stayed with Penelope last night. Communication had been sparse—in fact, the only time she'd answered any of my calls or texts was last night, and that was to tell me that she needed time.

If it weren't for Adam, I would've gone insane with all the silence in the house. Yesterday, I busied myself with stripping the mattress and tossing it all in the garbage—wishing like hell that that was all I had to do to get rid of my problems. I bought new bedding and then scrubbed the house clean as if I could remove the memories with some Clorox.

But that only helped pass a fraction of time, and I needed something to keep me from hurling myself off a cliff. Hence, calling my best friend.

We sat out on the back patio, finished beers littering the table. Drinking probably wasn't my best response, all things considered, but what else did one do when they could have impregnated a woman who wasn't their wife and their wife left them all alone to deal with the potential fallout?

"She still hasn't answered?" Adam asked, breaking the silence that had settled over us.

There may have been times before then that I wished for just a bit of silence when things got really crazy around here, but I didn't think I'd ever ask for that again. I'd have given my left nut to hear Natalie yelling about dirty clothes left on the bathroom floor.

I shook my head as I stared out into the thick trees that lined the edge of our property.

"The video is legit?" he questioned once more, so I slid my phone to show him.

Brooke kept her word and sent me a video of her taking the morning after pill. She documented everything, opening the package, swallowing the pill, showing her empty mouth after. She was still wearing the same shirt as when she left the house. The woman covered all the bases for us. I had no idea if she had anything to lose like I did with Natalie, but she was equally invested in making sure nothing permanent resulted from Friday night.

"She said she was on the pill too?"

I nodded. She also told me that she was due for her period shortly and was certain we didn't have anything to truly fear, but at that moment, I hadn't been willing to count out any possibility. I took another pull on my beer bottle.

"Have you told Natalie that she did this?"

The video was sent yesterday, and the moment I received it, I called her. I wanted to tell her that Brooke did was she said, and I hoped it would help bring her home. She didn't answer. I didn't want to text that kind of thing to her and I wasn't going to forward the video to her. That seemed cruel. Although, it didn't seem like Natalie was interested in not being cruel because what she was doing felt exactly that.

"I tried," I replied. My voice was dry and harsh.

Adam had the decency not to try to offer me some platitude about things working out.

We sat quietly, the rustle of the leaves on the trees in the breeze the only sound.

"I know this won't make you feel any better at the current moment," Adam said a few minutes later. "But at least the chances of this resulting into a child are slim to none."

He was right. It didn't make me feel better.

Nothing could have made it feel right except my wife coming home and being the rock I needed her to be.

Chapter Twenty-Six

Natalie

Matteo's name flashed on the screen as I exited the airport into the parking garage. I'd just landed in Seattle from a quick trip to Portland to handle some things for the gallery opening in two weeks.

I didn't bother to tell Matteo I was heading out of town for two days. Based on his text messages and voice mails, he was getting progressively angrier that I wasn't coming home or answering his calls or texts. Couldn't blame him. I certainly wasn't going to call him while I was in Portland. We weren't speaking and I'd just hopped on the plane, which was childish and rude, but him knowing it would have just made things between us worse. After I snuck home for a change of clothes while he was at work and couldn't get out of there fast enough, all I thought about was the idea that maybe a bit of distance between me and here would be helpful.

I'd have done anything if it meant finding a way not to want to crawl out of my skin every moment of the day. Anything to have those nightmares that were present whether my eyes were closed or not go away. All I could think about was Matteo and his new family. Adorable little Brooke and their sweet baby. Visions of their life danced in my mind like the goriest of all horror movies come to life.

Matt didn't deserve to be shut out. I knew that above all else, but I just *couldn't*. Not yet. A long, harsh breath blew from my lungs as I sent him to voice mail and drove home. Or my temporary home.

My emotions were all over the place, same as every day since the weekend. I was exhausted as I pulled into the driveway. Skipping dinner at heading right to bed sounded like the best thing in world.

I didn't have the energy to move. All I wanted was to hide away from the world until everything returned to normal. If anything ever returned to normal again.

Penelope peeked through the window again. She was either worried I was going to sleep in the car or that I was a burglar who liked to park in the driveway. It was the third time in the last seven minutes. I knew it was exactly seven minutes because I kept checking the clock as if I could just wish the time by. Wish my life into a place where all my problems no longer exist.

Everything was overshadowed by this looming doom. Food didn't have a taste. Things didn't have smells. Life just sucked. Fear and pain consumed me. My heart was heavy. My stomach flip-flopped with every turn I made that took me in the opposite direction of my home—where I so desperately want to go but couldn't. I was a coward.

Just then, the front door swung open and Matteo's form filled the space. Every inch of him shook with an intense something. I couldn't tell from my vantage point in the car, but I knew things were about to get real.

Matt was done letting me ignore him.

Part of me was thrilled to see him. I still loved him fiercely. But the other part, the vulnerable part, of me was terrified of this confrontation.

I gulped as I exited the car. Nothing felt worse than

knowing you were the problem but not having any way to fix it or make it right.

He wasted no time storming down the path to the driveway and the car. "Is this how it's going to be? It's been six days, Natalie."

I wanted nothing more than to tell him it was all going to be okay but with everything all unhinged, I didn't know if it was true.

Matteo was clearly exhausted. He was wearing his glasses, a tell-tale sign he wasn't himself. There was stubble lining his jaw. His dark hair was sticking up in all directions as if he'd run his hands through it over and over.

Penelope looked apologetic from her spot on her porch and I wondered how long Matteo had been waiting for me. And what they spoke about.

"Natalie . . ." Matteo sighed. His voice no longer filled with anger but rather desperation.

My emotions were on overload, I wanted Matt to wrap me in his arms and assure me that it would all be okay but then that evil picture of him and Brooke and their baby and our babies all smiling for a happy holiday photo crashed through that thought reminding me that everything wasn't okay and there was a chance it never would be again.

"I—"

He reached a hand forward in attempt to grab mine. but I stepped back. The hurt on Matt's face matched the hurt in my heart "Please don't finish that sentence with can't."

The first tear rolled my cheek. "I don't know what to do here, Matteo."

I could tell he wanted to grab me, hug me, or maybe shake me, but it was clear he wanted to be touching me. My stupid brain seemed to have wiped all memory of his touch and replaced it with visions of him coming in Brooke. Unprotected. Then the happy family photo sans me popped back in. Lather. Rinse. Repeat.

"We're supposed to weather this storm together." His eyes glittered with moisture. I've only seen Matt cry twice. The day the kids were born and when his grandfather died. "I cannot sit in the house all alone any longer." His voice grew a notch louder. "I can't sit around waiting for this to all work out. We're a team, Nat. That means we handle shit like this together. Not with you hiding out at Penelope's and leaving for Portland without telling your husband. Is that what we've become?"

His anger flared, igniting mine as well. My fist clenched around my purse. Angry tears streamed down my face. "This isn't easy for me either. You just don't get it."

"What don't I get?" He crossed his arms over his chest. "Because last time I checked this was just as bad for me as it was for you. Do you think that I like the fact there is a possibility, no matter how big or small, that another woman could be carrying my child?"

It might not have shown in my actions, but I knew that wasn't easy for him. I wasn't a complete idiot, but logic wasn't in control. I took a deep breath and tried to explain myself. "Of course, you don't. I know this was an accident. But it's like that movie when they're trying to kill Freddy Kruger and they pull him from the dream. They bring him into their world, and he starts destroying them. That was what it feels like happened to us. We dragged our sex-adventures into our private lives—into our home, our bed. We mixed our worlds, and they came crashing down around us. There was a real chance that you impregnated another woman, in our bed, while I watched. That is the stuff nightmares are made of, Matteo. I can't figure out how to separate the two worlds again. They are all knotted together. I can't stop imagining what they could mean for us, for the rest of our lives. We've been here before. We know all too well how reliable the pill can be. It's like deja-vu with Jackson and Emma but I'm not in the picture this time. "

"Nat—"

"I'm terrified and hurt and sad. I felt like my skin was crawling for the two minutes I was in the bedroom on Monday." My chest heaved as I battled to get a hold of my anger and pain. "It's all so raw. I'm not strong enough right now to do anything other than wake up in the morning and perform basic functions. I'm sorry. I know you deserve better, but I just don't have any more left to give right now."

It was a struggle to put one foot in front of the other. Subconsciously I think I knew it would be unbelievably hard to walk away from him which is why I stayed away. I was torn in two. One half of me wanted to run back to Matt and just pretend that nothing ever happened. Go back home and live our lives as if the last week never happened. But the other part of me knew just how much damage this whole thing had inflicted.

Chapter Twenty-Seven

Matteo

Natalie had just walked away from me. Again. I wanted to chase after her as she headed up the driveway to the front door and force her to talk with me, force her to act like a partner, but I had to be at an important dinner with my boss in an hour. Earlier that afternoon, he came into my office and told me he wanted me to meet a client who just hired us.

A part of me had a feeling something big was going to happen for my career tonight and I wanted to share it with Natalie. That just made me angry. Next thing I knew, I veered off the exit and headed toward Penelope's, ready to drag my wife home after almost a week of her hiding out here. Only, I hadn't expected her to be on her way home from Portland when I got there. I expected her to just be getting home from work as well. I thought it was the perfect time to catch her off guard. Not give her any time to hide from me.

My anger kicked up a notch when Penelope told me she had just landed back in Seattle after having been in Portland for the last two days. After learning that, I wasn't leaving without confronting Natale. I gladly sacrificed an hour of my time waiting for her to get home from the airport.

I didn't get what I came for. If anything, I just felt worse as I stared at the front door to Penelope's house a few moments past Natalie having already gone inside. Pen stood there looking at me with her eyes full of sadness.

Penelope was extremely empathic, and I knew this was hard for her. Even if she was Natalie's friend first, she was just as close of a friend to me as she was to Natalie. She had texted several times over the last few days to check in but left out that Nat wasn't there in her messages. It felt like a sucker punch to the balls to find out Natalie had flown out of town without so much as a word. She just up and left and I wanted to smash my hand through Pen's glass coffee table as she spoke while I waited.

Natalie's words sat heavy on my chest all the way home and to the restaurant. She couldn't separate the reality and the fantasy any longer. I knew the movie she was talking about. *Freddy Vs. Jason.* It was always part of the Halloween movie marathon that Jackson loved to watch every year.

Brooke brought everything from the darkness into the light. Natalie didn't want the two to mix, she didn't want to acknowledge that it all existed in the same room. That was what she didn't understand. Whether it was a dream or nightmare, it was *our* life. We needed to deal with the consequences of our actions together. Only then could we separate the two again. But truthfully, were they ever separate to begin with? We are who we are. We want what we want. We enjoy what we enjoy.

All of the want and indulgence tasted like ash on my tongue.

I was begging for forgiveness while Natalie acted as if I went out of my way to hurt her. When it felt like the exact opposite, like she was trying to punish me.

I couldn't put into words how that felt.

Each day I sat alone, painfully aware that I was one more day closer to knowing the fate of this awful situation, waiting, hoping for a call from Brooke telling me that we could put the monster back into the box. If the news was anything other than we had nothing to worry about, I wasn't sure my marriage would survive it. And, shit, did that hurt.

I'd been trying to convince myself that Natalie wasn't doing well with the unknown. I knew she was scared of history repeating itself. Nat was on the pill in college. We were the .01%. We knew all too well how anything could happen. I kept saying that, so long as Brooke didn't turn out to be pregnant, we could get through this. But if that wasn't the case, I was seriously starting to worry my life would never be the same.

BROOKE'S NAME FLASHED ON MY PHONE SCREEN. I SAT ALONE in my empty house the next day packing a bag to head out for a trip to meet with our new clients. Last night, my boss informed me that I was being promoted from consultant to senior consultant. We were heading to Florida for three days to meet with our new client, see their business plans, discuss policy options and rates.

Being bumped up to senior consultant and spear-heading this new client with Barry was a massive accomplishment for me.

One that could be overshadowed by the news of this call.

My heart hammered in my chest. I knew what this call was for. I'd anxiously been waiting for it. I just didn't know if I could handle the results. Logically, my brain kept telling me I knew she was on the pill, she took the morning after pill, and it was just a week ago tonight. She couldn't be pregnant with my child even if she was. Right?

I wanted nothing more than to turn to Natalie and confirm my thought process, but she wasn't here. My teeth gnashed together remembering how alone I was in dealing with this. Anger rose up from my gut, but it was squashed back down when the phone vibrating in my hand took over my focus.

A buzzing filled my ears as I answered the call. "Hello?"

"Hi, Matteo." Brooke's voice was light and airy, as if she didn't have a care in the world. Thank god she was great throughout this whole thing. The situation could have been a thousand times worse with someone else.

I swallowed the lump in my throat down. "How are you?"

"I'm all right," she replied. "I just wanted to let you know I started my period this morning. We don't have anything to worry about."

A numbness surged through my body. It was as though I was feeling so much leading up to that news that it all shut off as soon as I had my answer.

Relief was euphoric. The chains of uncertainty and purgatory released their hold on me. All I wanted to do was turn to my wife, tell her the good news, and pull her into my arms. As bizarre as it sounded, this was a moment I wanted to share with her. We could move forward without any tethering to our disastrous night.

Except she wasn't here. I loved her unconditionally, and the longer I didn't feel that in return, the angrier I got.

No. I wasn't angry. I was downright furious with her. It was time she heard how I felt.

The next morning, I stomped up to Penelope's door and knocked. I didn't give any thought to the hour. It wasn't early exactly, but if Penelope had just gotten home from work this morning, she was about to be woken up.

For a moment, I thought about coming over here last night, but I was mentally exhausted. I didn't want to confront

Natalie tired and angry. I had a lot to say and I didn't want to do or say something I'd regret.

The hushed whispering behind the door brought all that fury right back to the surface.

"Tell him I'm not here. Tell him I already left for work."

"I'm not lying to him." Penelope hissed.

I cleared my throat. "I can hear you. Natalie, open this damn door."

Chapter Twenty-Eight

Natalie

My heart sank as Matteo called out on the other side of the door. It was eight in the morning, and this early of a visit was the last thing I expected.

"What is wrong with you?" Pen chided as she looked from the door to me with disappointment painted across her face. "I'm not lying for you. Stop hiding here and fix your marriage. I would have killed to have Kevin care about fixing our relationship the way Matteo wants to work through your problems."

She opened the door and revealed an agitated Matteo. "Come in."

Her eyes bounced between us. "I'll be in the kitchen." She gave me a pointed look before leaving me standing in front of my irate husband.

Why did seeing him angry make me defensive?

My guard shot up, and I hated it. Matteo had always been my safe place, not somewhere full of unease and shame.

He cleared his throat. "I spoke to Brooke last night."

Her name sent my stomach to the floor next to my feet.

"She started her period. We have no pregnancy to be concerned about."

The anger in his voice was a contrast to the flood of emotions soaring through me. Relief. Exhaustion. Maybe a bit of anger, and something else I couldn't quite identify. Incredulousness, perhaps.

"Why do you sound so angry about that?"

His fists clenched at his sides and his nostrils flared. "I'm pissed because when I could finally breathe again, when I could feel my shoulders relaxing, when I finally felt a fraction of anything positive in a week, the only person who matters wasn't there with me. I sat there alone, again. When I really needed you."

It didn't matter whether or not he was right, my sensible side had taken leave and my mouth just started running. "And I'm still trying to figure out how the hell our perfect marriage got here—with my husband being relieved he didn't get another woman pregnant."

He grunted and stepped forward, forcing me toward the living room. "Jesus Christ, Natalie. How we got here doesn't matter! You're hurt. You're upset. You're angry. I get it. But there are two of us in this situation, in case you've forgotten. How I feel matters, too, damn it. Stop only thinking about yourself here and letting your feelings cloud your judgment. You're starting to really piss me off."

I opened my mouth to reply, but it was too late. Matteo stopped me. "You had your chance to talk. I've been begging you to speak to me for eight fucking days. I've always bent over backward to make you happy because I love you. I've listened to you say that you can't. You can't talk. You can't be around me. Can't look at me. All while you ignore the fact that, each time you say it, it cuts me open and I'm bleeding out over here. I'm barely holding it together, so now you are going to listen to me."

His words were laced with pain and the guilt flickered in my heart a bit. "I need you to stop playing the victim and be my wife. Be my best friend. Be my support. From the moment you reminded me that we were careless, and a child was a possibility, you've placed all the blame on me. I was the one held responsible. I had to discuss birth control and STIs with a woman who I'd met when I was drunk the night before. You stuck your head in the sand and left me hanging out to dry."

"I've been alone in this too."

He took another step closer. His stubble had grown out, giving him a very rugged look even in his slacks and collared shirt. "That's been your choice. Because you don't want to admit your mistakes and accept the accountability. I've owned mine. You haven't. You're upset and mad about mixing our worlds, but you're the one who did the mixing. I didn't invite that woman home with us. I followed all of your cues, let things play out how you wanted them to. I didn't hear any objections from you at any point. Yes, I forgot the condom, but so did you. There were three adults in that room, and no one thought about protection."

I knew that. I'd run this through my head so many times. If I did this, that that wouldn't have happened. If I'd made better choices. If I'd acted like a regular wife and mother, this wouldn't have happened and my marriage wouldn't be on the line with a love child potentially waiting in the wings.

Matt was right, but that didn't mean I was wrong. I had the right to be hurt and sad. But there was no longer a chance of my nightmare coming true, so what happened next? "I don't know where to go from here."

"Where exactly is here, Natalie?"

The huff drew from my lungs involuntarily. "Here is feeling so far from my husband we might as well be on different continents instead of standing next to each other. Here is seeing images of my husband having sex with another woman whenever I close my eyes. Here is me staying with my friend because I don't know if I can step foot in my bedroom without seeing it all again."

There was a lot in that statement. Before I could even try

to unpack it all, it was spilling from my lips. Matteo wasn't going to let any of that go.

His arms stretched over his chest as he crossed them. "What if something like this had happened with Adam? How would you feel if the situation were reversed, and I left you to deal with that all on your own?"

I shook my head, trying to ignore that Pen, who was no doubt listening from the kitchen, had just been inadvertently told that I'd slept with Adam. "I don't know." I shrugged, not wanting to admit I wouldn't like it. "But we didn't have to worry about this with Adam."

"And you'll never have to think about it because I took care of it ahead of time," he reminded me. "Adam and I discussed how the night would go. That night with Brooke wasn't planned."

Heat rose up my neck. My face felt flushed. "So, what you're saying is that it's all my fault because I was the one who said we didn't have to plan everything out and we could go with the flow? Is that what you're saying?"

He shook his head as my frustration reached an all-time high. "What I'm saying is that I don't think there should be any blame at all. We should be working on learning a valuable lesson and putting it in the past." He ran his hand through his hair. "At first, I was okay accepting your anger because I felt like I'd wronged you. But did I really? I made a mistake and was dealing with one of the most potentially life-altering situations I'd ever had to deal with, and I was doing it alone. Without my wife, without my best friend, without my partner. Did you ever stop to think about what *I* was coping with this week while you holed up at Penelope's? No, you didn't. I needed you to stand by my side, and you didn't. You left. Where was my understanding and support when I needed it?"

My lips parted, my mouth opened, but nothing came out.

Matteo sighed, defeat overtaking his rigidness. "You need to work toward letting me down from the cross, Nat. I've owned my lapse in judgment. I've told you how I feel. It's your turn to acknowledge those feelings instead of dismissing or invalidating them with your own shit. I know you were scared. I know that you think that our two worlds mixed, but there were never two different worlds. It's all one life, and when you can finally see that, maybe you'll see the destruction happening. Don't ruin our marriage over one mistake."

A tear slipped down my cheek. Matt's hand twitched as if he wanted to wipe it away, but he didn't come any closer to me. "We're supposed to work as a team to find a solution. Let me know when you're ready to do that. Maybe when I get back from Florida, you'll be ready to be the woman I love again. "

Wait, what? "You're going to Florida?"

"Oh, yeah, by the way, I received a promotion to senior consultant two days ago." His jaw clenched as I tried to digest his words. *Promotion.* "I head out in two hours to meet with a new client. Thanks for being there to celebrate with me. I've only been waiting for this for years."

He was leaving town. He finally climbed his way to the position he'd wanted for two years. "Senior consultant?" I asked as he took a few steps back toward the front door. He just nodded, his back to me as he grabbed the knob. "How long will you be gone?"

"A couple of days," he replied as he opened the door. When he turned backed to me, his eyes seemed haunted and despondent. "I'll give you a call when I return. Maybe then we can start to act like we're a married couple who loves each other again."

Chapter Twenty-Nine

Natalie

I'd been trying to make sense of the kaleidoscope of random thoughts and dichotomous emotions swirling inside me since Matteo left that morning. Everything I thought and felt kept butting together, making a bigger mess.

My mind was a muddled sea of confusion, and I had no one to help me work through it. No one could work through this jungle of a mess but me.

Stress, anxiety, fear, panic, and anger. I'd felt them all for the last week. Mostly at the same time. But they had become amplified to a whole other degree.

I'd never seen Matt the way I did earlier. He was callous and enraged. All I wanted was to be overjoyed. He had a new, well-deserved title. There was no longer a threat with Brooke.

Except, I couldn't process his words or rejoice in the baby that is no longer a possibility. Everything swan around in my head distorted and chaotically. I needed to make it all stop before I went insane. My job was the only thing keeping me grounded lately, so I threw myself into it. Work had become my safe haven, and that was where my attention needed to be today.

I didn't even mind when Bastien lost his mind over his

brushes or his wobbly easel or his paint colors being wrong. He spent an hour ranting about orange, and I was right there next to him, hanging on his every outlandish accusation about the supplier and sympathetically nodding my agreement when he decided it must be someone breaking in and switching his paints to sabotage his work. Focusing on someone else's issues was far easier than dealing with my own.

The paranoia was new for Bastien, but I rolled with it until Annetta stepped in and started yelling at him in French.

He stopped complaining after that.

A text came through from Penelope.

Penelope: Bateau 7:00pm. Dinner isn't optional. Norah and I will meet you there.

I knew immediately that they were staging an intervention of some kind. No way was Pen staying quiet after hearing everything that happened with Matt this morning.

My palms were sweaty when I parked at the curb and fed the meter. The day has started to catch up with me and I was exhausted. Even my hair hurt. Between Matteo, Bastien, the screaming in French, and my own subconscious, I felt as though I'd been through war. Battle after battle. I didn't know if I had another one in me for Pen and Norah.

Norah was waiting for me in the lobby when I arrived. She linked her arm through mine and guided me to the table. "Pen already ordered us some wine."

"Thank god." I breathed a sigh of small relief.

Norah looked me over with sad eyes. She was never one to hold back the truth. "You look worn thin, babe."

"I feel thin," I said as we joined Pen in the booth. "I feel like I am living in this . . . this . . ." I struggled for a way to put it all into words. "Cloud? Fog? As if I'm running in place and can't move."

As Norah and I slid into the booth, the waiter arrived with

three glasses of red wine. "Can you bring over a whole bottle?" I asked, knowing we were going to need it. Or at least I was. He nodded and walked away just as I realized that I couldn't actually drink the entire bottle because my car was here and calling my husband for a ride wasn't an option. I couldn't ask him to come get me or have him bring me here in the morning. God, that was so symbolic of the current state of our marriage—in two totally different places, literally and metaphorically. That thought stung deep.

Sliding the one glass I'd be allowed to have closer, I began to ramble and couldn't stop. "It's taking so much energy for me to try to keep my shit together. I'm mad. I'm sad. I'm hurt. I'm lonely. I miss him, but I still can't look at him the same."

"It's okay to feel all those things." Norah comments as she passes me a menu. "You are allowed to be all those things. What isn't okay is living in them. You need to move through them."

"After this morning," I tell her. "I think it's clear that I don't know how to do that. I don't know why his anger pisses me off and makes my guard go up. I don't know why he can't see how hard this is for me. That I couldn't just hold his hand and say that everything will be okay while we wait for word on his role of baby-daddy. I couldn't."

My chest heaved a bit when I finished. I didn't mean to say all that, but it just came spilling out, and I couldn't stop.

Our waitress arrived a minute later just as Penelope was about to say something. We ordered our meals and then Pen picked right back up. There were no pleasantries today. We dived headfirst right in.

"Have you spoken with Matteo since this morning?" she asked and leaned forward for a piece of bread from the basket on the table.

My teeth gritted together at her tone. "He texted to tell me he landed in Florida."

She shook her head. "A lot happened this morning, and

you guys leaving it like that, letting things fester seems like a really bad idea. You can't ignore it and expect it to heal."

"I'm not ignoring it. I wish I could. It's all that I can think about."

Pen took a bite of bread, so Norah jumped in. "You can take this however you want, but I've been biting my tongue for a few days and just can't do it anymore."

I drained my glass, knowing whatever she was going to say was going to piss me off. God, I didn't think I was going to make it through dinner without another glass.

Norah slid her wine over to me. "We came together, I'll drive your car home."

Finally, something going my way. I grip the stem of her glass, bracing for her words. "Thank you."

She nodded. "I don't think the punishment fits the crime. I don't even think there was a crime. Things got out of control, and I can't really imagine how you felt that morning. I also can't figure out why you keep shutting out Matteo as if he'd done something wrong."

"He—"

She held her hand up. "No. I'm not done yet. I get being upset about the situation, but it wasn't as if you walked in on him with his mistress. There was nothing nefarious going on. He didn't get drunk and bring some random woman home alone. From what you've told me, it wasn't even his idea. So, why have you iced him out?"

My fingers tightened around the glass and I had to loosen them before I broke it . "I'm a woman who had to imagine her husband having a baby with another woman."

"But there's no baby," Penelope interrupted. "So that isn't something to be worried about anymore."

"It's still a damn hard pill to swallow, Pen. What else was I supposed to feel but pain and betrayal?"

Her eyes were soft, and her voice withheld judgment.

"Feeling that way isn't wrong. But he didn't betray you. Unless there's something I'm not aware of."

I took a deep breath and hung my head. "No, there isn't anything else going on. But things are different. They feel different. I don't know why, but I'm scared. Our life could have been irrevocably changed."

Our dinners arrived, and after our waiter left, Norah turned to me. "Your life *could* have been irrevocably changed, but it wasn't—at least not by a pregnancy. You were rattled, which is natural, but she isn't pregnant."

"The crisis was averted," Penelope chimed in. "What you need to do is look past the fear of something that is no longer relevant so you can see the damage that fear and anger and hurt did."

"What on Earth are you talking about?" I glared at her across the table ignoring the pork chops sitting in front of me. "What damage?"

"Natalie, I love you, but you are the one who is making everything worse right now."

I opened my mouth to argue against that statement, but she held firm.

"Nope. You need to hear this. All I keep hearing is 'I' and 'me.' What about Matteo? I imagine he feels as if you abandoned him in the worst way at the worst time. Put yourself in his shoes for a second. You wake up to a strange woman in your kitchen and your wife fuming mad. Your wife tells you that you could have knocked the chick up and, oh yeah, by the way, you could have caught a disease that would make your junk fall off as well. Then, while you're still grappling with those bombs, you get the random woman to leave and make sure you and your wife have a plan. There is finally a second to breathe, a moment to sit with your wife and try to work through what happened, only your wife refuses to talk to you and then leaves."

I lived the picture she was painting. It hurt but looking at it through this lens seemed worse. I wanted to throw up.

"Are you done?" My voice was ripcord tight as I railed against the situation she just summed up in a handful of sentences.

"Not hardly," she whispered. "Did you listen to him this morning, Natalie? I mean really listen? To what he wasn't saying? He is falling apart. That man has always been there for you, no matter the cost to himself, and in what was probably the first time he really needed you, his wife and partner, where were you? He needs you. He's been telling you that he needs you even with how angry he is with you. And, yes, he has the right the be angry with you so stop getting all affronted when he shows you he is mad. But he's communicating his needs to you and you. Are. Ignoring. Them. He got a freaking promotion, one that I'm assuming is a big deal, and you weren't there when that happened. You're missing the good things because you can't stop focusing on the one bad thing. The one bad thing that can no longer hurt you."

She needed to stop. I wanted her to stop. I didn't want to hear this.

The first tear slipped down my cheek. "Pen. Please," I whispered.

Her voice softened, but she continued. "It isn't too late to fix it, though. Matteo wants to fix this. You need to work together."

"You can't live in this stage of regret," Norah said, pushing her entrée aside. "That's what this is—it's regret, and you need to push through. Move past this with Matteo, not alone. Let go of that fear about what could've been and focus on what is still here."

She makes it sound so easy. "How?"

"That's for you guys to figure out," Norah replied. "But I think that after fourteen years, he deserves for you to try—

unless, of course, that isn't what you want. Are you thinking about leaving him?"

Just the thought of that made my heart hurt. "No, I don't want to leave him, but I can't figure out how to stay with him either. I can't stop seeing what could have been in my mind. It's like a reel of torture that plays over and over."

"Well, like I said, the first step is moving past the fear. It's no longer relevant," Pen said. "Then I guess your second step would be to talk to Matteo. Be honest with him, trust that you two will do what you always have done and get through this together."

I nodded, completely exhausted as I picked up my fork and started in on the roasted potatoes on my plate. My stomach begged for food while also rebelling against the idea of it.

Norah and Pen transitioned the conversation from my problems to this week's episode of *The Bachelor*. I thought that show was dumb, and they knew it. They were giving me a few moments with my thoughts.

My dinner didn't have a taste. It smelled good, looked good, but I didn't taste it at all. My mind whirled with everything these two laid out for me and it made me sick to my stomach. Everything felt so impossible. All I could see were trees, there was no forest in sight for me. How did I get past the trees to see the forest?

"Nat?" Norah's hand slid over to cover mine. "Hey, you okay?"

I blinked and shook my head, trying to clear the mess. "I'm sorry, what did you say?"

"I'm going to get your car," she repeated. "I asked for your keys and where you're parked."

The waiter came by with the check, and Pen grabbed it. "I'll go take care of this and use the restroom. I'll meet you out front."

I hadn't realized we'd finished dinner. I didn't remember

eating or drinking the rest of the wine in the bottle. Digging into my bag, I pulled out my keys for Norah. "I'm around the corner."

She nodded. "I'll meet you back at Pen's."

My eyes landed on the last two or three sips sitting in my glass. Why not? I was going back to Pen's to think about how pathetic my life had become. I'm just grateful the kids are in camp and aren't here to see this mess.

"Natalie?" A gruff voice startled me, and my eyes darted over my shoulder to find the watcher from Immersion standing at the end of our table. For a second, everything felt surreal, and I fidgeted, trying to remember the guy's name.

Gerald? No. "Gerard?" I hoped that was his name.

He smiled warmly, as if my getting his name right was the best part of his day. He nodded. "Sorry to interrupt your meal, but I saw you earlier, and when your friends left, I couldn't resist checking on you to make sure you were okay."

Make sure I was okay? That was odd. This man kept getting more bizarre each time I crossed paths with him.

Hairs on the back of my neck rose at the strangeness of this conversation. "I'm all right."

He looked me over as if he didn't believe me. "I haven't seen you since that night we last spoke. I was worried that something had happened. Everyone okay? Jackson? Emma?"

I didn't like the way my children's names spilled from his lips or that he even knew their names at all. An eerie feeling settled over me. He was doing more than just watching that day in the sauna. He was listening, but more than that, he was cementing facts about my life in his mind.

"I'm fine. Just busy. My husband and I are taking a break right now."

Penelope returned, looking at me as if I'd grown a second head while she was gone. Gerard's eyes narrowed a bit and got a beady glaze to them. "I'm sorry to hear that." He glanced at

Pen and then back to me. "Well, I hope to see you again soon."

As he walked away, a chill ran down my spine, and I made a mental promise that if I ever ran into him at the club again, I would leave immediately. I didn't like the way he glanced back over his shoulder at me as he returned to his seat at the bar with a buddy.

I felt their eyes on me like a smarmy touch.

Penelope angled her face away from the two men watching us and asked, "Who was that guy? You looked uncomfortable talking to him."

Trying to match her subtly, I whispered, "A guy from Impressions."

Penelope looked shocked and a bit grossed out. "What did he want? Is he allowed to talk to you? Like don't you have NDAs and stuff?"

My fingers tightened on the strap of my purse as I slung it over my shoulder. I was ready to get out of there. I didn't like that my two worlds were colliding again. "I think that's why he waited for you two to be gone. He didn't mention the club but did say he was concerned because he hadn't seen us in two weeks."

She practically choked on her spit. "You haven't done anything with that man, have you?"

"Eww, no." I shook my head. "But he has watched us have sex a few times. It's open to whomever wants to watch."

"Okay, I think we should get out of here," she said. "I don't like the way he's looking at you."

The interaction with Gerard left a cloud of unease that followed me back to Penelope's. The urge to call Matteo niggled at me. He would make me feel better. Tell me things were fine and there wasn't anything to worry about.

Penelope was right when she had said that Matt had always been there whenever I needed him for whatever I needed.

Was I really making things worse? I knew that silence and distance weren't going to help, but I was stuck in this . . . I didn't know perpetual nightmare of what-ifs and regrets. I wasn't ready to tackle going back home yet, but maybe talking to Matt was a smaller step to start with. Maybe smaller goals were what would help.

Pulling out my phone, I brought up the text message about his arrival in Miami. It was late there. Too late to call. Or at least that was what I told myself

Natalie: I'm sorry that I haven't been there for you. I am in my own hell, and this is the only way I can deal. I don't know how to handle all of this.

My thumb hovered over the send arrow. I hesitated. Matteo said so much this morning, and then with the girls piling it on, my apology felt pathetic, but it was all I had.

Still, I wouldn't blame him if he didn't respond. When the three dancing dots appeared, I let out a slow breath.

As his text appeared on my screen, I'd wondered if perhaps no reply would have been better.

Matteo: I know. But it still doesn't change anything.

He used my own words on me. Damn, I didn't like it. I knew what they meant. The damage was already done and it was hard to erase it.

Chapter Thirty

MATTEO

When I turned and walked away from Natalie the other morning, it was a thousand times harder than it seemed. I had to, though, because, while I would do anything to fix my marriage, I needed to remember to also take care of myself. I needed a time out even if Natalie looked as if she needed a hug and a thousand questions answered.

Rather than focusing on learning all I could about the client we were meeting with and the things his company was looking for from us, I was absorbed in thinking about all the ways I'd been naïve about this whole situation. I'd thought as soon as I was able to tell Natalie that we didn't have any permanent ramifications or reminders from that night to deal with, the switch inside her would flip, we could heal, and things would start to return to normal.

Instead, her accusation of my being upset that Brooke wasn't pregnant lit a fire inside me. I didn't know whether she said it just to be a brat or she truly thought that, but either way I couldn't stand there a second longer, telling her all the ways I needed her without her being able to understand.

While her text may have been the spark of a match in a dark cave, it still didn't begin to make anything better.

I began to understand what she meant when she said that our regret didn't change the past. She was sorry for her actions, and I was grateful for that, but it didn't do much to help me justify or understand how she reacted.

Knowing that someone was remorseful for their actions didn't make it all better. It didn't change the event that transpired. Natalie could be sorry that she shut me out, but it didn't change the fact she cut me off. It didn't sooth anything.

This entire two weeks had been exhausting. My head ached. My heart hurt. I felt so empty. My emotions were shifting and not to a good place.

The last three days had actually been a much-needed reprieve from my life.

Our new client, Diego Rosa, wanted to form an insurance company that sold a unique insurance product—a legal services product, which is being considered insurance in the state of Florida. He wanted some help, some actuarial help and actuarial credibility, to figure out how much he would need to charge for this product in order to make a fair and reasonable profit, how to document those calculations, and justify it to the state of Florida, so he hired our firm to go through that process with him.

A lot of work went into something like that. Financial statements had to be developed along with balance sheets and income statements. These were our best estimate of the future financial condition of the company based on the anticipated revenues and expenses of the company. These are necessary to submit to insurance regulators as part of the licensing process for a new insurer.

Diego asked for my help in preparing an insurance rate filing for all this, plus communicating with the insurance department in an effort to get the department to approve the licensing of the new insurer and their proposed rates.

The beauty was all in the detail of numbers. They didn't lie. They were what they were and you either accepted that or didn't. A new project was exactly what I needed to get lost in to distract myself from the hell of my home life.

Our flight back from Florida landed just before ten, but with the time change, it might as well have been three in the morning. Barry and I spent the flight reviewing what was still left to be done to complete Diego's profile, noting deadlines for submitting the required statements to the state, and a few other things he wanted me to take on in my new role. We exited the plane and made our way to the luggage carousel.

"Thanks for all your hard work, Matteo," Barry said as he grabbed his bag and we turned toward the exit. He was heading out front for a cab and I was making my way to the parking deck. "I just wanted to ask, is everything all right? While your work is as impeccable as always, after spending the last three days with you, you don't seem as happy as someone whose career was just elevated to the next level should be."

Barry was a nice guy. I'd been working under him for about four years, and while I wasn't going to spill all my guts to the man, I also knew I needed to let him know that nothing was going to affect my work in my new role. "Thanks, Barry. I appreciate your concern. Everything is good."

He nodded. "Okay. Have a good night. Get some sleep. Or drink some bourbon."

I couldn't say whether either of those would help, but I replied nonetheless, "Will do."

Even with my frustration and disappointment in her actions, for the past couple of days, I'd been tossing around the idea of surprising Natalie with something I felt was necessary in order to move forward. We *needed* to move forward. Even my boss knew my life was in some kind of upheaval. It was time to start putting everything back together.

My phone was still in airplane mode, so I reached into my pocket to turn it on, attempting to see if I could get the ball rolling with the idea I started discussing with my uncle after I left Pen's house the other day. My uncle owned a general contracting business and was willing to help me with what I wanted to do.

My phone let out a torrent of chimes, beeps, and dings as it came back to life.

My eyes zeroed in on the voice mail notification. It was from Natalie.

I clicked the button, and her voice filled my ear. She sounded desolate and slightly tipsy.

Her voice was calm as the message started, but I could tell her mind was anything but with the way her sentences all ran together. She barely took a breath as she said, "I know that we should have this conversation face to face, or even over the phone, but it's on my mind and I can't turn it off, so I need to leave this message now." She paused for a breath. "It took me some time to realize that I wasn't the only one hurting. I didn't think about how you felt because I was too encapsulated in what I felt."

The bitterness and resentment I harbored couldn't let me wrap my head around how she hadn't considered that. "I also think it was too hard for me to see your side of the situation, and that maybe I didn't do the best job of explaining why I'm having such a hard time with it all. Why I can't just wrap my arms around you and smile because there is no child with Brooke."

My palms moistened as my heart rate picked up. I'd never be able to thank my lucky stars enough that those words never became a reality.

I wasn't sure how much more I could handle after the week I'd had. All the talk about not knowing how to fix things made my skin crawl, and I didn't think I could sit around and listen to any more. Nat was sorry for her response to the situation, but that didn't mean she wasn't still looking for a place to throw blame to relieve her guilt or justify her actions. I wasn't in the mood for any of that at the moment. I wanted to get across the parking garage, into my car, and head home.

She took a deep breath, and I swore I held mine as she spoke. "When I woke that morning and Brooke was in the kitchen making breakfast, it annoyed me from the moment I realized what she was doing. I'm not sure why since it was a rather nice thing to do. Then I walked past her clothes on the floor, and all I could see was her with you from the night before. When you met us in the kitchen, she looked at you the way you look at someone you know intimately, which she did. But you are my husband, and she had no right to look at you that way. That was when I realized there hadn't been any protection. I was suddenly thrust into this parallel universe. It was like she just inserted herself directly into my shoes, into my whole life, overnight. Sleeping with my husband. Cooking breakfast for my husband. Potentially carrying my husband's child. And it was all happening in my own damn house. It was too much. I snapped. I was consumed with rage and jealousy. It seemed as if she was trying to steal my life right from under my nose, and I let it happen. Then it all morphed into a cloud of sadness and fear that I didn't know what to *do* with. We can't take it back. I can't find my way out of the cloud."

Holy shit.

That I didn't see coming. I had to sit on the bench outside the elevators of the parking garage to try to absorb it all. Natalie felt insecure. I had no idea she felt threatened in that way. I understood how the idea of Brooke ending up pregnant scared her, that was common sense, but she never said anything about the jealousy. And I never suspected. I'd assumed that she felt as steadfast in our relationship as I did.

"What is it that you want to take back?" I asked to no one but still genuinely wanting to know. I'd be lying if I said I didn't enjoy the experience, but I wanted to know why Natalie hadn't. That was something we were going to need to discuss.

A wave of pure sadness washed over me as she continued trying to explain. "When I woke up the next day, everything felt wrong. But it didn't feel wrong until after. We had fun. I enjoyed myself during it because you were enjoying yourself. I wanted to give you something I assumed you wanted as you had done for me so many times."

Wait what?

That was a volley of arrows piercing my heart. I never asked for that. I didn't need it.

"I know what you're thinking, and no, you never asked for that night with Brooke, but you're a man and what man doesn't want to see his wife with another woman or have a threesome? I guess I figured it would be like that night with Adam, so why not give you that experience?"

My heart pounded in my chest as I thought about what she was implying. Did she plan that night with Brooke ahead of time?

She answered my thought in her next confession. "I didn't set out to find a woman to bring home with us for anything, but Brooke was kind of into me and she was definitely attracted to you. The idea popped into my head and I ran with it. Let it all play out once things started moving in that direction. I didn't plan it, but I didn't stop it. Everything is fun when you're drinking, and it doesn't really register as something that is happening in real life. How do I live with this mess I've caused? How do I live with this jealousy and regret? I thought I could handle it and be strong like you, but I'm not."

The sounds of her swallowing interrupted her words, which were becoming a bit more frazzled and her pitch grew higher as the words tumbled out faster. "This whole thing is *my* fault. I know that. I started us down this path with my stupid desires. What the hell am I supposed to do now? I can't take it back. It happened, and now I have to live with it. I couldn't have just been happy with a normal sex life like all the other married couples? I had to want more, and now I've ruined everything."

By the end, she was crying. And hiccupping. I stood from

the bench, wanting nothing more than to wrap my arms around her whether she wanted them there or not. "It's eating me alive, Matteo. The sadness in your eyes, the images I can't get out of my head, the regret. I just can't."

The beep over the line signaled that the message had ended. "Oh, love, nothing is necessarily ruined. You just needed to have told me this about ten days ago."

If I had known the root of the problem for Nat's behavior, I would've known how to better handle the situation. We both needed to find security and safety within one another again.

She left that message about an hour ago. It was after ten, but I pressed the call back button as I made my way to my car any way. It went to voice mail as I had a feeling it would.

I pulled up Penelope's number, knowing she'd answer, and I could at least check on Nat.

"Hey," she answered on the third ring.

"How is she?" I asked as I hit the button on the remote to open my trunk. I tossed my suitcase inside. "She left me an emotional message about an hour ago."

"She's going to have a bit of a hangover tomorrow." Penelope sighed. "I was pretty hard on her the day you left. She's coming around but is riddled with guilt and regret. The wine started as soon as she got home from work today. She cried for about twenty minutes after her phone died during her message. She's passed out now. She also spoke with Jackson and Emma today, and I think that made things worse for her. With you all being apart, she is really spiraling."

I knew I needed to follow through with my idea and start to piece our life back into place. One of us needed to take charge, and Natalie certainly wasn't in any condition to do so.

Taking a deep breath, I exhaled slowly. "We'll get through this, Pen. I've got somewhat of a plan, I think. Just keep an eye on her for right now, all right? Now that there is no baby for her to focus on, I think she is coming to terms with everything she said in her message."

Chapter Thirty-One

Natalie

It was amazing how fast and deep we fell from grace. One day, everything was chugging along just fine, and the next, I found myself leaving long rambling, semi-drunk messages on Matteo's voice mail because it was easier to say what I needed to a machine than the man himself.

It wasn't easy for me to accept my responsibility in this situation. I knew it was my fault. I knew I needed to accept that in order for us to move on.

```
Matteo: I got your voice mail. Can we meet
later to talk about what you said last night?
```

The Metro Portland opened next week, and I was finding myself constantly pulled between the two locations. Tonight, I'd head down to get things finalized because Bastien's showing opened Tuesday evening.

```
Natalie: I'm leaving for Portland tonight for
   an early morning walk through. I need to
          leave for the airport at 8.
```

Matteo: How about 6?

I'D BEEN PUTTING OFF PACKING FOR MY TRIP TO THE LAST minute because I didn't want to go back to the house for my suitcases or clothes. Penelope was great at sharing her to-die-for closet with me, but I needed to suck it up and get my own stuff.

Also, I needed to face my bedroom, and I hoped that would be easier to do alone.

The entire drive home, I gave myself a pep talk about how it was just a room and I was strong enough to block it out. This was our home, so I had to find a way to get over it. My lunch rumbled in my stomach anyway. A huge rock of discomfort sat in my chest.

When I pulled into my driveway, Adam's truck was parked in it and there was a pick-up truck with construction supplies in the bed parked along the curb.

Curious and a bit worried, I trotted up the path to the front door and let myself in.

Adam was on the couch in the living room, flipping through a sports magazine. He looked up at me and smiled softly. "Hey, babe." He rolled the magazine in his hand and stood to give me a hug. "How are you?"

He obviously knew about what was going on between Matteo and me. He had a hundred questions swimming in his eyes, but I had a more important one. "I'm all right. What are you doing here though? Did something break?"

He looked torn. His eyes darted toward the hall as he bit his lip in contemplation.

"If he didn't tell you, then I think maybe it's supposed to be a surprise."

There was a good chance I'd never enjoy a surprise again. Recently, I'd developed a strong appreciation for things being planned and organized. Nothing could come and mess things up that way.

I didn't see anyone working from where we were in the living room, but I heard the sound of work being done somewhere inside. "Adam, I'm going to find out either way. I'm here."

He gripped the back of his neck. "Listen, I don't know much about the whole plan. He just asked me to fill in for him here to let the crew in. I don't think he was expecting you to stop by."

What difference did that make? "Probably not. But what does that have to do with anything?"

Adam looked torn. "I don't want to ruin any plans he may have with this. Why are you here anyway? Are you sneaking in whenever Matteo isn't here to avoid seeing him? That's so messed up, Natalie."

I shook my head and dropped my bag to the floor. "No, not avoiding him specifically. I'm avoiding all the memories that come rushing back to me when I step through the door. I'm heading to Portland tonight, so I need my suitcases and more clothes. I can't put it off any longer."

The sounds of ripping masking tape filled the air. The smell of latex tickled my nose the closer I got to my bedroom. When I stepped into the threshold, the first thing I saw was that all the furniture was piled in the middle and covered with a tarp. There were two guys in the room, painting the walls a dusty rose. The taupe carpet had been replaced with dark walnut hardwood. A ceiling fan replaced the old light fixture over where our bed used to sit. The operative phrase there was *used to* since there was no longer a bed in the room.

"He pulled some strings with his uncle and got a crew to come in to redo it." He looked down at me. "They've been at it since around eight this morning."

Tears welled in my eyes. We were both mad, but even at

our lowest point, he still thought of me. He still tried to make things better for me.

Adam wrapped his arm around my shoulders. I laid my head against him and sighed. Why couldn't I shove all this in the past and move on? Why was it so hard for me but Matteo made it look so easy? Why couldn't I decide if I was mad or not? My emotions were flopping around like a fish out of water.

"Why won't you come home, sweetheart?" Adam asked as we watched the man paint the neutral color on the walls. "What happened?"

I looked up at him. "How much has he told you?"

"I know the chain of events." His words were soft. "I've heard Matteo's version, but that isn't the same as yours."

My lungs burned as I sucked in a breath and held it in for a few beats. I exhaled slowly, savoring the sting in my chest. "It wasn't like the night with you. With you, it was an experience, and then we went right back to who we've always been. We didn't spend the night together. I don't mean this offensively, but you were an added bonus to an experience between Matt and me."

That didn't seem to bother him. "And with the other woman?"

"When I think about it, I feel jealousy and regret. It seems I have a problem with him being intimate with other women."

Adam chuckled. "If you think Matt wasn't jealous when we were together, you were either not paying attention or were too distracted to see. We talked about everything beforehand so he knew what was coming every step of the way. I knew my place, and Matteo knew that I did, which made it easier for you to trust and enjoy. But that didn't mean he wasn't ticked off at the way you fell apart on my tongue. Why do you think he wanted me to see how he could make you come?"

He made sense. Matteo had drilled me with a ton of questions when considering the threesome with Adam. With

Brooke, clearly nothing was planned. "I was trying to give him something cool, and it backfired."

Adam smiled as he squeezed me tighter. "Next time, you should ask him. That is, if you ever consider trying something like that again. Don't be so quick to swear off all girl-on-girl action." He waggled his eyebrows like a typical dude. "You just need to find the right partners and maybe have a discussion before all the clothes come off."

I doubted I'd ever have another threesome, but his advice was logical.

"Can I help with the suitcases?" He looked at my outfit, which was a maxi-skirt, crisp white T-shirt, and chunky brown belt, and then turned to the bedroom. "I doubt you want to risk getting paint on yourself."

Or risk Penelope's wrath if I ruined her clothing.

"Thanks."

He smiled. "It will all work out, Natalie. I've never met a stronger couple than you and Matt. Don't give up."

Chapter Thirty-Two

MATTEO

Natalie was seated on Penelope's porch swing when I pulled up. She looked the same as she always did but different at the same time. She looked calm, yet still a bit unsettled.

I hated that we were still so far apart emotionally when we couldn't seem to stay in the same city for more than a day or two at a time this week. I had no idea how we were going to pull off parents' weekend with the kids in two days if we didn't get to talk through all the things Natalie left in her message.

I wanted to plan a way to have this conversation where things weren't rushed and we could talk it all through, but it seemed our work schedules had other plans for us. I had to take what I could get. We couldn't continue to push this aside.

Natalie looked nice as I stepped onto the porch. Her dark hair was swept off to the side, and she had on a navy-blue dress. Her eyes seemed a bit brighter than they were in the beginning of the week.

She smiled weakly before adverting her eyes. "Hi."

"Hi," I replied as I sat next to her.

She kept her focus out on the front lawn. "How was your trip?"

"Fine," I responded, following her lead with the small talk. "How are things with the gallery?"

In the midst of everything going on, I'd kind of forgotten about the Portland opening.

"The final inspections are tomorrow morning," she said, picking at some invisible lint from her skirt. She still hadn't made eye contact. "The painters will come in after and the set-up crew will be in with all the fixtures to start hanging things when I get back on Sunday."

She wouldn't miss parents' weekend on Saturday for anything short of the world collapsing. "Are you flying back in tomorrow or Saturday morning?"

"Tomorrow." Natalie finally turned toward me. "I saw the bedroom."

Again, I nodded, not knowing what response she wanted from me. Was she upset that I had the bedroom redone or relieved?

"It was supposed to be a surprise."

I nodded for a third time.

"Why?" It was several questions rolled into one. Despite this chasm between us, I could still read between Natalie's lines.

I dug the corner of my nail into the wood of the arm rest on the swing. Which why did I answer first? "You made it clear that you didn't think you could ever feel comfortable in our bedroom again. Selling the house would be a drastic decision, so I decided to see how this would help first."

"Why didn't you tell me about it?" she asked.

"It was easier," I said shrugging. "If I just redid the room and showed you, I'd hoped that it would make things less hurtful. I didn't want you to think about the reasons we were redoing it. Just that it was a whole new room with new memories to be made."

By taking all the decisions away from Nat, I thought she wouldn't have to think about everything with Brooke anymore. The whole idea of this was to move past what went down that night.

"Knowing that you had it remodeled makes me feel . . ." She paused to think about her words, and my body braced for a battle. Maybe doing major home renovation without speaking with her first was a mistake. "Loved."

Her words slammed into me, but for an entirely different reason. "Loved?"

She nodded.

"Had I not made you feel loved before?"

She shook her head and my face fell. "It isn't what you're thinking." She rushed out. "What I mean is that when I saw that you changed everything about our room, it felt like the night all this began. It was that first night when you arranged a whole dinner and sex. I mean I get that I said I didn't think I could return to the bedroom, but, to me, it felt like you were taking care of me when I couldn't do it for myself. Even though I didn't truly deserve your empathy and compassion. You knew I'd struggle so you shifted the burden from me to you. The room looks pretty and new. I love it and I hadn't even seen the finished project. Now, when I think of the room, I can focus on the pink on the walls and the fan I always said I wanted during the summer. I can see you loving me even at my lowest."

I'd always had an understanding of what Natalie needed before she did. It was part of the connection we had. It was part of what made us work so well together. It wasn't hard to see that we needed to make some drastic changes to get the ball rolling in the right direction.

"I'm glad that you like it."

"But?"

My eyes searched hers. "But we are ignoring the elephant in the room."

"Ugh." She groaned and slowly blinked, shaking her head. "Drinking and feelings and cell phones don't mix."

My hand instinctively went to her thigh. Her skin burned under my palm. "You needed to say all that, Natalie. You should have unloaded it days ago. It would have been a little easier to understand your behaviors. I didn't know that you were feeling jealous of Brooke. I thought you were just angry and scared. If I had known you thought that Brook was just going to walk into my life and replace you, I could have assured you that would never happen. No matter what the situation."

"Just because you say it doesn't mean that I would've accepted it." She sighed heavily. "Everything is a mess up here." She tapped her head. "I can't seem to cope with the fact that I did this to us. I can't seem to see how to go back now?"

A sheen of wetness coated Natalie's eyes, but she blinked it away quickly looking back out to the lawn.

I squeezed her thigh. "If we want to move forward, together, you are going to have to speak up about your feelings. We can't live two separate lives and expect things to fall back into place. It's killing me, Natalie."

The wetness thickened in her eyes and collected in the corner. "I . . ."

She needed to understand that we couldn't heal separate. We needed to heal together. "I'm a family man. My life is rooted to my family. I love my children. I love my wife. But for almost the last two weeks, it's just been me. On my own. It's like living this life I don't want is sucking the life out of me. I feel like I'm a boat out to drift with no anchor. You're my anchor Natalie. I couldn't ever have a life that isn't rooted to you and the one we've created."

"How do we fix this?" She swiped a stray tear from her eye. "How do I accept everything I've done and move on? How do I live with this?"

All I wanted to do was pull her into my arms, stroke her hair, and whisper in her ear that we do it together. We put one foot in front of the other. We carve out time each day to have conversations. About our day, our feelings, the damn weather. Anything to show her that nothing is ruined, and we can be us again. Distance isn't the answer.

It was difficult to tell what she was thinking. Her face was a mix of different emotions. Worry, sadness, and a pinch of happy. "I really do appreciate what you did with the bedroom."

"You're welcome."

What else was I supposed to say?

She tucked her hair behind her ear and fiddled with the ends. It was something she did when she was nervous. "Maybe we could go for dinner when I get back."

We sat there discussing a possible meal together as if we hadn't been married thirteen years. I didn't know whether to punch the wood I sat upon or cry. I was hoping that since Natalie let out her deepest insecurities and I'd reassured her of just how irreplaceable she was to me, she would come back home. Not offer to schedule me in for dinner the next day. But I guess it was a positive step and I needed to recognize she was trying.

"Yeah, sure."

Natalie looked upset with my apathy in that moment. "Look, I don't like this any more than you do. I'm sorry. I thought I could be like you and give you everything you wanted, but I'm not. I wasn't strong enough. But I won't lose you because of it. I've been selfish. I've been stubborn. I've made mistakes. I'm not perfect. But I *am* trying here, Matt. I'm lost too."

"So, come home." I tried not to grit my teeth as I spoke.

She sighed as if coming home was the biggest inconvenience of her life. "I know I need to come home, but I need to get my head straightened out first. Before I can concentrate just on that, I need to get through this opening. I just need to tackle one stressor at a time."

I understood what she meant, but the words still seemed like a slap in the face. *Tackle one stressor at a time.* Our marriage and home had become a stressor for my wife. Wonderful.

Just when I thought we were taking a step forward, it felt like with those words, we took three steps backward.

Chapter Thirty-Three

MATTEO

The doorbell rang, and I called out, "It's open."

Adam was joining me for wings, beer, and baseball tonight.

It was a stark contrast to my typical Saturday night, which was running around with the kids or going to Immersion with Natalie or even dinner with her. Instead it was ordering wings, stopping at the liquor store, and watching the baseball game.

If we didn't get our shit together, this could be all my future Saturdays starting next month. I didn't get to have dinner with Natalie Friday or have the opportunity to talk in the car on the trip up to see the kids on Saturday. There was some kind of crisis in Portland.

The gallery failed inspection for some kind of electrical issues. Insults were hurled, egos were bruised, and crew were fired all for the inspector to fail the building rather than giving a conditional approval and coming back to check. Without an approval from the city's board of planning, Metro couldn't open on Tuesday.

Natalie had to find a company to come in and fix the issue immediately while trying to sooth the inspector and beg him to come back the next day. She was stressed to the max and couldn't leave the place unattended.

Instead, she FaceTimed with the kids while I was up with them. It wasn't the same as her being there in person, but I could tell she needed to see them even if just through a camera.

Adam's larger-than-life presence filled the room as well as the scent of buffalo wings. "Man, you look like crap."

I nodded my agreement. "I feel pretty stellar, too."

He passed through the kitchen and then sat next to me on the couch. The wings were deposited in the middle of the coffee table, the tops of two beers were popped, and the first batter struck out.

"Natalie and I spoke on Wednesday."

This was news to me. Natalie didn't mention Adam during our chat. "Yeah?" I had a bunch of questions. "Were you with her when she saw the bedroom?"

He licked buffalo sauce off the tips of his fingers. "She thought something was broken and came in panicked. I tried to talk her out of it, but you know Natalie."

Yes, I did. "Thanks for trying."

He tipped his beer back and settled into the corner of the couch. "She looked surprised in a good way."

I tried to change as much of the room as I could for that specific purpose. The further away it was from its previous setup, the better. "She said she really liked it."

He took a drink of his beer and then hung his arm over the side. He was intently focused on me. "When are you going to bring your girl home?"

Not for a few days, at least. "She's in Portland until Wednesday."

"What's she doing in Portland?" he asked, bringing a wing to his mouth.

"The gallery is opening a new location there."

He took another swig of beer, washing down his chicken. "When?"

"Tuesday."

He frowned. "Isn't that like a big deal?"

I nodded and sat forward to grab a wing.

"Are you going?"

I shook my head and took a bite. Damn, these were good. "I wasn't planning on it."

His forehead scrunched. "Seriously?"

"Yeah, why?"

He leaned over and placed his beer down on the table. "You guys are fighting to put shit back together, and yet, you aren't going to show up to something you know is a big deal for her?"

"It isn't as if she invited me or asked me to come."

He looked at me with disappointment. "Matteo." His voice was firm. "Natalie's dealing with jealousy and regret, she's worried that everything has been ruined. You aren't showing her it isn't. Don't you see that? You put more effort into planning a night for us with your wife than you are putting in to trying to fix your marriage. Come on, dude, you're better than that."

"She doesn't want me there. Her words were something along the lines of wanting to handle one *stressor* at a time."

He grunted. "When did you become a pussy?"

So much for watching baseball and hanging low with my buddy. "What's that supposed to mean?" I snapped back.

He scoffed. "Two months ago, you asked me if I was interested in being a third with you and Nat. No hesitation. No fears. Just straight-up honesty. Now, you're afraid to piss off the wife you're trying to win back by supporting her?"

My jaw stiffened, and my teeth clenched. As much as I missed Natalie, I also just wanted a night of not thinking, of not wringing my brain dry.

I ran my hands through my hair. "Listen. I'm tired. I'm tired of playing guessing games as to what may or may not work. I asked her to come home, and she told me not yet. That she needed to get through the stress of opening the new gallery first. Isn't that a clear message that she wants these two parts of her life separate?"

"Or"—he tilted his beer toward me and raised his eyebrows—"everything goes off without a hitch, and Natalie looks around, taking in all of her hard work, and can't really enjoy it because you aren't there to share it with her. You, the person she loves the most, will be the guy who couldn't be bothered to put aside the argument and be there for her. Weren't you pissed about the same thing with your promotion just this week? How is she expected to believe that nothing has been ruined then? How can she feel secure in that?"

Fucking Adam.

"Would you be there if everything were right in your world?"

The answer came without any conscious thought. "Yes."

He sat back and smirked. "Then there's your answer."

My mind started weighing each side. Pros and cons. What could go wrong? What could go right?

"Don't think so hard," Adam said. "I'm off for the next three. We can head down tomorrow if you want or even Tuesday morning. Road trip. I'll keep you from losing your mind on the way down. I'm sure Natalie wouldn't mind the extra celebrant. Too bad we couldn't get Trev to come. Hey, what does the other married guy say about all this?"

Trevor laughed at me. He couldn't wrap his head around trying to do something like we did with his wife Audrey. "He told me I better grovel until Natalie said it was enough."

Adam made it sound simple. Just hop in the car, hang with my bud, and go see my wife. As if it would fix all our problems.

"So, what do you say?" he asked. "Do we need a Road to Portland playlist?"

Seattle hit a home run, and cheers erupted from the speakers. I took it as a positive sign. Three weeks ago, I was desperate to get my wife back. I needed to tap back into that guy. "Let's do it."

Chapter Thirty-Four

NATALIE

THE PAINTINGS FILLED THE ROOM with a tidal wave of color. Bastien's work wasn't about objects and figures but shapes and colors. This new focus was gorgeous splashes of vibrancy that told a story. The canvases started out with blacks and gray and transitioned through the color spectrum into orange and yellow.

It was titled *Life in Reverse*.

The thing I loved about abstract art was that you couldn't lock it in a box. It meant something different to everyone who looked at it. I had no idea what Bastien was envisioning when he painted these, but when I looked at them, I saw a story of life.

The yellows and oranges blended to represent the brightness and innocence of new life. We experience so many events and emotions during our time on Earth but then we fade into the black as we come to an end.

Or I could flip it and see it the opposite way. We start life in the dark and grow into the light. Things become bigger and brighter as time passes.

The serenity I felt taking it all in washed away the obnoxious amount of stress I felt this weekend.

"No!" Bastien shook his head and stomped his foot like a three-year-old, drawing my attention away from the painting. "This isn't how they go. The canvases are too far apart and this one is upside down. *Putain!*"

He was in rare form the rest of the morning and found sadistic joy in making everyone's heads spin.

I didn't envy the people tasked with rehanging or Annetta, who was the one who got to calm him down. With the rest of the gallery being mine to get ready, I slipped away, blocking out Bastien's diva moment.

One of my favorite parts of my job was this. Today. Seeing it all come together. I'd spent months securing other pieces to house. Countless hours spent tracking down muted pieces that wouldn't interfere with Bastien's vision for his collection. It hadn't made a lick of sense until he unveiled his own pieces.

My fingers flittered over the smooth dark marble of a sculpture I was able to procure from a Turkish artist. It was one part of a perfect array of pieces to complement the main focus.

It took me about two hours to double- and triple-check all the piece plaquettes, history blurbs, and program orders before I was positive everything was set for tonight.

In the main event room, Bastien was finally signing off on the setup. Ten pieces hung as the focal of the space. He played with lights for a moment, and when he switched on the spotlight, it was as if the canvases came alive.

"It's breathtaking," I told Annetta. It made all his crankiness and outbursts from the six months wash away in favor of the warmth I felt looking at the paintings.

She nodded. "The asshole has more talent than he knows what to do with."

Her eyes traversed the room and landed on me. "Everything is wonderful. You did a magnificent job, as always."

"Thank you."

She checked her watch. "I'm going to grab him, feed him lunch, ply him with a few glasses of Champaign, and go over his speech for tonight. We'll see you at five."

Annetta ran a tight ship, and no one knew how to handle Bastien Bisset like his sister. Their duo was unparalleled.

As I stepped into the warm heat of Portland, I pulled my phone from the pocket of my pleated shorts. I was making a concerted effort to reach out to Matteo, especially since the chaos here cause me to miss our dinner plans on Friday. I sent texts about my day. Thoughts of this and that. I knew he wanted me to come home, and deep down, I wanted to too. I was hoping to unscramble my brain as soon as this building opened tonight. I'd fly back to Seattle tomorrow with the gallery set and the showcase in full swing.

Then I would unwind these fears from my mind.

Matteo had looked so withdrawn on Thursday, and I knew I owed it to him to try harder. He typically held this ownership of himself, and it was clearly missing last week. He seemed defeated and basically admitted as much. He was tired. I wasn't making it easy to love me, I knew that. My inability to deal with my regret was destroying my husband.

I was working on changing my perception of the situation. We tried something new, and I didn't like it. Like trying a new dish or perfume or sexual position. It didn't work for me. I enjoyed it in the moment, but I had no desire to do it again. That was it.

There was no need for me to dwell in the negative.

What I needed was to find that mind scrubber from *Men In Black* to eradicate the memories that followed from the next day. Then I'd be good.

Cigarette smoke wafted through the air, tickling my nose

as I walked toward my hotel, which was a block away from the gallery. Looking up, I spotted a man who looked eerily like Gerard from Immersion.

There was no way that could be. My mind just kept finding new ways to torture me. If it wasn't glimpses of Matteo's non-existent second family, it was the creepy guy from the club who unnerved me the last time I saw him.

I just couldn't keep my two worlds apart.

With each step closer I took, the better I saw the figure. My mind wasn't playing tricks on me. What the hell was Gerard doing here? In Portland? At the same hotel I was staying at?

My stomach dropped to the sidewalk as I noticed that his focus was on me as I approached.

"Natalie?" He feigned shock as if he hadn't just watched me walk two hundred feet. My skin crawled with the way his beady eyes looked me over. "What a small world. What are you doing in Portland?"

He crushed the end of the cigarette between his thumb and index finger before dropping it into the ashtray on the top of the garbage can. "Work. We have a new gallery opening."

I instantly regretted giving him that much information because there was something about running into him here that didn't feel so innocent. Something about the way his eyes sparkled that made me want to step back. "You work for Metro?"

Goose bumps danced across my neck and I forced myself to nod. "I do."

His lips spread into a strange smirk. "I didn't know you were involved in the art world. I'm also here for Bisset's new collection. I'm in the market for a new piece of art."

I tried to keep my smile tight, not too inviting because I didn't want to spend any time near him tonight. But he was also a potential buyer, so I had to maintain my professionalism around him. "It's going to be great."

"Where's Matteo? Is the family coming to see the big reveal?" he asked as he searched the space around me as though he were truly looking for Matt.

All my spidey scenes fired off warning shots, screaming at me to get away. I never told him Matteo's name. He never spoke to Matteo.

Relax, Natalie, he has seen you two together. He's heard you call out his name.

"He'll be here later," I lied, not caring if there was a reason for how and why he knew Matt's name. It would be easy to say something came up if he asked again at the show. At the moment, all I cared about was getting inside my hotel.

"Well, see you later." He shrugged as he turned and walked into the hotel as if he were staying there too. I waited until he disappeared around the corner before I went in. Something in my gut told me that man didn't need to know I was staying here as well.

A feeling of dread stirred in my belly. Things felt . . . off. I wished Matteo were here. Remembering my phone in my hand, I pulled up Matt's name and called as I walked to the elevator banks. His voice mail picked up, so I left a message just before I entered the elevator car. "Hey. I'm on my way back to my room then I'm heading for lunch before I have to get ready for the showing. Just wanted to call while I had a minute. See you tonight."

It sounded stupid, but just hearing his voice helped wash away a bit of my unease. That was definitely a good sign. The paranoid part of me made sure to keep up my lie because I didn't know where Gerard slunk off to.

The cloud of apprehension he cast over me followed me down the hall, but I reminded myself that my brain was on overload and I was probably just trying to find some new way of distracting myself from dealing with my issues.

I stopped outside my room and slipped the keycard from my pocket. As I slid it into the lock, my head was shoved forward, my face slammed hard into the door. Everything stopped for a moment as pain reverberated throughout my skull. A sharp sting burned across my forehead and an agonizing throb emanated in my cheek.

My bag and phone fell from my hand to the floor. I tried to focus so I could scream for help, but a hand that reeked of cigarettes covered my mouth. Gerard. I knew it deep down. Something warm trickled down my face. Blood—either from my forehead or nose, I wasn't sure—mixed with the disgusting taste of the dirty skin pressed against my lips.

"Shh."

My fears ratcheted up about a hundred notches. My heart hammered so hard in my chest I was terrified I'd have a heart attack. Gerard's other hand reached down to turn the handle, and he forced me through the door to my room. The contents of my purse scattered across the floor as he kicked my bag in with us.

Tears trickled from my eyes thanks to smashing my nose, my forehead burned with agony, and a deep-seated fear rose up as the latch clicked shut behind me.

"Help!" I yelled as loud as I could the second he released his hand from my mouth. "Help!"

I ran to the side of the room as far from him as I could. He charged forward, and the sound of him backhanding me vibrated off the walls. The right side of my face pulsated, and I felt it start to swell, but I didn't have a second to focus on it before Gerard yanked me to him and covered my mouth again. His other arm curled around my throat as he put me in a headlock. "I am here to help you," he snarled as if I were an ungrateful hag. In the distance, I thought I heard my phone ringing.

His hold tightened around my neck, squeezing until I was barely hanging on to consciousness. He released my mouth. It wasn't like I could yell as he choked me. My fingernails clawed at his arm, trying to get him to let go, but he wasn't deterred. He stepped forward, pulling me with him.

Panic gripped me tight as he grabbed one of the thigh-highs hanging from the side of my suitcase and jammed it into my mouth. His dirty fingernails scraped the roof of my mouth in his haste to push the nylon between my lips, and then his palm was, once again, pressing over my lips. I retched and did my best not to vomit around the gag.

"We have a special connection, Natalie," he whispered into my ear before he licked the side of my face.

Don't throw up! Don't throw up! If you throw up, you will choke on it and die!

Genuine fear for my life spread through my veins like wildfire. I couldn't breathe through my nose, making me think he broke it when he shoved me into the door. His hold around my throat hadn't loosened. I wasn't sure if he was aware that he was strangling me, which was scariest of all. He was in some kind of state of delusion.

"I felt it that first night I watched you fall apart in front of me. He might have been the one inside you, but I was the one you sought out with your eyes as you climaxed. It was such a beautiful thing to watch, love."

The way he used Matteo's pet name terrified me. It meant he paid closer attention to us than I thought. Only, I had always been so engrossed in whatever Matteo was doing to my body that there was no way in hell I was ever connecting with him. He just happened to be there when it all exploded.

He let go of my neck and yanked me up by my hair. My scalp was on fire as he gripped a handful of it by the roots. He glared at me with hard eyes as his voice grew angrier. "But then you closed me off. You teased me."

He leaned in and ran his nose down my cheek not the least bit deterred by the blood no-doubt now covering the side of my face thanks to the burning gash on my forehead. My body revolted in repulsion. "You allowed me in and then cut me off. He told me all his plans and painted an erotic picture that I wanted to see. Then he went and closed the door."

His hot breath skated across my jaw and down my neck. He was starting to breathe a bit heavier. The idea that he was getting revved up for something big, something I definitely wasn't going to like, sent terror barreling through me.

He jerked my head back and smirked with sleazy confidence. "Was I too much competition for him? Could your husband feel me lulling you away from him?"

His grin was absolutely sinister as the next words passed his lips. "Is that why you stopped coming to the club? Is that why you two separated?"

My stomach tightened. How could he know that?

My gut knew this wasn't a coincidence. I wasn't imagining things or being dramatic.

A tremor ran down my body, and I squeezed my eyes shut, trying to control my emotions.

He was stalking me

Had been for weeks at least. Black spots hung on the outskirts of my vision as dizziness started to take over when I thought about him following me all summer. Did he know where I lived? Had he followed me to Penelope's? Is he following Matteo too? What if he'd killed Matteo and was here to drag me away?

Was it possible to actually be scared to death? Because everything inside me turned off. My vision blurred. My ears rang. My whole body felt as if it were missing feeling.

I was off kilter when he shoved me onto the bed and snatched the sash from my robe lying on my pillow. I felt as though I had no control over myself. I was seized by terror.

He approached me with the sash and some adrenaline finally kicked in. Blood smeared across the bedspread as I tried to roll away from him. No way was he going to tie any part of me to something. Not happening.

He snagged my ankle and pulled me back toward him. I

attempted to grab on to the bedspread, but I couldn't get purchase. My head throbbed as Gerard flipped me over and yanked me. His eyes appeared feral as he dragged me to him and looped the sash from the robe around my ankle. "No fret, dear Natalie. I've watched you enough to know just what you like. Even if you did dangle that juicy plan with the sex swing in front of me in the sauna and then shut me out, I still know how you like to be touched."

His hand trailed up the inside my thigh, inches away from my core, and it was as if his touch rendered me immobile. I froze. He was going to rape me. I wanted to kick him in the face. Then punch him in the throat. And the balls. But I couldn't move. All I could focus on was this unwanted touch.

Disgust washed over me as he slipped his hand into my shorts. A wave of nausea crashed down on me as he flicked my clit. Another tear leaked from my eye down my cheek.

I heard the sound of my phone ringing again. Then it all hit me.

Snapshots of the kids and Matteo shuttered through my mind.

The kids on their last birthday.

Their faces when they showed me all their hard work at camp.

Matteo the day we got married.

Matteo's smile the day we bought our home.

The children giggling on Saturday mornings when they made breakfast with Matteo.

My last image of Matteo would not be the look on his face when I told him I couldn't come home yet. That wasn't how our story ended. This wasn't how I ended.

Over my dead body would I allow this man to touch me. I'd fight him to my very last breath.

He was not going to take that or anything else from me. A wave of courage and strength pulsed through my veins as I jerked my foot back and put all the power I could muster into shoving it into Gerard midsection. I couldn't allow him to tie me up. If that happened—I didn't want to think about it. The kick was hard enough to knock him off his balance. He tripped over the luggage rack and fell.

Quickly, I yanked the stocking from my mouth, but before I could belt out a cry for help, a fist smashed into my sternum. The breath was ripped from my lungs. A dull buzz filled my ears as I dropped to the ground. My head thudded against the floor as pure fire burned through my chest. I couldn't get air into my lungs. I gasped and gasped, not feeling any relief.

Gerard loomed over me, rage oozing from his body. He swung his leg back and kicked me in the side. A sharp stab ricocheted in my chest cavity. "That wasn't very nice."

I rolled to my side trying to cope with the assault of agony raining down on me. He shoved me onto my back with his foot and straddled my torso. He dropped down, kneeling over me. He covered my mouth with one hand, making searing pain blast through my face and my vision flicker to black, and pinned my hands over my head with the other. He leaned down until we were nose to nose, and when my vision started to focus, all I saw was the unhinged look in his eyes.

One way or another, my life may never be the same for me after this.

My phone was on a continuous ring out in the hall. It was like a sign from above telling me to hold on because someone was looking for me. Hang on as long as I can. Survive however I needed to.

"That fucking hurt, Natalie." Spittle flew from his mouth as he snapped at me. "I can see why he ties you up. You're a wild one. You're going to be so much fun."

He leaned down and bit the swell of my breast as I cried in agony behind his hand.

Using everything I had, I jerked my hips, attempting to dislodge him from me. Nothing mattered other than getting him off me. All my efforts got me was a hard tweak of my nipple. Another wave of sobs tore from my chest with each nonconsensual assault of my body.

I heard a deep voice in the hall, but my phone had stopped ringing.

It could be the only chance I got for help. I couldn't waste it.

Chapter Thirty-Five

MATTEO

THE THREE-HOUR TRIP WAS actually a blast from the past. It was something I needed. A few hours on the open road, with my best bud, heading to get my girl back was food for the soul.

Adam made a playlist on his phone just like we did for road trips back in college.

We stopped at a diner just outside Seattle for breakfast.

It felt more like heading to an out-of-town baseball game with my buddy.

We didn't discuss my marital issues. It was understood that this was it. I was winning my wife back tonight. Instead, we talked about Adam; about his possible promotion to lieutenant, how the Seahawks were going to do this season, whether he should trade his truck in for something new.

We drove inside the city limits of Portland just after lunchtime, which was when Adam finally broached the subject.

"What's the plan?"

"I was thinking we could start with all of us having lunch."

Adam glanced over at me. "You don't have to include me in your plans, man. I'm here for moral support and to be a road partner. I'm okay with spending the afternoon on my own."

"I was kind of hoping you could maybe be a buffer. Ease a bit of the tension and discomfort."

He didn't hesitate. "Sure, but if lunch goes all right, you should ask her out on a date tonight. Not one of your date nights of late, either." He gave me a pointed look as he followed the GPS's directions downtown. "You'll be dressed up and it would be romantic to take her out. Remind her that she is the only lady in your life. Always will be."

My phone rang and Natalie's face popped up on my screen. My lips stretched into a smile. Seeing her face on my screen took away some of the anxiety that was starting to stir in my stomach. Adam lowered the music, but I shook my head. "I'll call her when we get to the hotel. I don't want the GPS to giveaway the surprise."

Even though I wanted to hear her voice, we didn't know where we were going and there was a ton of traffic. I'd call her back in five minutes.

Natalie was staying at the Nines which was on the same block as the gallery. It was also booked when I tried to make a last-minute reservation for a room. Instead, Adam and I grabbed a one at a hotel a few blocks over.

Ten minutes later, we were checked in, but something felt wrong. I'd listened to Natalie's voice mail and she sounded unsettled or concerned. She said she'd see me later. She had no idea I was coming down here. I tried calling her back several times, but her phone kept going to voice mail.

That was fifteen minutes ago. I kept calling as Adam and I decided to walk over to her hotel since that was where she said she was headed.

"Maybe she was tired and fell asleep," Adam offered as we crossed the street, one block closer to Natalie.

"Maybe." I sighed as I got her voice mail again. "But the

ringing would've woken her up. She isn't that heavy of a sleeper."

I had to have called at least twenty to twenty-five times already. She wouldn't have slept through that.

"Shower?" Adam suggested instead trying to ease the growing alarm in my chest.

Shaking my head, I pressed call again. "She said she was going to lunch. And that she would see me later. She doesn't know we're coming, but it was the way she said it, Adam. It was in the shake of her voice. Something was upsetting her. Now, she isn't answering. That isn't a good sign."

As the Nines came into view, the ringing in my ear stopped and a male voice replaced it. "Hello?"

My heart was in my throat. "Who is this?"

"I'm one of the security guards at the Nines," he replied not doing a damn thing to ease my worry.

I picked up my pace, running down the street toward the entrance of the hotel. "Where's my wife?"

"I'm not sure, sir. This phone was laying in the hallway," he said. "Someone complained about the constant ringing."

My insides twisted into a painful knot. Something was very wrong. "I'm in the lobby," I rushed out as I sprinted in. "Which floor did you find it on? Something is wrong. You need to find my wife."

"Third floor," he answered. A second later he was calling out, "Is everything okay in there? This is hotel security."

"What's going on?" I yelled into the phone.

My legs weren't moving fast enough to keep pace with the fear in my gut. I ran past the elevators and straight to the stairs.

"Matt, what's going on?" Adam asked, right behind me.

I was taking two steps at a time, but it still didn't seem to be moving me anywhere. "I don't know. Nat's phone was found in the hallway by security."

Chapter Thirty-Six

Natalie

Despite Gerard's hand covering my mouth, I yelled. I projected my voice as loudly as my lungs would carry it. Someone was on the other side of that door and knew that something was wrong inside the room.

Gerard pinched my nose closed, and a pain so intense exploded from his touch. A thick evil laugh filled the air around us as he let go and did it a second time taking sick pleasure in the way my terror and agony leaked from my eyes down into my hair.

Foregoing a third squeeze to my nose, he shimmied his body closer to my face as he worked his belt undone with the hand not covering my mouth. The sound of the metal clinking had the blood in my veins turning to ice. "I've got something that will keep your mouth occupied for a bit."

Absolute, undiluted, panic surged through me. I knew what his intentions were, and I couldn't let that happen I just couldn't. A burst of adrenaline hit at the exact moment I needed it to. With as much force as I could gather, I tossed my hips from side to side, trying to get Gerard off me. I could feel his erection against my chest as I thrashed. Deranged bastard was enjoying this. His eyes sparkled as he grinned down at me.

Rising up on his knees, he worked the button of his pants. Those few inches seemed to give me just enough room to get him where I knew it would hurt most. *His* yelling would still alert the person in the hallway.

Trying to ignore the immense pain that assailed my head and face as well as the fear rapidly bubbling from my gut, I raised a knee up, aimed at his balls, and drove my knee into them. I must've hit some part of them because Gerard fell over. Half his weight landed on me and the other half on the floor.

I was able to slip out from under him and scramble to my feet. "Help!" I screamed as loudly as I could to the person on the other side of the door. My voice was rough and raw. I opened my mouth to yell, but I didn't get to before he grabbed my ankle. I reached the table and clutched the leg to try to pull my foot free, but I couldn't. There was a sickening pop and then a blazing pain from my ankle as Gerard yanked hard enough for me to lose my grip. "He—"

I grabbed the phone cord, pulling it with me as Gerard tugged me across the floor using my injured foot. My fingers scrambled for the receiver, and I grabbed it, turned, and slammed it into his head as hard as I could.

"You fucking bitch," he bellowed, releasing my foot, which felt hot as it pulsed and swelled, and gripping the side of his head. A maniacal smirk curled on his lips as he pinned me with a malicious stare. "We could have been great together, Natalie. You just had to go and be an ungrateful bitch, though. While I'm still going to have fun with you, I don't think it's going to be so much fun for you now."

I scrambled back, trying to pull myself up using the desk, as Gerard rose to his feet. Pure malevolence radiated from him.

There was a commotion and some yelling on the other side of the door, but I didn't turn toward it. Gerard was a beat too slow finding his footing, and before he was steady on his feet, I went for it and grabbed the iron I'd left on the desk this morning just as he straightened and swung.

The sound of metal hitting skin had my stomach turning and bile rising in my throat, but I hit him again and again . . . and again. By the time the door to the room slammed open, my arms were ablaze from the exertion and my lungs raged with a fire that echoed the ones in my ankle and face. I struggled to drag in air as a scorching burn consumed me with each gasp.

I spun, blinded by rage, and raised the iron as I tried to blink clarity back into my foggy brain.

The man was in a uniform.

His hands were extended, his voice calming as he said, "Ma'am"—he stepped forward—"I'm with hotel security, are you all right?"

The iron was still clutched in my fingers. My hair was disheveled, and my face was sticky with blood. Oh, and there was a man unconscious and bleeding at my feet. I was fucking peachy!

The adrenaline drained away as fast as it had crashed into me. My body deflated, the iron dropped with a hallow thud, and my hands shook as hard as my lower lip trembled. There was more noise in the hallway. More people.

The reality of what just happened smashed into me harder than all the physical damage Gerard had inflicted. My body trembled with the force of at all as I sank to the ground

He stalked me. Followed me here from Seattle.

He attacked me. He wanted to rape me.

He was possibly going to kill me.

I fought back.

I beat him with an iron.

"Natalie!" My name echoed out in the hall. "Natalie!"

Matteo barreled into the room, shoving past the security guard in the doorway. His face was a mask of fear. He looked so frantic that I barely noted Adam behind him as my husband dropped down and pulled me into his arms. His eyes roved all over my face and down my body, taking in all my injuries.

A moment later, a flurry of people invaded the hallway. Police officers, EMTs, hotel management.

A thousand questions were thrown at me, yet all I could focus on was Gerard's unconscious body being loaded onto a stretcher and wheeled out of the room followed by two police officers.

"Ma'am?" I heard someone say as he or she touched my arm.

My body recoiled from their touch as the room began to fade out. The sounds muted and my vision tunneled as I heard Matteo call my name.

It was as if the moment Gerard was no longer near me, my body and mind could relax. But with that, all the pain, fear, and anguish of the past twenty minutes rushed back in, and I shut down.

Everything went black.

Chapter Thirty-Seven

Natalie

"SHE REALLY GAVE HIM HELL," someone with a husky voice said. "She should be proud of herself. Fighting back takes so much courage."

Matteo's reply was garbled to my ears, but his voice was clearly identifiable.

"We'll swing back in a few hours," the other person told him. "Hopefully, she'll be awake and feel up to giving a statement. Then you guys can head back to Washington."

Flashes of my time with Gerard in the hotel room assaulted me in rapid secession. The beeping from something beside me started blaring rapidly.

"Natalie?" Matteo said from my side. When I attempted to turn my head toward him, I was met with sharp pain everywhere. "Natalie, can you hear me?"

I blinked my eyes open as people rushed into the room. A bright light was shined in my eyes one by one as I voice my displeasure with it.

"Natalie," a strong feminine voice called to me. "I'm Dr. Kurtz. Can you hear me?"

A mangled mashup of sounds left my mouth as I

continued to fight the light trying to blind me. Hadn't I been through enough?

Fingers entwined with mine at my side. "It's okay, love. You're safe now."

The beeping slowed, and the light turned off. I blinked my eyes slowly open.

"Welcome back," Dr. Kurtz said. "You've been asleep for a few hours. That's nothing to be too concerned about after all you've been through. How do you feel?"

In the ten minutes that followed, I learned the extent of my injuries.

It took five stitches to close the gash in my forehead. I had a small hairline fracture in my cheekbone, which should heal on its own. I hadn't seen the swelling so much as felt it, but she assured me that the swelling would go down after a few days. My ankle had been dislocated, and I had one broken rib. My nose also had to be reset.

When the doctor left the room, Matt twisted his fingers through mine. "I need to ask you something, love."

With slowness and precision, I turned my head toward him, trying not to upset the dull ache lingering in the back of my skull. He shifted forward and pressed his lips against my knuckles. "What about the kinds of things we can't see?"

My heart thudded. I knew what he was asking, and I didn't want to think about Gerard's filthy hands touching where he wasn't welcome. My voice was horse and strained. "He—" I cleared my throat. "He touched me." I swallowed down the bile rising from my gut. "He bit me." I shuttered thinking and the white-hot pain I felt when he sunk his teeth into my breast. My body started to shake involuntarily.

Matt stood from his chair and sat on the bed, trying to pull my battered body into his. I scooted to the side as far as I could to give Matt enough room to lie next to me and pull me into him. I didn't care how much I hurt. I needed his comfort as the tears began to leak from my eyes.

Everything was just too much for me for the moment.

"I'm going to head to her hotel and gather her things." I thought I heard Adam as I came back to consciousness. "I'll bring them to our hotel. We don't need her going back to that place."

"Thanks," Matteo replied. His chest rumbling under the hand I had resting on his chest. He was still lying on the bed holding me like he had been when I'd closed my eyes. "Can you pop into the gallery and see how everything went with her boss? I know she'll want to know when she wakes back up."

"Will do," Adam said. "How's she doing? Did she say anything when she woke up?"

Matt didn't say anything, and a thick silence coated the room. "Understood, I'll be back."

Warm lips pressed to my head as the door to the room clicked closed. "I know you're awake."

My eyelids felt heavy as they opened, and I took in the room. We sat in silence for a few moments as my fingers toyed with one of the buttons from Matt's shirt.

"How are you here?" I asked him, remembering that he was here in Portland when he was supposed to be in Seattle.

He inhaled deeply. I felt his heart hammering inside his chest. "I wanted to surprise you by coming tonight."

Images of him barreling through the crowd into the hotel room flashed in my mind. "But how did you know where I was and what was happening?"

He ran his hand over my tangled hair. "I knew something was wrong because you sounded upset in your message. When you didn't answer any of my hundred calls back, Adam and I made our way to your hotel to see if you were all right." He dragged in a ragged breath. "We'd just gotten into town when you called. The security officer answered your phone just as we got outside the hotel. I'm sorry, Natalie."

I tilted my head up, ignoring the stings that came from moving my head too quickly. "What for? This isn't your fault. You weren't even here."

A haze slipped over his eyes as his jaw clenched. "If I'd just answered your call when you called, this may not have happened."

I attempted to turn onto my side to face him. He held no responsibility for this, and he needed to know that. "You couldn't have stopped this from happening," I told him. "If it wasn't now, it would have been another time. He followed me here and back at home. He knew we weren't together. He knew the kids' names. I was targeted, and there wasn't anything either of us could have done because we had no idea he was stalking me."

He tipped my head back gently and stared into my eyes. "I'm so incredibly proud of the warrior you are. I know that you must have been terrified while that animal had his hands on you."

Not too sure about being proud that I beat a man with an iron, but I was damn grateful I did. I had so much more to live for. So many things left to do. For the first time in weeks, wrapped in Matteo's arms, everything felt safe again—as if it were all going to be all right.

Tears glistened on my lower lids as I thought about what Gerard had planned to do to me. "For a moment or two, I wasn't sure I'd ever get to see you again."

Matteo's fingers dug into my upper arm as he cradled me against him. He pulled back and looked down at me again. Concern and anguish colored his face. "I've never felt fear like I did for those ten minutes, love."

Exhaustion was beating me down and a dull ache radiated throughout every cell of my being. It seemed as if I'd lived an entire life in the time since I'd left the gallery earlier that day, but I had something important that needed to be done. It couldn't wait a second longer.

I looked up at Matt. "There's something that I need to tell you."

His brow scrunched and worry screamed in his eyes. "What? What is it, love?"

"I was so, so wrong." The words were thick as I spoke them, laced with regret and shame as he listened with rapt attention. "The way I acted after our night with Brooke wasn't fair to you. I acted like an angry child and left you when you needed me most."

"You did," he nodded woefully. "It was awful for me. You were the only one who could truly help me battle everything I was feeling, and you weren't there."

Tears slipped from the corners of my eyes. He didn't try to say anything further. He didn't try to make me feel better about his brutal truth. Instead, he gave me the moment I needed to form my words and continue on as I swallowed the lump lodged in my throat. "You needed me. You told me you needed me. You begged for me to help you through it, and I ignored you like an ungrateful bitch. I'm so damn sorry. I'm sorry because all you've ever done is try to make me happy. You've always been whatever I needed whenever I needed it, and I repaid your love and dedication by treating you horribly the moment things didn't go my way. I was selfish and don't deserve you, but I hope that you can and will forgive me."

The wetness on his cheeks hurt me more than anything Gerard could've ever done. "I know you're sorry. I know you weren't doing it to hurt me, but you did. Badly. I'm not saying we can't move on, but I need you to know that you eviscerated me. That cannot ever happen again, love. We always need to be on the same side."

I nodded, laid my head back on his chest, and closed my eyes, feeling far more secure than the events of the day should've allowed me.

Chapter Thirty-Eight

MATTEO

My heart had crumbled when I stepped into that hotel room and got a good look at my wife. Before I could even fully assess what the hell had happened to her, she had passed out. Blood and bruising covered her face. There was an alarming amount of swelling from under her right eye to her jawline. I had no doubts she had some serious damage to her nose or cheekbone.

I'd died a thousand deaths in the span of those few minutes. It was like being nauseous, suffocated, and punched in the balls all at the same time.

While we lay together —for the first time in weeks—in that hospital bed all night, I couldn't stop staring at her. Drinking her all in. Thanking my lucky star that she was brave enough to fight back and I had the chance to hold her once more. She relaxed against me in sleep, and some of the cracks in our foundation filled and settled. When something as scary as yesterday happened, it made us reevaluate our priorities and remember why our relationship was worth fixing.

Her apology and my being able to hold her all night were all I needed to vow to forget about the past two weeks and move forward. We'd learned some hard lessons, but we couldn't let those lessons hold us back.

My eyes stayed glued to her as she laid in that hospital and napped. I was afraid that, if I blinked, she'd disappear and be back in that room fighting for her life and her safety. She was being released shortly. The detectives had left about half an hour ago with her statement, and Adam was collecting our things from the hotel we were staying at.

Annetta and Bastien fretted over her when they stopped in earlier. They came with a large arrangement of vibrantly colored flowers and jokes to cheer Nat up. "We could take care of him for you," Bastien offered. "We've got 'friends' back in Europe who wouldn't think twice about making him disappear for you."

Annetta smacked him and said, "Don't make promises you can't keep." She turned to Natalie. "I'm the one with the friends, you just say the word."

When Annetta tossed in the wink, Natalie laughed and, even though we still had so much left to go through, it was music to my ears.

Someone tried to attack her. Hurt her. She beat a man with an iron to avoid being raped and or killed. She fought off a man who stalked her here from Seattle. She was strong and elegant and brave. She never left my side, and nothing could've made me happier.

I'd be calling the owners of the club first thing tomorrow. Immersion was supposed to have top-notch vetting and client security. How Natalie found herself with a stalker from there was unthinkable.

Listening to her statement to Det. Jiménez wasn't easy. I had to fight back the bile with each detail she revealed. We were told Gerard would stay in holding, waiting to see a judge at some point in the near future for arraignment. They were charging him with assault, forced entry, and sexual assault. When we arrived back in Seattle, we'd file a restraining order and push for stalker charges. We wanted to make sure he stayed in prison for as long as possible so he could never do this to someone else. We also wanted to make sure that, if by some miracle he was release on bail, he couldn't come anywhere near Natalie without penalty.

"Watching me sleep is creepy when my face doesn't look like this." Her voice startled me. "But staring at this swollen mess is even more disturbing."

I laughed, which felt foreign in my chest. "I can't help it." I shrugged. "The nurses are getting your paperwork ready. Want me to help you get changed? Adam is collecting all the rest of our stuff from the hotel."

She nodded as she pushed herself up in bed. "Thank god for him taking care of that for us. Thank god, he took this trip with you too."

Natalie was straightening her shirt when the nurse came in with her discharge papers. She couldn't get it pulled down fast enough for me to miss seeing the welt on her breast that made my blood boil to a rage.

The nurse went over a few things with Natalie, fitted her for crutches since she couldn't walk on her ankle for at least four weeks, and sent us on our way with a smile.

"You guys ready to head home?" Adam asked, popping his head into the open door. "Your chariot awaits."

Natalie looked up at me from where she sat on the edge of the bed and smiled. A warmth settled over us as she said, "There's no place I'd rather go."

Chapter Thirty-Nine

Natalie
One Month Later . . .

Dr. Alexa Morgan smiled as Matteo and I sat next to each other. "How are the two of you doing this week?"

The two of us glanced between each other, a smile tugging at the corners of our lips. "We're doing well."

It felt so good to be able to say that.

The past month had been a bit of a wild ride. Between healing my body, my mind, and my soul, there were days I wasn't sure I was going to make it through intact.

Nightmares haunted me. Aches and pains assaulted me. Fear made me afraid to be alone.

I was strong and brave. I knew that. But just because things didn't get to where Gerard wanted to take them, didn't mean that I made it out whole.

Part of my soul was left back in that hotel room.

But a tiny weight had been lifted when we started seeing a therapist last week. She specialized in marriages and traumas.

She clicked her pen, ready to jot her thoughts as she listened. "Would you like to tell me about your positives this week?"

Warmth was evident in Dr. Morgan's expression as we explained that the nightmares were less this week. We even went back to Immersion. We didn't do anything there except have a drink, but it was still a big step for us. We had thought we'd never step foot in there again. Matt was Switzerland. He didn't care whether we ever went back or not, but I knew I needed to at least try once. Even if it was just to prove to myself I was strong enough.

"Wow," she said when we finally got to the end. I bet that wasn't what she was expecting to hear this evening. "First, Natalie." She directed her attention to me. "What you went through was a terrible and frightening ordeal, you were incredibly brave, and you still are each day you wake up and work toward the future."

"I was petrified when I realized what was happening. I saw him outside the hotel smoking right before and seeing him was unsettling. It didn't feel like a coincidence that he was staying in the same hotel as I was for the gallery opening. This was the second time I'd seen him outside the club, and it just felt fishy. I never expected him to attack me, though. As I was fighting him off me, snippets of memories with Matteo and the kids flickered in my mind, reminding me I had things to do with my life and this man wasn't going to take those things from me."

Matteo squeezed my hand. His strength and support encompassed me like a caress. He leaned in and kissed my temple. "I'm very proud of you. You're incredibly strong and resilient."

Dr. Morgan motioned between us, using her pen as a pointer. "That you still can experience true positive affection between the two of you is an encouraging sign."

Matteo nodded. "That man may have tried to take from Natalie, but instead he gave us something. What he did reminded us of what we were fighting for." He smiled at me. It was almost as bright as it was three months ago.

"It's just sad that it took something so horrible to show me the truth," I added.

The doctor shook her head. "Do not sell yourselves short, Natalie. You had started to reach out to Matteo before the attack. That call to him because you were feeling uneasy probably saved your life."

We switched gears after that. "Natalie, how has being back in your home been?"

When I had walked into my house after we returned from Portland, I'd been prepared to be bombarded with snapshots of that night with Brooke, but they didn't come. Rather than remembering that, I found myself fixating on all the memories with my family.

"I almost feel as if I was worried for nothing," I admitted. 'The bedroom came out gorgeous. It feels like an entirely different room. As I sat in the living room the first day back, I wasn't thinking about the mistakes we made that night but rather last Christmas morning and the joy on the kids' faces when they opened their new phones."

After everything that happened with Brooke, I'd been practically blinded by my fixation with the negative. I couldn't direct my attention at anything other than all the things we had done wrong.

I couldn't see that we did so much right.

We had something special.

That there wasn't anything Matteo and I couldn't overcome when we played on the same team.

We tried something new, and it didn't work for us.

We lived, we learned, and more importantly, we loved.

Even when we didn't think we could, we loved harder than we knew possible.

Because no one could ever love me the way that Matteo did. I didn't want anyone else to.

No one would ever love Matteo the way I did. I couldn't

ever make up for letting him down when he needed me most, but I'd never stop trying.

No one could ever replace me in his life.

We were made for each other.

Epilogue

MATTEO

IF IT WERE UP TO me, we wouldn't have to come back here ever, but I was following Natalie's lead. We had been here twice since the Gerard fiasco. Once for drinks and once where we wandered around as voyeurs.

There was no telling what we were here for tonight.

Natalie had been through a lot all those months ago in Portland. After four months of therapy, she was doing so much better, *we* were doing much better, healing.

If she said she never wanted to come here again, that would be all right with me.

Sure, a part of me missed the way Natalie melted under my touch the times we had been here before. When we were here, Natalie entered a head space that was difficult to get into at home. Not that I was complaining. I just missed the way Nat used to lose herself in her desires. Only because it was due to shame. She felt shameful that her need to try new things brought so much pain and strife into our lives.

We grabbed drinks at the bar and took a seat in the lounge area. Max de la Cruz made his way over to say hi. The three owners made sure to check in with us every time we scanned in. It must have been some kind of alert in the system. They were extremely distraught about the chain of events that happened and kept trying to make it up to us. We understood that they couldn't have known that Gerard was going to snap. He had a clean record, and they had no reason to deny him membership to the club prior.

He was currently serving seven years in prison for what happen back in Portland.

"What do you think the odds that one of the swing rooms is unoccupied are?" Nat asked.

Her eyes twinkled in a way that I hadn't seen in months. A warmth flowed through my veins. She was ready to embrace that side of herself again. My dick twitched at just the thought.

I didn't want to get too excited. Natalie could still not be ready considering where this road led last time. "We can certainly go take a look."

She nodded eagerly.

We stood from the lounger, and she leaned in. "I was just thinking back to how you owned my body the last time we were in there. I'm so wet."

My cock throbbed against the zipper of my pants. "Is that so?"

She pulled her lip between her teeth. "Think you can do it again?"

I cocked a brow at her. "Is that a challenge?"

The corners of her mouth tipped into a devious grin. "It is. It's been so long since you've taken me there. I almost can't remember what that feels like."

She remembered exactly how good I could make her body feel. "You're itching for a nice little spanking, aren't you, love?"

She grinned and threaded her fingers through mine. She walked toward the hallway where the swings were located with a little extra sway in her hips. "Maybe."

Oh, she was going to get it.

"Careful, love. My alpha is always simmering just below the surface."

Her laugh went straight to my dick.

She was definitely going to get it.

Acknowledgments

THERE'S ONLY ONE PLACE TO start here . . . Matteo! Sigh! Matteo is by far my favorite hero I've written. He's understanding, accepting, supportive, and loves with all he has. Did you find yourself hating Natalie at the end? Yeah, me too! I strongly dislike Natalie at the end even though I 100% understand her position and her inability to just move one. She was riddled with shame, regret, and jealousy. I don't think I could imagine myself in her shoes.

That said, I think we can all sympathize and feel for Natalie in the beginning. As moms and wives and employees we can lose ourselves and the spark in our marriages. This story is about exploring new things with your partner and discovering new things about yourselves and growing, which is important. We don't have to do it in the same manner Matt and Natalie did, but we should do things for ourselves, things that make us happy.

We can all learn a lot from Matteo and Natalie.

Onto the thank yous!

Bloggers and Readers.... Thank you for your support. Thank you for posting about my books. Thank you for joking with me, chatting with me, and hanging out at events with me. I met some really great people in this book world, and I just want to say thank you! It's because of you I'm putting out another book!

My hubby... Your unwavering support is the most beautiful gift in the world. Sometimes I can get so wrapped up in these stories that I completely forget the world around me. You never complain. Not when the laundry doesn't get done, not when we've had takeout five nights in a row because I can't stop working to cook. Not when my brain's fried and I want to throw in the towel. You just tell me it's okay and I can do it. You listen to me prattle on about fictional characters like they're in the room with us with a smile. You come to all my signings and are the best support in the world. I love you!<3

My children... Thank you so much for being so understanding about mommy's 'working.' Thank you for asking about my books and how many there are and congratulating me they're finished. I love you guys, and everything I do is for you, even if it may not seem like it. <3

Ashley... Thank you for loving Matteo as much as me. Thank you for reigning me in when I want to hurt Natalie in the worst ways. I don't know what I would have done without your input to make this book as fantastic as it is now. Your patience with my lack of time management is greatly appreciated as is our banter and conversations You're a Rockstar!

Tiffany... My slutty, dick-loving, country bumpkin! God, are there even words to express my gratitude for you, your work, and your loyal friendship? Thank you for EVERY single thing you do for me. I push and push and you always come through, surpassing my expectations with a smile on your face. (Like I'm about to do with formatting this book at the 11th hour!) Thank you for your friendship. True friends are hard to find, and the luckiest girl in the world with your annoying ass <3

Isabelle... Even with your always overflowing plate, you find a way to be there whenever I need you. Whether I need a shoulder to cry on, a voice of reason, or someone to tell me I'm wrong, you're my girl! I honestly have no idea what the hell I would do without you. Thank you so much for being you <3

I'm so sorry if I forgot anyone, but please don't think you're unappreciated. I love each and every person who has been stood behind to rotted for me.

XoXo
Kimberly

About the Author

BY DAY, KIMBERLY IS A high school English teacher who also happens to have four beautiful, insane children who keep her in running a million different direction on a daily basis. At night, she tries to get all the steamy stories in her head down on paper or computer screen so she can eventually share them with her wonderful readers, but more often than not, falls asleep in the process because sleep is life. She's a Jersey girl at heart and that is where she currently calls home with her husband, children, and two cats.

When not writing or being a taxi driver for her kids or napping, she can be found curled up with a good book or watching her beloved New York Jets or drinking coffee. Lover all things romance, including a little M/M action as well as the dark and twisted, she enjoys video chats with her best friends and always loves to hear from her fans on social media.

Connect wit K.A. Berg!
www.bergbooks.com
FACEBOOK FAN GROUP: Kimberly's Knockout Fangirls
NEWSLETTER:—http://www.bergbooks.com/newsletter.html

- facebook.com/authorkaberg
- twitter.com/AuthorKABerg
- instagram.com/AuthorKaberg
- bookbub.com/profile/k-a-berg
- goodreads.com/authorkimberlybracco

Also By
K.A. BERG

THE UNINHIBITED SERIES

Inhibitions

Unrestricted

Freed

THE APPREHENSIVE SERIES

Fallacy

Irrefutable

Unpredictable

THE "ONE" SERIES

One Taste

One Regret

One Love

STANDALONES

My So-Called Perfect Life

Indulgence

LEARN MORE ABOUT K.A.'S BOOKS

https://bergbooks.com/books/

Made in the USA
Middletown, DE
21 October 2021